The first JJ Sto

The Stoner stories #1-5 ı
thriller, *SPECIAL RELATIOI*

An action-packed antl
operative JJ Stoner, who uses sharp blades, blunt instruments and his innate persuasiveness to discreetly resolve tricky situations for the British government

This collection contains the first five JJ Stoner short stories plus an all-new, previously unpublished stand-alone quick thriller and other bonus material

FIRST CONTRACT: JJ Stoner was a soldier who killed people for a living and made no bones about it. On a scorching day in the Iraqi desert, when British blood stained the sand, he over-stepped the mark. Faced with a dishonourable discharge and accusations of murder, Stoner accepted an offer from a stranger who represented an intelligence agency. Suddenly, Stoner found himself about to execute his first private contract...

TWO WRONGS starts with great sex and ends in sudden death. US Navy SEAL Stretch McCann believes he's met the girl of his dreams. Trouble is, she's married to someone else; another military man not inclined to suffer rivals lightly. Enter JJ Stoner, covert investigator and occasional assassin. Stoner offers Stretch an opportunity for action...

THIRD PERSON: A target is being stalked through rain-soaked city streets. Someone seeks JJ Stoner, independent operative, covert investigator and occasional contract killer. Caution is advised: with Stoner you often get more than you bargain for and this is Ireland, not so very long after the Good Friday agreement. Someone plans to put a cat among the peace process pigeons...

FOUR CORNERED: Stoner needs to prove to his boss that he's more than a one-trick pony whose only skill is delivering an abrupt ending. But when a static stake-out abruptly escalates into live fire, JJ is distracted by two killer women. What should have been a 'routine conversation' with a disenchanted weapons inspector veers into violence with fatal consequences...

FIFTH COLUMNIST: A bent copper is compromising national security and needs to be rapidly neutralised, but none of the evidence will stand up in court. That's exactly why men like Stoner operate in the shadows, ready to terminate the target once an identity is confirmed...

SPECIAL RELATIONSHIP: When Stoner returns to the USA he's treading on sensitive territory. No Englishman is exactly welcome in Louisiana so soon after the international oil rig disaster. Stoner claims he's visiting New Orleans for the annual jazzfest, but the agents sent to intercept him have a hard time believing this...

Feedback from reviewers:
'Gritty story-telling at its best, with graphic (but well-written) sex and a plot that fires from the hip.'

'It launches you straight into the mayhem and, like its protagonist, JJ Stoner, takes no prisoners.'

'Oh my, this book surely packs a punch. The writing is bold and blunt, with horrific things said in a matter of fact way. It sends a shiver down your spine.'

'Wildly witty and effortlessly accomplished. Stoner is a virtuoso with both his hands and with silenced firearms.'

'The tightly-written prose has more than a touch of the Elmore Leonard about it – sparse, sharp and often witty as well.'

'There is hardly time to draw breath in this fast-moving adventure introducing a frighteningly capable executioner.'

'This is fine writing wrapped cunningly around a totally credible character. JJ Stoner is a man you'll hope to meet again. Just not in a dark alley.'

'Five stars. The author is a professional with poise and we look forward to reading his next piece.'

'A brilliant read, along the lines of Jack Reacher.'

'The dialogue is snappy, the characters are sharply developed, and the plot moves effortlessly forward.'

'Intelligently written, with excellent characterisation, sharp wit and punchy back-n-forth dialogue.'

'Sophisticated story-telling, written in a mature style, and targeted at a mature audience.'

'Move over Ian Fleming, JJ Stoner could replace James Bond...'

'An hour's intrigue and entertainment: tight, humorous, direct, logical, philosophical and a bit scary.'

<< oOo >>

All material by Frank Westworth

This anthology first published 2016 by Murder, Mayhem and More, an imprint of The Cosmic Bike Company Ltd
PO Box 66, Bude, EX23 9ZX, UK

www.MurderMayhemandMore.net

Please be advised: this publication is intended for an adult audience. It contains explicit language and scenes of a sexual and violent nature.

THE STONER STORIES

FRANK WESTWORTH

FIRST CONTRACT

CONFUSION. INSTANT CONFUSION. Where there should have been order out of the chaos of war there was only chaos and further chaos.

Sudden movements of several bodies disguised the flight of the blade. The sound of the blade's impact was disguised by the grunt of the target as it landed. The source of the blade – the exact source – was disguised by the movement of all the bodies concerned and by the bleeding grunt of the target; all eyes were on him, not seeking the source of the blade.

Blood spurted as the blade sliced a vessel in the target's neck. Either a remarkably skilled and accurate throw, particularly so since the movement had been so effectively disguised, or a singularly lucky throw. The spurt of the blood was stemmed immediately to a restrained flow by prompt action on the part of the soldier standing next to the victim. The transformation from target to victim had been accomplished with exquisite ease; the screech of static from a radio confirmed that the instant call for immediate medical assistance had been acknowledged, so attentions shifted to the source of the attack, a group of five local civilians all wearing the same beards, soft hats and loose clothing, all of the clothing the colour of the scrubby Iraqi desert, no helpful insignia nor useful signs from the heavens above to indicate which if any of them was formal recognisable military or which of them had thrown the knife to such immediate and remarkable effect.

One of the three standing, uniformed and therefore formally identifiable soldiers strode with purpose and plain intent to the group of Iraqis, spread out his opened palms before them and asked them to reveal who had thrown the blade. With a certain inevitability, the same pidgin English which had always been entirely comprehensible for the many non-military transactions of a soldier's life in a faraway land – procuring and negotiating life's little luxuries to ease a tour's burdens and lonelinesses – was now entirely mysterious to the five locals; they rolled their collective eyes in shared anguish at the catastrophe which had befallen the stricken soldier, but plainly considered that the knife's flight was the result of heavenly intervention and that they were all witnesses to a miraculous act, rather than a clever murderous attempt.

The solo soldier, a sergeant, and plainly a senior one, looked back at his stricken comrade. Dressings and pressures had been applied, a medevac chopper promised, but heads were being shaken – heads out of the injured soldier's sightline – and more British blood was leaking pointlessly into the desert sand.

The sergeant repeated his demand for information, speaking gently but with sufficient force for his words to carry to all ears present, to native and invader alike. His tone was one of weariness, resignation, no particular aggression and certainly no violent intent. His words produced only more theatrical incomprehension, much shaking of heads, much shared and plainly sincere regret at the tragic leakage of life before them. The name of Allah was invoked more than once; he was either to blame or was offering comfort and forgiveness, it was difficult to recognise which in the sadness of the moment. Five sets of open palms were paraded before the sergeant; all of them as innocent as the other, was the suggestion.

A single shot interrupted the stage grief; one of the Iraqis sagged from seated to fallen, his dark blood draining from his exploded head into the sands of his native home. The sergeant held his smoking handgun in plain view, spread his arms wide to express his regret, his masculine sorrow. He looked towards his fallen comrade, a friend maybe, certainly a military brother. Heads were shaken. A body was stretched out onto the sands, sunburned British hands reached for weapons; the sergeant shook his own head, turned back to the four remaining prisoners, and spoke once more, revealing his sorrow at the pointless tragedy which had befallen them all, his regret at his poor mortal inability to judge his fellow men, and how he shared the belief of the men before him that their deity was indeed most merciful, most powerful and all forgiving. Particularly the latter; a fine constant in such unpleasant and uncertain times. A comfort in the dark days of this life. He fired again: the nearest prisoner; once in the head, an execution, probably painless, death certainly instant.

Screams of protest arose from the remaining three men, two of whom scrambled to their knees before him, wails of supplication thrown before him for his attention. The third man wailed but he did not kneel. The sergeant once again shot the nearest prisoner to him; more blood, more brain tissue decorated the desert. Shaking his head sadly, he walked to the remaining supplicant, who was gesturing at his seated companion; plainly blame was being allocated and mercies entreated. In decent English. A miracle. The sergeant nodded his understanding and shot the supplicant through his left eye; death was instant, the brain reduced by the bullet's passage into something less than it had previously been. The desert once more reddened around them, and was nourished.

The sergeant stood before the sole survivor, who sat cross-legged and relaxed, holding his gaze with dignity and patience. No histrionic displays of terror, simply acceptance.

'Salaam,' said the sergeant and shot the prisoner through his left eye, as before, without waiting for a response. He turned to face his comrades, joined them in listening for an approaching helicopter; none was in earshot. No words were necessary; the three men dug five graves, one for each of the native dead. Their own dead companion they wrapped in a bedroll, and they began their trek back to their temporary desert residence. In the distance they could hear the double pulse of a twin-rotor chopper, the unmistakeable call of the Chinook coming to carry them home.

oOo

'These things are always a crappy business, Sergeant Stoner,' the non-military man with the military bearing remarked. 'Have you admitted anything to anyone yet? I've read through all the statements – including that of the lonely goatherd who could see misdeeds at a remarkable distance and who we cannot actually place with any certainty anywhere near your patrol. However,' he sighed a sigh of profound weariness, 'we have a pile of Iraqi bodies which appear to have been transported to their next lives by single shots from your very own service weapon. They appear to have been executed, and although our political masters think nothing – less than nothing – about indiscriminate city bombings which kill plenty of unarmed civvies, they do appear to hold a dim view of the execution of disarmed murderous soldiers. It's a mystery to me. Always has been. Anyway; have you admitted to anything?'

The sergeant remained standing at ease before the civilian. 'No. Should I be calling you "sir", by the way? I must have missed the introduction.'

'Call me what you want. You've admitted nothing. Good. Your troops are as exceptionally loyal as I'd expect and their own statements are entirely confused and contradictory. Great works of fiction every one, the addition of a few avenging angels or marauding aliens would have added only a little to the entertainment value and couldn't detract from the absence of verifiable facts. Apart from one common theme; your saintliness and high moral fibre, stuff like that. Leadership quality, they call it, also charisma and several psychobabbling terms beloved of shrinks everywhere.

'But you've admitted nothing. Your troops have backed up that particular nothing with another nothing of their own. The unsubstantiated nothing from that lonely goatherd will doubtless be withdrawn with the right incentive.' He paused. The sergeant's expression eased towards the quizzical, a little. The civilian continued his musing. 'Very unreliable, these native witnesses. One day they swear they can lead you to Saddam's massive underground bio-warfare factories and nuclear launchers, the next they've never even heard of Saddam and always thought that nuclear energy was a sort of decadent Western toothpaste. It's a challenge for intelligence analysts everywhere, let me tell you.

'We're going to have a meeting, probably tomorrow if I can get the charges dropped and provided you agree to that meeting in advance. No agreement, no meeting, and I lose interest and go pester someone else. Tomorrow's meeting will be in a place where no one's recording our conversation.' He looked levelly at the sergeant, who looked back in the exact same way. Both men nodded.

'The ordnance,' asked the sergeant as the civilian prepared to leave. 'The bullets from my… from the weapon involved?'

'All fired by the same Browning, I suddenly understand. Nothing to suggest they came from a Smith &

Wesson, a Beretta or even a SIG Sauer P226, as you carry, I believe.' His gaze was level, his voice calm and a little amused. 'Military police will try to connect that missing weapon to a missing person, but this is a warzone, nothing's easy. Things ... weapons get lost and stolen all the time. Thriving black market, mercenaries and the like. Crappy business, wars. Except commercially, obviously enough. See you tomorrow. I'll send a driver once we've sorted the paperwork.' He dropped his own paperwork into a thin briefcase and turned for the door.

The sergeant snapped to full attention, but it was lost on his companion, who left the room without looking back. Before the door closed completely, it opened again, this time to admit a gaunt full colonel. The sergeant remained as before, at full attention.

'Easy,' said the colonel, waving at a chair as he fell into another. 'Take the weight off. Look casual, you'll be a civvy tomorrow.'

'Sir?'

'So, Stoner, currently but not for too long one of her majesty's heroic sergeants, decorated and blooded; what do you make of the Hard Man?' The gaunt colonel dropped his beret on the desk between them, leaned back and undid a few shirt buttons.

'Sir?'

'The military monosyllabic interrogative,' remarked the colonel. 'Easy to learn and to use, gives away nothing and is always polite.' He grinned, suddenly and unexpectedly, revealing gaps in his stained teeth. 'You've just passed your interview with the Hard Man, Sergeant Stoner. I think he liked you, though he's such a lying, dishonest shit of a pig that it's not always easy to tell.' He grinned even wider, revealing further dental absenteeism. 'You understand what you've agreed to? And you can speak plainly, the recorders are switched off, though the Hard Man would tell you to ignore that statement as every potentially positive statement is a lie in any theatre of operations. You'll get the hang of his world. If you survive it. You should flourish in it, Stoner, man of your intelligence and clear vision.'

'He's a spook, sir?'

'Well done. Yes. And a horribly senior and horribly successful one. Full colonels fetch and carry for him.' He spread his arms modestly. 'As seen here.'

'I said nothing, colonel. He spoke, I listened, I said nothing. I agreed to nothing. What have I agreed to ... without saying anything?'

'It's his way, He talks all the time and says nothing – almost nothing. You'll learn how it works if you survive working with him. He'll talk endlessly around a subject, discuss the weather, the cricket, the state of tractors in the Ukraine and such, and then you find yourself with a mission, with resources to carry it out, and you'll either carry it out, fail to carry it out or expire in the process. That's the most likely outcome, but you might succeed. People do.'

'Missions to do what? Sir?'

'Kill people, mostly. Not always, but mostly.'

'Like life as a regular then?'

'No. Not even a bit. Excuse me.' The colonel pulled a cell phone from a leg pocket of his fatigues, thumbed a button and listened to it. Closed it again. 'That was quick. You're free to go. He really must like you. Kindred spirits, maybe.' He smiled again, slid the phone across the table. 'This is for you. Instructions will arrive as text messages – usually – very occasionally as a straightforward call or voicemail. Take a look at the screen, and you'll get your first lot of directions; where and when to meet. Don't tell anyone – including me – it's safer to know nothing when he's involved.

'Oh, and welcome to civvies, former-sergeant Stoner. Your tour is complete, you're discharged with a full pension, which means something, and honours, which mean nothing, your billet will be cleared and your personals will get sent back to the UK as soon as there's a gap on a flight. Straight to whatever address we have as your home. Or anywhere you'd prefer – tell me now.'

'Whatever, sir...'

'No more of the sirshit; I'm just another colonel to you now. You don't see your troops or your oppos, I'm afraid. Not until after you've carried out your first contract for the Hard Man. That's how it works. If you succeed, you're in the clear.'

'If I don't?'

'You have an imagination; use it. You OK for money? You'll need some at first. After that it gets a lot easier. Usual provisos about success, failure, things like that. OK?'

'OK. I'm fine for money. If I'm under cover, do I still use my own account?'

'Get it straight, Stoner. You're not undercover. You're a civilian; behave like one. You'll get all due pay, but you won't need it. Not after your first contract. It's much easier than you think. If the Hard Man wants you undercover, he'll tell you and that's what you'll be. Easy as that. Go find a hotel, say nothing to anyone, and meet him where and when he tells you and do what he tells you. Do that and your future is bright.'

Stoner and the colonel stood up together. 'What will you tell the troops, colonel? They're bound to wonder where I've gone.'

'I'll tell them you were beamed up by aliens. Not too far from the truth...'

oOo

'Got much baggage?' The Hard Man dropped into the seat facing Stoner. He snapped his fingers and glared and a waiter came running, took his order and left, returning within seconds to serve them both some of the delicately diluted molasses which the locals graced with the title of coffee. The Hard Man took a sip and winced.

'Fuck,' he said. 'You'd not need to be very wicked to be insomniac after drinking this.' He took another sip, searched out the waiter and nodded to him, dropping a large cash note on the table and pinning it with an ashtray. 'That,' he remarked, 'was a cunning play upon the idea of there being no rest for the wicked.'

'I got that.'

'Good. Smarter than the average pear.'

'Bear.'

'That too. More pears than bears in Bagdad. Marginally. Pairs in the chesty accessories sense totally absent. A pit of a place. Baggage?'

'None. Nothing I need. Chap can buy a toothbrush anywhere these days. It's the relentless spread of civilisation.'

'It is indeed. So, Mr Suddenly Civilian Stoner, why are we here?' The Hard Man sipped his coffee and grimaced appreciatively.

'The great existential question confronting all of humanity, or just you and me, here in this desperate café wondering whether the coffee is survivable or a war crime in itself?'

'You choose, former sergeant Stoner, all else will follow.' The Hard Man leaned back in his chair, shrugged the heavy shoulders inside their lightweight suit.

'I'm going to kill someone for you, after which you will add money or its equivalent to my fortunes and then we see where we go from there. If anywhere.'

'This doesn't bother you? The killing someone? You're approximately correct, by the way.'

'No. Why would it? I've been doing little else for the last several years, apart from marching up and down various hills, sharing social diseases and painting coal white, soldier stuff. Also oppressing various minorities or even majorities, depending on the whim of American presidents.'

'You're not bothered about duty to your country, comrades, colours for the trooping of, Mister Stoner?'

'Should I be?'

'No idea. Most soldiers are. Killing strangers isn't a problem so long as your queen and country tell you to do it, or even some grinning American president as you put it, but when the order comes from some fat bloke in a sweaty tropical suit attempting to pretend that he's man enough for this astonishing coffee sometimes – usually, even – they can't hack it. That's my question on this fine sunny morning.'

'Don't care. Who, where, when and how? And ... there's always an and ... what next? After that. It has crossed my mind that I could easily be a one-trick pony for you, a one-time single-shot sort of thing, disposable after use. Wolves for the throwing to. You get the idea.'

'Now you're being clever. I'm unconvinced that cleverness is a good idea in a hired gun. But... we'll get back to that. Maybe. One-trick pony? No. It's not worth the hassle setting up a suddenly and unexpectedly ex-military man to avoid the long fall, peer disapproval, breast-beating letters to The Guardian and the like, just to use him once. I'm straight, Stoner. So long as you're straight with me, I'm straight with you. I'd not survive long otherwise; I'm sure you can work that out for yourself.

'So, moving along and expressing appropriate thanks on behalf of a grateful nation for your acceptance of a new job without any mention at all of its terms and conditions, I can reveal that you will be leaving this vale of tears exactly as soon as I can get your departure sorted and facilities in place for your first murder.'

'So I'm your private murderer now? Charming thought.'

'Don't fret about it. I don't do euphemisms, even if I knew what they sounded like. You were correct; you're going to kill someone for me. No law permits this, so it's murder.'

'Technically murder? Can you flag me down another coffee? It's actually delicious, and your big brown eyes work wonders with the waiter boys.' Stoner shunted his empty cup and its saucer across the rickety table, tapping it with his fingertips until it collided with his companion's crockery. The Hard Man looked at him with amusement, flapped his fingers in an apparently aimless way and coffee appeared before them. As did a hookah with two pipes and mouthpieces. Stoner looked across at his companion and raised an eyebrow in silent query.

'This is god's country, Stoner,' said the Hard Man. 'It is frowned upon for chaps like us – or any chaps, really – to consume alcohol, fermented grape juice or whatever, but it's perfectly OK to get utterly wrecked on the local dope. Which is...' he wiped one of the mouthpieces on a handkerchief, '...remarkably pleasant. Conducive also to good sound non-aggressive negotiations. You need a company. A limited company.' He took a long, slow, deep draw from the hookah, deep liquids bubbled within, and he sighed. 'If you don't know how to set one up, I'll make an introduction for you.'

'There's really no booze in this part of town?' Stoner wiped the other mouthpiece on his civilian sleeve and took a slow draw from the hookah. 'The bases are full of booze.'

'Dulls the thinking and makes life an endless search for toilets.' The Hard Man was calming, noticeably. 'And I've never understood why the white man has this thing about wiping mouthpieces on a shared pipe. Any decently communicable disease is going to be above that kind of useless gesture. It's why we fit in so badly in this part of the world and why all our efforts at bending the wily native to our will fail. Which they do. I'll be glad to get home.'

'Which is where? The UK, presumably?'

'It'll all come out in the fullness of time. At the moment, your life wouldn't be enhanced by an appreciation of my domestic arrangements. It's all part of my control freakery. I'm a true believer that if I know all the dirt about you and you know no dirt about me, then we'll get along swimmingly, the world our muscly mollusc, that sort of thing. Good dope, no? Did you know that the next war will be in Afghanland, and the excuse the political shitwits will use will be that we need to stop them growing poppies, recreation for the use of? Idiots. The world needs more relaxation, not less. Idiots. Your turn to speak. I'm feeling sufficiently mellow to be a little useful to you.' He drew more from the pipe, then sipped at the replenished coffee, nodded his appreciation to the waiter and added a second slice of paper money to the first.

'Company. Why do I need a company?' Stoner absorbed more coffee than fumes; the waiter refilled his cup again. 'I do your dirty work, you pay me. Why a company?'

The Hard Man's gaze was wide-ranging, no focus obvious. 'It's bureaucracy. You need a company which can invoice whoever we decide you can invoice for services provided. You'll need an accountant, too, most likely. Everything's legal, above board.'

'OK. So I invoice someone for security services or something, then I get paid. Is it really so simple?'

'Yep. Be a little imaginative about what you're billing for, so that when it crosses my desk I can make sure the papertrail leads only to endless meaningless forms deep in the morass that is any government. We'll work it out if you survive your first contract.'

'I might not survive it?' Stoner seemed more amused than concerned by the idea.

'You should. There's no mileage in recruiting incompetents. I didn't hack all the way from leafy England to this shithole to recruit some dimwit target who's likely to get popped before he even takes a shot. Your jacket's impressive enough. When you got flagged up I thought you were worth the trip. Even though the in-flight amusement on a Herc is rubbish in the extreme. Worse than the BBC.'

'Jacket?'

'Military file. You're going to Ireland, land of dark unpalatable beer and about the same number of murderous religious nutters as this place. You've been before. One of the reasons I was attracted to you.'

'And I'm going to kill someone? Who?'

'No one you know, and yes.'

'You going to tell me who he is?'

'Why? Is it important to you? Do you actually want to know? Would it help you? Would it make you more effective? Motivated?' The pipe had burned out, and the Hard Man waved away the offer of a fresh one.

'I don't care.' Stoner appeared to be looking at himself. He inspected his fingernails with some care. 'Should it help? Should it matter more to me whether I'm drilling holes through a patriotic Arab with sunburn and an impossible language in a hot country, or a paleskin patriotic Paddy who prefers eating sheep to goats and worships his own gods in his own ways in Latin?'

'I don't think they do the Latin any more.' The Hard Man blinked. 'I think they've worked out that any deity capable of creating the entire everything is probably also capable of understanding several languages. I think this passes for revolutionary thought in some places. I'll give you a little background. You can ask some questions if you want, and after that I'll find you once the job's a done job.'

'Just like that?'

'Just like what?'

'You've not mentioned exactly what you want doing or how I'm supposed to do it, resources, weapons, cover story, contact details. All that spook ninja assassin stuff.' Stoner appeared more amused than concerned.

'Yeah. True. You're a man of perception.' The Hard Man reached within his clothing and produced a cell phone, which he laid on the table between them. 'This,' he announced with added drama, 'is your direct line. Only you have the number. It's in the phone you've already been given. It's speed-dial number one. Easy to remember. Everything I need to tell you will come to you down that phone. Get another if you want to call up the girlfriend, arrange nights out with the boys, dial a pizza, so forth. Keep that one just for me. You don't need anything else. You call me, leave a message and I'll return the call. If I call you, you call me right back. We don't do offices or safe houses and until you've passed the audition we don't actually do much recognisable spook stuff. It's really simple. As soon as you're back in the UK, book a nasty cheap hotel using your usual credit card. Book it for a week, as close to a ferry to Derry as you like. Within twenty-four hours of your booking in, all the details you'll need for the hit will be delivered to your room, including where you can find the weapon we'll provide for you.'

'You do provide support? Evac, things like that?'

'No. You go in, you find the mark, you take him out as quickly and as cleanly as you can, and then you return to your cheap hotel in the UK. I'll contact you as soon as we have verification, pat you on the back, give you a shiny coin or two and you return to your new civilian life.'

'And then?'

'What "and then"? There is no "and then". This is not a career. This is not the army. What little "and then" there might be depends entirely on how well you perform. It really is as simple as that. You'll have a complete life if you want one, you can have a proper job if you want one, though I don't think you're the sort. Are your ears burning?'

'What?'

'Stop saying that. It makes you look like an idiot. Your ears should be burning because you've got a pile of data on your cell phone. It's a clever cell phone, so clever that it can handle a lot of words. If you're a very good boy I'll give you one that does pictures, too. The relentless march of technology. The data on your phone now tells you which plane you're catching.' The Hard Man tipped his own phone towards himself and read its screen. 'In about an hour. Have a great flight. Say hi to Bernie for me.' He lifted off from his chair like a rocket attempting to gain orbit, called a couple of sentences in convincingly incomprehensible Arabic to their waiter, who nodded, and the Hard Man was gone into the crowd.

Stoner picked up his new cell phone and started to learn its ways.

oOo

Airports are usefully frantic, Dublin as rushed as others of its size. Stoner passed through security with no more than an amused question about his notable holiday sun tan to interrupt his progress. He carried only an overnight bag and was at the head of the queue for taxis.

The hotel was more comfortable than he'd expected, and certainly more comfortable than the motel-style establishment he'd been favouring in England. Whoever had handled the booking had been in a generous mood, he felt. Stoner checked in, confirmed that his reservation was for a big room for a week and that the bill would be collected by the London booking agency. He shared comfortable amusement with the receptionist about the dimensions of his expense account, confirmed the underground whereabouts of the hotel's secure car park, dropped off his single bag in the big room he could now call home, returned to the taxi rank and hired another cab.

'Not a destination I get every day,' the soft tones of the cabby's Irish voice shared further amusement. Stoner was happy to be spreading a little laughter with every conversation; a good goal to compensate for a life of professional violence. 'Dublin Harley-Davidson. You going to buy a motorcycle, bud?' The cabby gunned his vehicle into the frantic traffic.

Stoner smiled some more, stroked the black goatee beard, which contrasted strangely with the bleached stubble on his scalp, and nodded vaguely without comment.

The cab driver made a final attempt at conversation. 'My brother has a big motorcycle. It's a Honda. A big one.'

His knowledge of motorcycles exhausted, he fell silent, a sensible reaction to his passenger's good-humoured silence.

oOo

'Rentals? Sure. What did you have in mind, sir?' The Harley salesman ushered his potential customer across the showroom, ranks of gleaming muscle machinery, all leaning to the left, each motorcycle with its front wheel on full left lock, each motorcycle resting solidly on its kickstand. 'Touring our beautiful country? Do you want luggage? Throw-over bags? Have you held a motorcycle license for more than three years and is it clean?' He smiled in a conspiratorial way. 'It needn't be entirely clean, if you see what I mean, sir, just clean enough.'

'Many more than three years,' Stoner smiled in an accommodating manner. 'And entirely clean. Offence-free, that's me.'

'You ride too fast to be caught, sir!' Salesman and customer laughed quietly together in the manner of old friends sharing a familiar joke. Fast riders rarely ride Harleys. Harleys are many, many things; fast isn't generally one of them. The deal was done, rider and motorcycle introduced.

Stoner's cell phone shook in the breast pocket of his shirt; at last, contact and hopefully some directions. He dug it out, leaving the dark blue-green motorcycle idling under him, and examined the phone's small screen, nodded to himself, replaced phone, zipped up the jacket, kicked up the stand, engaged a gear and rolled seamlessly into the thunder of the evening traffic.

oOo

The leather-bound biker scooped his bottle from the bar, ignored the glass which had arrived with it, and seated himself at a quiet table in a quiet corner facing the door. The evening was early, a band was assembling around a small stage in a distant corner, tappings of drums and tunings of strings providing a vaguely exciting harmony to the overall hubbub. Stoner tipped his bottle to his lips, merely moistening them rather than drinking, and watched. And was watched in his turn, a stranger conspicuous in a boozer more accustomed to its regular clientele, regulars who would bring guests by invitation and who regarded tall, dark mystery men with some caution – and more than a little suspicion.

'You're very early!' A soft handbag landed hard on the table, disturbingly close to the open bottle. The bottle was unconcerned, as was Stoner, who looked up and raised an eyebrow in what may have passed for a welcome.

'Is it yours? The Harley? Big bike, big man.' She grinned and continued her greeting monologue. 'Long time no see. Glad you could find us OK. I'll get a glass. You OK for a drink?'

Stoner rose to his feet, waved her to a seat next to his own. 'Hi,' he said. 'What'll you be having?' His hard Belfast consonants cut cleanly through the softer southern brogues surrounding them, silencing some conversations, which resumed again after their participants absorbed the presence of the foreigner and his strangeness, a strangeness made more acceptable by the welcome from his female companion, and explained by his choice of transport and his northern tones.

'It's on the counter,' she told him, pointing to the bar, where indeed there stood a large whiskey and a small jug of water, as well as a second bottle of Bud for the biker. Stoner collected them, forging a return path to his small table through what was quite suddenly a crowd, and remained standing after passing the whiskey and the water to tame it to his lady of the evening. With no introduction, the band struck up and conversation ceased, replaced by steady drinking, flirting and the humour of misunderstanding which connected the two. Stoner's new lady friend sank several whiskeys but went light on the water; he wet his lips from time to time and watched as he was discussed by several of the harder-faced men around the bar.

His lady friend leaned into him and bellowed by his ear. 'It's in the bag. When you're ready.' He slid the bag onto his lap and squeezed it, familiar fingers recognising the ordnance it held. Glock, by the feel of it. Ideal for close work. Two men joined them, uninvited. The leader of the two presented the lady with another glass, and a bottle of Bud joined its companions in front of Stoner.

'You're new.' Shouted over the hubbub and not very aggressive. Not yet. 'Not seen you here before. 'Call me Paddy, if you like.' Stoner raised a bottle and drank from it, an entire mouthful of light beer which had been standing for so long that it was both warm and flat, rather than sharp and cold. Pancake beer.

'Paddy,' he said. 'John.'

'Just John? You here for a reason, Just John?'

Stoner surprised them all by standing, draining the bottle, wiping his lips with the back of his hand, and leaning into the very private space of Paddy, his new friend, his lips ending up as close to Paddy's ears as was possible without actual intimacy. 'You've either a poor memory, Paddy, or you've not been drinking here for very long. Either way, what the fuck I do is of no concern to a man like yourself.' The sharp Belfast consonants and short vowels landed like artillery rounds in the mud of the surrounding conversations, which fell silent, nervous casualties of what sounded like an opening salvo in what appeared to be at least a skirmish.

Stoner rested a large brown, very brown hand on Paddy's shoulder. 'I'm here for the music, man. What else?' A wide grin split the goatee and Stoner bounded over to the stage, where the casually familiar band were taking a break, the musical silence adding to the rippling currents of club conversation and bar banter. He spread his arms wide in greeting and chatted to the band's unobtrusive guitarist, with much gesturing and surprised laughter from the latter. Then he returned to his table and his seat, scooping up a bottle as he sat once more, and drinking from it.

'Seems like I might give you a tune,' Stoner smiled. 'Been a while since I played around here.' His three companions stared at him.

'Are you, like, famous?' Paddy's junior companion spoke for the first time.

Stoner shook his head. 'No,' he said. 'Just loud and offensive. And full of shit. What're you having, boys? What can a man from the wasteland get for you hospitable Dubliners in these peaceful days? And then would you everso kindly fuck off so I can get along with the seduction which is so dear to my own heart and the real reason I'm braving such a distance from homely comfort.' All three men laughed, the single woman looked away in distaste.

And once they were alone at their table once again, she asked him to identify himself. 'Just John will do for you too.' His Irish accent appeared to be thickening with the pouring of the evening. 'Who is the lucky man to benefit from my attentions tonight? Point the way with those fine Irish eyes of yours and with that sweet Irish voice, not with your fingers, please. Be accurate, be exact. Mistakes can be difficult to rectify later. I can't offer a warranty in case of mistaken identity.' No smile accompanied his words. The band was reassembling, the leader waved to Stoner, a broad smile on his face. Stoner assumed the reflected expression and waved back, offering a bonus thumbs-up as encouragement.

Stoner confirmed the identity of the man described by his companion; twice, to avoid embarrassment. He was part of the same loose social group as Paddy and his friend, appeared as calm and no noisier than any of his circle, and within moments of the identification confirmation, the target rose and headed for the door, the outside door which led to the outside yard and the outside toilets. Stoner followed, signalling to the band his intention to return and to make music just as soon as the demands of beer pressure had been released.

Grunted greetings as men line up to leak. Just the two men in front of him, occupied with matters in hand. The target was loudly savouring the traditional male release, his companion's response inaudible over the sounds of splashing. The companion left, first in, first out. Stoner walked silently behind the remaining gent, his target, reached around and expertly spun his neck for him, piss spraying uninterrupted as the pisser died in his hands, and continuing to splash as the dead heart continued to beat and the living brain continued to die and Stoner lifted him into a cubicle, sat him down, glassy amazed stare to the fore, tucked his dribbling dick into his pants to keep at least a little cleanliness next to the dead man's approach to an assumed godliness, and locked the cubicle door from the outside – an easy task for an old soldier.

Beaming broadly, Stoner took a seat with the band. His lady companion, gun-laden bag beside her, watched with some surprise as Stoner changed the tuning on the borrowed acoustic guitar, acknowledged a generous introduction from the leader of the band, then launched into a medley of furious Provo protest songs, familiar to all in that Catholic bar, all with their choruses to share. After that single long song closed and brought the entire house to its feet, Paddy and his companions prominent among the approval-shouters and the chorus singers, Stoner asked for and was given a little moment of quiet in which he was allowed to recall his fallen brothers in arms.

After bowing his head, looking sombre and raising it again, he offered another, shorter song, another medley of outraged Irish words set to American slave music, played with a slide, a black tubular device he produced from a pocket somewhere, which replaced the fingers to extract the notes from the guitar's strings, and to considerable effect. Paddy, his circle, Stoner's woman companion and several others in the audience grew steadily aware that the bottleneck, the slide Stoner was playing with, was in fact a silencer for a pistol, a suppressor which muffles the bellow of the gun when used to clandestine effect. They applauded more, and pointed it out to their own friends. The house, as they say, was brought down.

And as the cheer rang the rafters, Stoner walked tall and silent through his crowd, now singing inebriate songs of its own, collected his black crash helmet and his black leather jacket and left, through the main door, to where his blue-green Harley-Davidson sat on its kickstand awaiting their shared departure. It was a formidable exit.

oOo

'Great performance, Mister Stoner. I wish I'd been there to witness it for myself.' The Hard Man's voice was crisp and clear, even through the cell phone's small speaker. 'The newspaper headlines were clever, too, how the boozer's clientele were distracted by a stirring performance from an unknown Belfast singer while persons unknown murdered some unfortunate in the bogs out back. Do you know who the dead guy was, by the way? Anyone you know? A private vendetta, was it?'

Stoner's spine crawled. 'Say again,' he managed, weakly. 'The guy I killed was the guy your girl pointed out as the target.'

'Ah.' The Hard Man poured insincere sympathy down the telephonic airways. 'There's the rub. Not my girlie. Not mine at all. Mine was there, watching and waiting for the man whose pictures she'd been sent, loaded with the passwords, secret signs and the like and the identity of the target. The right target.' He drew a deep resonant breath and was silent.

Stoner was recovering. 'Sorry, then. The woman approached me bang on time, made the right introduction, had brought a Glock and knew exactly who I was and why I was there.'

'You've grown a beard, dyed your hair and look like a biker.'

'Men grow beards, my hair is natural, and I ride a bike. It's a Harley, and it's in the hotel's car park even now. I hope.' Stoner was becoming more confident as the conversation progressed. 'I'm not sure how the fuck-up was mine, but whatever, I don't care, sort out your girlie or whatever, and I'll take another shot. Who was the mistake, though? An innocent nobody?'

'No one important to me.' There was a pause. 'Not yet. You're booked into the hotel for another several days. Is there any sign of surveillance on you?'

'Not that I've seen. But I've not been anywhere, done anything – apart from the odd bit of murder and mayhem – so I'd not see a tail if there's a tail to be seen. Was the target – your target – actually in the pub?'

'You talked to him. According to my girlie – the right girlie – you even bought him and his best mate a round. According to both her and the independent observer, he really enjoyed your provo performance, too.'

'Independent observer?'

'I'm a cautious man. I believe in bets being well covered, in case of mishap.'

'Like the wrong guy taking the fall?'

'It's not the first time it's happened. Some operators get messy and collect collateral. Sometimes only the collateral actually gets topped. It can be a cruel and heartless world.'

'So the guy called Paddy – which I doubt is his real name, and who I thought was an objectionable asshole – he was the target? OK. Tell me where, and I'll go find him.'

'Just like that? You have a gun of your own? As well as the suppressor? Nice touch, by the way, the suppressor. Newspapers loved it. And it deflected any bad ideas that you – an obvious gunman – might have snapped some no-mark's neck. Clever.'

'If accidental.'

'That too.'

'I can always find a gun in Ireland. The entire island is a floating gun store. Is it safe to talk like this on a cell phone?'

'Entirely. The only persons capable of recording the conversation are those listening to it.' The humour in the Hard Man's voice was unmistakeable, even down the phone lines.

'Which may or may not be just you and me?'

'Exactly. Tell me about the notable Irish accent, Mister Stoner. It made a deep impression upon the lovely

Bernie. She said it brought tears to her ears – or something – to hear the Belfast blarney. Said she could almost hear the whole Harland and Wolff thing, rivets and hammers, bad breath and endless insults aimed at the papacy. Stirring stuff, she said.'

Stoner dropped a pause into the conversational flow. 'Who's Bernie? You've read my record; I did more than one tour in the fine city of Belfast, some of it under-cover, all of it brilliant. Magic city, great people. Shame they waste so much time killing each other. They'd inherit the earth if they'd stop killing each other and killed other wasters instead.'

The Hard Man's amusement drifted through the ethers. 'That's why we evil English like to keep them fighting. Compensates for the lack of birth control.'

'That's the other part of Ireland.'

'There's no difference; fools are fools because they're fools, not because of geography. We can talk about it over a good bottle of something, sometime, assuming you can actually complete the contract, kill the right person and avoid getting killed yourself.

'Special concession time,' the Hard Man pulled them both back to an approximation of the matter in hand. 'Do you need support? Speak up if so. And – I must say this – I was impressed by how well you handled yourself in an alien situation. Irish bars are a lot different to Iraqi souks. Very creative approach; find an opportunity and exploit it. If you can survive this, you could go far.'

Stoner pretended to give the suggestion some thought. 'No need. All I need is an accurate target ID and room to move. Will Paddy the Paddy be suspicious after last night?'

'Shouldn't be. He will be confused though, because you kindly took out one of his more vocal opponents. A rival. He'll be confused because he would have known about any action intended by his own fine boyos. But he shouldn't be able to make you for the killing ... not with any certainty. If he set up the wrong girlie to set you up, then he would have expected you to use the Glock and to take the fall for it. You might even avoid suspicion entirely. Did you speak with either him or the girlie before vanishing? Bernie said you did neither.'

'No. No further contact at all. Deliberate. In like Flynn and out like an Englishman. But I don't want to see either of them again, not together. They'd place me and I'd get hurt, which is unappealing. The downside of being conspicuously invisible is the conspicuous bit of it. Great smokescreen, great misdirection, hard to do encores.'

'You sound too familiar with this, Mister Stoner.'

'Read the file again. You get the complete version? The version with the undercover shit?'

'Were you Military Intelligence? An odd notion, but always possible, I suppose? Your basic file doesn't say that ... but I suppose it wouldn't. One of the darker MI bodies?'

Stoner laughed gently. 'Nope. Applied twice and got turned down. Twice.'

'Fuck. That's almost poetic,' said the Hard Man. 'Finish this easy little job and we can have a good chat. I'll have read all about you before we meet. Bernie will be in touch with you as soon as we hang up. Been great to chat. Kill the right guy next time, Stoner. And try to avoid the suicidal remorse thing too; your Catholic upbringing might induce terminal guilt, or something equally pointless. Cheery-bye.' And he was gone.

Stoner's cell phone rang immediately. A woman's voice. 'Let's try to do this properly. We need to meet.' She hung up before he could reply. The phone buzzed again to announce the arrival of a text message, complete with both a time and a place and the suggestion that Stoner should keep his current appearance.

oOo

The blue-green Harley-Davidson leaned on its kickstand snug against the wall of an Irish bank. Its rider, all mean beard, mirror shades and black leather, leaned on the Harley-Davidson. They could have been a statue; no movement was apparent. There was an area of absence around them; despite the busyness of the street, an invisible barrier somehow kept the passing pedestrians away. An unremarkable woman wearing unremarkable clothes braved the no-go area and approached the silent, motionless tableau.

'Can we go now?' Stoner maintained his apparent fascination with the endlessly passing crowd. 'I am busting for a slash and there's no easy cool way to do that standing here. Great bikes though these certainly are, they don't come with a restroom.'

'You've been here too long, then?' The question was amused and rhetorical. 'I'm always punctual. Never late, never early.'

'Laudable. I'll never forget it. I still need a leak. If it starts to rain there may be a flood. You OK on the back of this thing? It's a little loud, but it's very comfortable.'

'I don't have a helmet, and I am wearing a skirt.'

'Cool. You'll feel soothing breezes on skin that rarely knows them, and you can wear my lid if it fits. If it's too big it'll be no use to you and it's better if only one of us wipes their brains across a bollard.'

'Your head is far bigger than mine. Is that what you're saying, Mister Stoner?'

'If the cap fits. And your name would be?'

'Bernadette, Mister Stoner. Do you not recall me from last night?'

'I was preoccupied with the wicked ways of the world.' Stoner's Belfast tones stretched and compressed the breathing air between them, as he swung into the Harley's saddle, kicked up its stand and gestured for her to climb up behind him. 'You were wearing a great set of black jeans and a great set of tits, too. I always remember a great set of black jeans. Wrangler, by the cut of them. Tap me on the shoulder when you've arranged yourself. Hope you're wearing knickers. Doesn't do to scare the natives.' He fired up the big engine, which coughed into vocal activity, settling to the deep staccato off-beat grumble of such things.

She tapped his shoulder, easing back and sitting on her hands. 'You remember the jeans not the tits, Mister Stoner? Impressive in a man your age.'

He grinned away from her and rode off along the pavement. The crowd of pedestrian civilians parted before their steady loud progress, with hardly an overt glance in their direction. They were the object of all the attention at that time, but no one saw anything other than the bike ('It was a Harley. It was black – night black.') and the riders were hidden by the presence, the character of that bike itself ('There were two guys. There were a guy and a girl. There was just one guy and he was covered in tattoos. They both had beards. Huge black Harley…'). Stoner bounced the big blue-green machine off the pavement and rode the wrong way up a one-way street, ignoring the outrage of the oncoming cars, then pulled out into the faster traffic flowing on a major route, where he opened the throttle wide, fracturing the city traffic hum, buzz and hoot with a burst of artillery impressions from the Screamin' Eagle exhausts, their unsilenced roar reverberating from the tall glass fronts of the tall glass buildings.

Out of the city proper, pausing at Dublin Harley-Davidson to equip Bernadette with leather jeans, jacket, gloves and a helmet, and to equip the motorcycle with a tote bag to carry her civilian clothes. Stoner handed a plastic card to the cheerful salesman.

'Bike going well? And it's Mr Stoner, right?' The salesman chattered happily as he punched buttons on a card reader.

'Stoner's the name on the card, I hope.' The big man smiled in a vaguely menacing way. That salesman was unfazed; he met far more menacing types than this every day. He was happy in his work, was the salesman.

Then out into the country, the big motorcycle loping across the folded green countryside with the relaxed ease of a machine designed to tackle the American vastness, leaving a trail of thunder as it passed.

'You're not involved in this at all, are you?' Bernadette's opening gambit came as something of a surprise to Stoner, who had parked up and collected refreshment and had even paid for it. The motorcycle's hot and heavy metal ticked in quiet cooling conversation with itself.

'Involved with what?' He sipped at a bottle of weak beer. 'You're going to show me a man. Paddy appears to be his name. I'm going to kill him. That's as involved as I can get with anything. Hard to see how there could be much more involved than that. Frankly. Good ride, too, don't you think?' He sipped some more, admired the bike in the sunshine. 'They have a spirit, don't they? Some motorcycles, I mean. Some of them are almost ... I don't know ... animate.'

'You make it sound as though you're more affected by motorcycles than by people,' she sounded bewildered.

'Mostly, that's true. But in the same way that most people are just plodding, just padding, just ... pointless, so most motorcycles are the same. Some motorcycles, some people, just ... are more real. But yeah... seen from some viewpoints I prefer the company of motorcycles. Like this one. This one makes me want to climb back aboard and take a long ride. Lakes, loughs, beaches and mountains, maybe forests. It'll take us anywhere. People just disappoint. Just let you down. A motorcycle doesn't lie to you, pretend anything. It does what it does. Just like me. I'm here to kill a man, Bernadette, not to learn to love him nor to travel with him through the long halls of the night. Just to kill him. He's called Paddy. You know him somehow, I don't want to know how. I just need you to tell me where he'll be, and to get me there so I can pull the trigger, slide the blade. Whatever.'

'You make it sound so easy.'

'It is easy. It's extremely easy to kill a man. The reason we're wearing all this dead cow and Kevlar is because we are extremely easy to kill. Falling off a motorcycle can do it easily enough. D'you want another?' He gestured at her empty glass. 'I'll not drink much if that's OK. Need to stay sharp until the job's done. Which will be when, by the way?'

Bernadette stared at him. 'Are you truly so callous?'

'I'm not callous at all, Bernadette. Not at all. Paddy is nothing to me. He isn't an individual. He's just a target. There have been lots of targets down the years. Maybe Paddy's had lots of targets of his own, too.'

She paused. Then; 'Yes. He's responsible for...'

'I don't want to know, Bernadette. Truly. Thank you for trying so hard with me, but I truly do not care whether he's a second coming of Hitler or Mother Theresa reincarnate. He's just some guy, and I'm going to kill him. If you need some form of justification, that's great and I'm cool with that, but understand that I do not. I don't need it and I don't want it. I have no immortal soul. Tell me only what I need to know. I'll do the job and go home.'

'Back to England, that will be? Despite the voice, you're another bright Englishman come to interfere?'

Stoner shrugged, and sipped a little more. 'Whatever, Bernadette. If you won't tell me because I'm some stinking English pig, that's OK with me. Just tell the guy who tells both of us what to do and I'll take it from there.'

'It really doesn't matter to you?' She sounded increasingly amazed.

'We've been through that. How soon?'

'He'll be speaking at a club.' She passed a folded sheet of paper to him.

'And this would be where? Can you give me directions? Better yet, can you tolerate my company and the back seat of the bike and take me there?'

'Easy as that?'

'Yeah. Look and learn. If you want. I can buy a map if you prefer? Though you need to stay with me, in sight, at least.'

'You don't trust me?'

'How could I? I don't know you. I trusted that the girlie last night was who she said she was and look where that got me. I doubt that the boss will tolerate two identical mistakes in rapid succession. I doubt that he's where he is because of his generosity of spirit and sweet Christian kindness.'

Bernadette held up her hand, silencing him. 'Did she actually tell you she was me? Did she use my name?'

Stoner considered. 'No. Not that I remember. I walked in where angels fear to tread, frankly. But she knew who I was and why I was there.'

'You sure?'

'No. She's... she's not easy to remember. How's that, I wonder?'

'Could you recognise her? Again, I mean?'

Stoner leaned right back and drained the dregs of his drink in one single swallow. 'No. No. I can't picture her face and her voice is ... just like yours. That is truly strange. I have a fine memory, for faces, facts, for lots of things.'

'You've met Blesses and lived. Congratulations, Stoner.'

'Met what? You doing some religious nonsense now, Bernadette? Blesses? What's that when it's home? Benedictions from a man in a frock and a pointy hat?'

'She's weird. Simply that; weird. I could identify her; she used to be around a lot, in the troubles. Wherever she was there was a lot of trouble, always.'

'She's not alone in that, sister. But weird in what way?'

'When guys talk with her – and it's always guys, not girls – she just makes them believe her. Whatever nonsense she comes out with, they take it as God's own and act on it. Exactly like you did. Big eyes – what colour, by the way?'

'No idea.'

'How was I wearing my hair last night?'

'Tied back in a ponytail. Point taken. Fuck me.'

'Kind offer, graciously declined. Try to watch her from a distance if you see her again – if someone points her out, of course. Be careful. Just don't stare into her eyes. She's weird.'

'Like hypnotism? Some witchcraft like that?'

'Maybe. Do you trust me yet?'

'Nope. Less if anything. Mad story like that.' Stoner checked the time. 'Let's groove. Better to find the place in the light. Then if zombie-girl is there you can warn me.'

'I have to go with you?'

'Afraid so.'

'If I don't?'

Stoner shook his head. 'Bad question with worse answers. Imagine what you'd most like not to happen and that's what happens if you refuse. And then imagine what you'd most like to happen, and that's what will happen once the deed is done.'

'You mean what I think you mean?'

'Of course. Women are aroused by violence and demand the attentions of a demon lover to calm them afterwards.'

'You flatter yourself, Mr Stoner.' She smiled, shaking her head.

'Someone has to.'

oOo

By the book. They rolled into the evening, birds pausing in their evensong while the bike passed, resuming their celebrations as its mechanised thunder faded once more. Parked up. Left helmets locked to the motorcycle. Loitered.

'It's amazing. If I'd not seen it, I'd never have believed it.' Bernadette tied her long brown hair back and tucked it inside the leather of her jacket. 'It's like we're invisible.'

'Not really.' Stoner ran his hands through the short thick hair of his scalp, removing the sci-fi pattern left by the helmet's lining. 'They can see us perfectly well. They're just ignoring us. Because we are biker scum. It's great. I did this a lot in Belfast. It's a stunt, just like the stunt pulled by your pal Blesses. Is she really called that? I was thinking about her as we rode over. Need to meet her again. It'll bother me otherwise.'

'Some things do bother you then? You're not the unfeeling man of steel emotions you say you are?'

'Many things bother me, Bernadette. Killing assholes of no value to me isn't one of them. Not yet. Maybe it comes with maturity, like a fat gut and arthritis. Something to look forward to. I like to understand things. I think it's part of being more human and less ape. That and a passion for pizza. Stand you a pizza afterwards if you like?'

'You serious? You're going to kill someone and take me out for pizza afterwards?'

'You have a problem with that? Why so? Hang on, enlightenment needs to wait a while. Here's your pal Paddy.'

'Do you have a gun?'

'No.'

'What're you going to do? He's got, what, two bodyguards.'

'Two. They both have guns. I'll just borrow one.'

'How?'

'Men can be generous. Stay here. Please stay here. I'm being polite. Dream of pizza. I'll try not to be long. Don't let anyone near the bike. If anyone goes near the bike, rock it or kick it or something; the alarm would waken the very dead.' And he strode into the gathering crowd, approaching the bodyguard, a man of much meat and muscle and a shining bald head, who had remained outside after Paddy and the other muscle had entered the building. There was a short conversation, they walked around a corner and vanished from Bernadette's field of view.

Stoner reached into his pocket, pulled out a crumpled piece of paper, rummaged some more and produced a pen. He waved them at the hulking bodyguard. 'Paddy watched me play last night in the city and asked me to catch up with him.'

The muscle man nodded slowly. 'You did all the provo hymns. I heard about that. Yeah.'

Stoner swung a right-handed full-knuckle punch to the guard's temple. He staggered. Stoner's left hand provided a balancing blow. The guard fell back against the building. Stoner swung out his arms like wings to either side of him, brought the two hard fists in together, one to each temple. The guard's eyes bulged and rolled in different directions. He slid gracelessly down the wall and his head fell forward onto his chest. Stoner stepped back, balanced like a murderous ballet dancer and swung his heavy biker-booted foot, catching the guard's chin with his toe, breaking the jaw at its hinge with the skull, and driving the man's head backwards into the rough red brickwork of the wall. Silenced. Permanently.

He patted down the deflating corpse, removed a black SIG Sauer from its shoulder holster, removed the magazine, weighed its contents in his hand and replaced it, walked around the building in the glowing shadow of the evening, checking its emergency exits, in case of emergencies and a need to exit. As he completed the lap, passing the recumbent and lifeless guard where he'd left him, Stoner met the remaining guard, who was heading his way, presumably in search of his colleague.

'Have you seen...' was all he managed, before the black SIG Sauer in Stoner's right hand spat the first of its shells into the large man's heroic stomach, the sound of the shot effectively dulled by the naturally sound absorbent material which is body fat. The guard stared at Stoner in utter confusion. Reflecting that there was an argument for employing bodyguards who could think and react, rather than merely appear menacing, Stoner planted the muzzle of the black SIG Sauer beneath the guard's heroic multiple chins and fired the second of its shells upward and through the cranial cavity, a space usually occupied by a brain, although in the case of the guard that was a theoretical occupation rather than an proven fact. Once again, the sound of the shot was absorbed by Nature's generous fatty suppressor. Stoner caught the second corpse a little before it understood the revised nature of its condition, and helped it to settle next to the equally lifeless first guard.

A professional military career induces a certain level of tidiness and even a little respect in many men, and while Stoner was arranging the two guards neatly, so that they might possibly appear to be resting, drunken rather than deceased, a hand landed on his left shoulder. Before he turned his head, his right hand had refilled itself with the black SIG Sauer, and he rose rapidly to his feet, his outstanding soldier's hand / eye co-ordination seeking a suitable target for a third shot.

'Easy, tiger.' It was Bernadette.

'Weren't you staying with the Harley?' There was no stress to Stoner's speech. A simple enquiry, that was all.

'Blesses is here,' said Bernadette. 'You need to know that, and you need to remember to keep away from her.'

'And to avoid her basilisk stare?' Stoner smiled a grim smile.

'More Medusa than basilisk, man.'

'Yeah, whatever. Is she with Paddy-boy?'

'Not when I saw her. She was in the lobby, checking out the faces of the faithful.'

Stoner paused only for a second. 'Would she recognise you in all your newfound biker-chic finery, Bernadette?'

'I'd doubt that. We're not friends at all, now are we?'

'How would I know?' Stoner was plainly hatching a plan of some sort. 'OK. Go in, be inconspicuous as you can, find either of the two fire exits at the back of the hall and open the door. I'll go in through there and do what needs to be done.'

'And this fine pair?' She included the two men in a single gesture. 'They're out of action for the duration?'

Stoner nodded, checking his watch as he did so. 'They are. No worries here. Go now.'

'And if the fire door's alarmed?'

'Then there'll be more noise, more confusion. None of this is a concern. Noise, more noise, less noise, I don't care. I care about bullets and blades – and your zombie-bitch, Blesses, if she's as dangerous as you say.'

'She is.'

'Then keep an eye on her. And go now. Time marches.'

Only a few minutes later, the fire door nearer to Stoner and his silent audience of two banged open, framing a slightly breathless Bernadette. 'This biker gear is hot,' she panted.

'It's supposed to be, remember?' Stoner passed her, entering the building at a brisk walk and punching the handgrip of the black SIG Sauer into a red fire alarm switch as he passed it. Bells rang at once, impressively loudly. Stoner ducked through a curtain into the main hall, spotted his target standing by the stage's single microphone, dropped to his knee, braced his right arm with a triangulating left arm, steadied the black SIG Sauer and fired. One shot, two shots and a third for symmetry. Paddy the target was dead from the first impact, the second completed the destruction of his handsome head, and the third shell was lost somewhere in the madness and pandemonium of it all.

Stoner turned to leave, quietly calm among the chaos, to be confronted by Blesses. And her knife, a long shining blade which she sank into his midriff with all the strength she had. Stoner folded around it, wincing, as Bernadette seized his assailant from behind, pinning the attacker's arms to her side, although the knife remained in her grip. Stoner smacked the pistol against the side of Blesses' head, once, twice, and she dropped the knife and slumped to her knees. Bernadette stared at him, astonished that he still appeared to be living and breathing, not ruptured, bleeding out and generally dying in front of her.

'How...?'

'Kevlar. In the jacket. Can't beat it. And the pants. Bike gear is good like that. I'll have a hellish bruise, though. It hurts already. What do you want me to do with your friend? Quickly now, there are sirens and we need to leave.'

Bernadette produced a pair of stout plastic zip-ties and strapped Blesses' two hands behind her with them. 'The sirens come at my call, Stoner. I'm police. Weren't you told that?'

Stoner grinned widely. 'Sister! Excellent. How excellent is that?' He reversed the pistol, wiped its body and grip down with his scarf and fitted it into Blesses' right hand, passing her forefinger through the trigger guard, squeezing all together, then letting the weapon fall through her limp fingers to the floor. 'You'd be doing me a favour if you'd wipe down the clip at some point. Good to work with you. Hope we do it again, Bernadette.' He planted a kiss on her forehead and was gone, out through the emergency exit, as uniforms entered through the front of the hall, leaving Bernadette waving to attract their attention to her and away from him.

oOo

'You enjoyed the motorcycle, sir?' The Harley-Davidson salesman had accepted the return of the hire bike, and was checking it over, inspecting for signs of falling or abuse.

'Loved it.' Stoner's response was quiet and considered. 'I've always wanted one, somehow, but somehow never owned a Harley of my own. How much is it? This one? This very one?'

The salesman displayed no surprise. 'I can't sell you this exact machine, sir, but over there is a new one, a model mostly intended for Europe, baggage and screens, hardly any chrome, all black. I can have that ready for you tomorrow, registered, and taxes paid.' He named a figure. Stoner passed him a plastic card.

'Take the money from that, if you please. Your part of Ireland's a lovely fine place indeed. I've a few days spare, would rather ride back to the North than take a plane. Know what I mean?'

The salesman nodded. 'Coffee?' he asked. 'Let's do coffee while I take down your particulars. It won't take long. Not long at all.'

<< oOo >>

Two Wrongs

BACK THEN...

'Is this a habit or a hobby?' The mountainous black man aimed his question at the more conventionally proportioned white woman. 'Do you often date your husband's buddies while he's away?' Spoken softly and with a gentle smile, but a serious question nonetheless.

'There's a first time for everything.' She smiled right back at him.

'Indeed there is, but the real question is whether this is that first time?' The mirrored smiles were moving easily and steadily into a world of flirtation. She looked down.

'Not exactly.'

'Thanks for that. We should aim for a little honesty here. At least between the two of us.'

She sighed, with dramatic intent.

'Weren't you with the MPs before all the SEAL stuff? I should've known that dinner with a cop – even an ex-cop – would be all about questions, questions, questions. Can we order a drink yet? That's if you can slide one in between sessions under the bright lights.'

'One more question, just one, and then we can call over the guy with the shy waiter look and demand that he exchange our good money for his bad drinks. One question, OK? Then that's it.'

'Ask away.'

'You leavin' Davey? That's it. That's the question.'

'No.'

'Cool. I had to ask, Rose. I can't do a relationship right now. I'd be lying to you if I pretended that was what we were doing. The beautiful babe, big bad guy thing? That is one hundred percent good. I do so like that. And you are one beautiful babe, babe.'

'And you are the big bad boy, huh? So mean kick-ass bad-ass big bad black man that you need to act like Mister Policeman before buying a lady a drink? Hey... what's that all about? You never were much of a Puritan.'

'It's not that, baby Rose. It's just taking a recce before entering a minefield. Know what I mean? I gotta know what we're doing ... before we do it. No headroom for fuckups right now. Combat tour ahead. Bad dirty stuff. I ain't leaving no-one behind me. No-one grieves for me.'

'Not without your very own say-so?'

'You got it.' He pointed a hard stare over her shoulder, aimed and fired. The waiter arrived, at the double. Took his orders like a good dumb waiter and left to fulfil them.

'You always in charge?'

'You betcha. The only way to stay alive. It's the way I am, crazy lady. That way you can rely on me and ... I can rely on me.'

'Yes sir! You Navy guys all act like this?'

'Like what, exactly?' He paused. The waiter appeared with drinks, wondered about a food order, and agreed that it could wait for a few further minutes while they discussed the menu. A menu neither of them had even picked up yet.

'Like some insane control freak, is what. You ask a lady for an evening out and before you've even bought her a drink you're making with the terms and conditions, sub-clauses and provisos and what-ifs and dark hints about future consequences. It never occurred to you that this lady might just have wanted to have a good time, to get laid maybe? Can we have some old-fashioned bad boy bullshit soon?'

'Yes ma'am. Chief Petty Officer Stretch at your service, ma'am. Glad to oblige.' They both laughed. He reached across the table, took her hand.

'What say we read the menu and choose some food? Shore us up for the night ahead. There may be stormy waters, and we need to be prepared.'

She flicked open the menu. 'What do you fancy?'

'You call it, ma'am Rose. You lead and I will surely follow.'

'But only as far as the bedroom, is that it?' Mockery smouldered in her eyes, but still she smiled.

'There is no further than that, sweet princess. So far and no further. Are we going to eat any time soon? Choose something for me. Plan ahead. This big bad body of mine demands fuelling if it's in for a long haul.'

'Do you do the long haul, Stretch?'

'Surely do, ma'am. Depending on the stamina of the company of course. The long march is a Navy tradition.'

'Isn't it armies that march on their stomachs? Don't you Navy guys have ballast or bunkers or something? And why are you asking about Davey? You bothering about him in this? You best buddies, something? If so, speak now, soldier. Sailor.'

'Seals march on their bellies. It's their only way. Just watch one next time you meet one.

'As for Davey... No. Hardly know him. I just can't be tangled up in wreckage right now. That's just how it is. Nothing noble. I promise you there's not a noble bone in this sailor's body. Any case, no noble man would set sail leaving a lovely lady like you, ma'am, waiting in port. It would be a terrible distraction, I reckon.'

'You reckon?'

'I do so believe, ma'am. Just imagine, some asshole towelhead raises his RPG intent upon my immediate personal disadvantage and this sad sailor here remembers that he forgot to send you some flowers that day. Terrible thought. Easily distract me from dodging incoming, then ... boom! That is your fatal charm.'

'You so do not do flowers! Are you telling me that you send flowers? To your women?'

'I can see that your life will be a long voyage of discovery, Rose. Can we eat yet?'

oOo

'These are a true wonder of Nature.' Stretch cradled a breast in each hand. 'A delight. Beauties.' And indeed they were.

'Hmm... More a tribute to the silicone surgeon's subtle art, sailor. But thanks.'

'Really? I would never have known,' he lied easily, the small dishonesty as perfect as the breasts in his hands. He stepped back, features carefully composed into an expression combining stunned admiration, wonder and awe. Rose beamed at him, slid his hands down her body until his thumbs hitched up with the waistband of her panties. With a sigh, she returned her own hands to her own breasts, squeezed them softly; his hands, elastic attached, continued down to her ankles, and she stepped from the last of her clothes, Stretch kneeling like a supplicant before her.

He rose again to his full height, towering a full foot above her, his hands now resting on her bare shoulders and holding her at arm's length.

'Let me pause for a moment in appreciation.' He looked her up and down. 'Thank you O Lord, for thy bounty, thy wonders to behold.'

'Oh hush now!' she laughed with delight at his shameless flattery. 'Arms up, sailor boy,' and with some effort she reached high enough to lift his T-shirt from him, threw it aside and ran her hands over his massive chest. He reached for her then, but she pushed him away, gently.

'Look at yourself, sailor.' Her lips pursed, her fingernails tracing the neat tracks of well-stitched scars, first across his left bicep, then around his left side, between two ribs, stopping before his heart. 'Lucky sailor boy,' said quietly. He nodded, said nothing. She reached for his shorts, lowered them, stepped back...

'Jeez. Us. Sweet holy Jesus and all His saints. What is this?'

'We call this the torpedo, ma'am. We call this the black torpedo.' He watched her face, shining white teeth splitting his shining black face. 'Appears he wants to be your own special friend.'

'This...' she wrapped both hands around him, one above the other. Moved them apart along the length. Then further apart. Marvelled at how she could almost close the tips of her fingers to within an inch of their thumbs. Maybe more. She squeezed a hand experimentally, aiming to touch finger and thumb together. That distance between fingertip and thumb grew by maybe fifty percent. 'This is why they call you Stretch, Stretch? Because I do believe I can understand the reason why. Fuck. Me.'

'That is the idea, I guess. Now would be the time to change your mind. No dishonour in a negotiated surrender.'

'Change your own mind, sailor. I'd not miss this for the world. Be a ride to remember, I guess.'

'Maybe so.'

'All your own work?'

'Pardon me?'

'Men can do implants too, I'm told.'

'Is that so? No ma'am, I am one hundred percent me.'

'No ... chemical assistance?'

'No need. Not yet. Great things come in threes, and I am sure that this will be a great thing.'

'Threes.' She looked up, looked right into his eyes. 'This comes in threes?'

'The black torpedo has been blessed by a higher power with both stamina and staying power.'

'A higher staying power?'

'Mine not to reason why, Rose. Mine just to rise to the occasion. And to ensure that my lady receives everything she deserves. Even if she be my lady for just one night.' He stood away from her, strode to his discarded jacket. 'I have of course thought of everything and I have brought with me suitably dimensioned precautionary countermeasures. Reinforcements. Do you have a colour preference, ma'am?'

Despite her attempt to maintain a straight face, Rose burst into rattling coughs of laughter; healthy, bumper-sized snorts of amusement. Her eyes shone with delight.

'A colour preference?'

'You may find a gentle pinky shade less ... ah ... terrifying than one hundred percent black man. Ma'am.'

'Do other ... girls ... find preference in pink?' She spluttered less, though her smile grew wider.

'Not so far, Ma'am, but I am prepared. This is the navy way.'

'I am an army wife, Chief Petty Officer, and I have countermeasures of my own in place. I can repel my own boarders. You can leave off with the pink plastic. Jeez. Can we stop negotiating and just fuck? Do you never stop talking?'

Stretch rose to his full six and one-half feet and flexed his pecs and his biceps; his cock stood proud like the icebreaker it was.

'I should just read you your rights, and maybe a short version of the Treaty of Utrecht, whereby you gain permission to occupy this particular rock...'

Rose caught his right hand and slapped it between her legs. 'Shut it, sailor man, and do your duty...'

oOo

'Just stay still, Stretch. Just lie there beside me, inside me. I want to feel this big boy relax, to leave me quietly as he dozes.' She squeezed her thighs around him.

'He won't doze, Rose. He's just waiting for his new best friend to have a rest.'

'No joking, sailor. Let's just...'

'No joke, Rose.' The huge sailor flexed his hips and squeezed himself into her again. All the way. 'And no rest for the wicked.'

She smiled into the pillow, away from him. Eased herself around him, feeling the internal hydraulics, pressures and pleasures.

'We been wicked, then?' she mused. His huge hands closed over her breasts again, caressing gently, arousing her once more with their easy controlled power, restrained strength. Mounting pressure from the palms of his hands, gentle light stimulus from the tips of their fingers. Her pale skin shading to red beneath the movement of his black fingers.

'We need to be diligent, be vigilant. We need to practise more. That way we can attain true wickedness. The path to enlightened wickedness...'

'Stretch?'

'Uh-huh?'
'Shut up.'
'Ma'am.'

oOo

'Rose?'
'Hmm?'
'I believe that I have met my angel. My own angel.'
'Shut up.'
'Rose?'
'Hmm?'
'Can we do this again?'
'Hmm. Oh. Stretch?'
'Rose.'
'You've had your three strikes. I'm out. So shut up.'
'Ma'am.'

oOo

NOW

'Got plans for your leave, you?' Canteen clatter, canteen chatter, three CPOs, dressed in neat clean fatigues, cell phones before them, all switched on for the first time in ten weeks. Stretch McCann, like the other officers, scanned through the accumulated mass of messages, voicemail and clutter, listening, reading, replying, deleting and occasionally saving as he went. He sat back, stretched his arms, linked his big hands behind his big head and heaved. Muscles bulged, tendons cracked, joints re-seated themselves.

'Time in the gym. Time on the range. Maybe play some piano ... if I can find one.'

'Sounds more like time with the unit than furlough, you. She not called, your special one? She not calling for more of the torpedo?'

Stretch worked the big muscles in his neck. 'Nope. Maybe baby don't love me no more.'

'She got a sister?'

'There's always a sister, Bru.' But he was surprised and saddened, he had expected to find something from Rose. A welcome note. Even a warning that she was required for family duties would have been something. That was, after all, the way it was. But nothing. A big zero. Plenty from other friends, other lady friends, but zip from Rose. Invites for drinks, for bar trawls, for jaunts ... for some musical adventures carrying him away from Little Creek, Virginia.

'Got an invite here to play some bad jazz in Nawleenz, Bru. May do that. Always love that.'

'If she don't call?'

'Yeah. If she don't.'

''Cause you don't call her?'

'Yeah. If I don't call her.'

'And you won't. Either you got big pride, Stretch, or she got another man, and you know 'bout it and you ain't interfering. That's 'cause you are a good man.'

'Can't be because I am a good man. Never mind me, what you doing for ten days furlough, Bru?'

'Remindin' my wife that she married to a sailor, remindin' my kids that their pop is a sailor, then whorin' and drinkin' til the Navy send an MP to collect me from my dereliction.'

'Ain't no MP alive could haul you down, Bru.'

'Oh yeah. Every plan has a flaw. If I made good plans I'd be an officer by now.'

Both men laughed, the shared knockabout of veteran buddies.

'You ever fancy takin' a wife of your own, Stretch?'

'Not while others leave their own deserted, Bru. They occupy my time.'

'Now. Now you don't mean that, Stretch McCann. You just ain't encountered the correct lady. Not yet. But you will.'

Stretch smiled. 'I already did. I already met her. I met several hers. They all married off to good men. I am proud of the fine taste displayed by my fellow men. I salute them all.'

The third man, their Master Chief, spoke. He spoke quietly, as was his way.

'You don't find it flat-out exhausting, fucking the wives of other men, McCann? You don't find it demeaning? Demeaning for all concerned?'

Stretch reached for his jacket, lifted it, dropped it back onto its hanger. Flicked invisible lint from its shoulders. 'Sometimes.' The banter had died in his eyes. 'Sometimes, Master Chief. But...' his voice trailed for a moment. 'It ain't always what it seems. No offence intended.' The Master Chief's wife of a few short years had deserted him for a civilian while he was serving overseas and out of mind as well as out of sight.

'None taken, McCann. You don't worry about the hearts you break? You're a reliable man. Dependable. A good brother in the long fight. But you steal the wives of other serving men? You enjoy that? You feel good about that?'

'I do, Master Chief.' Stretch lifted the jacket, shook it gently and furled it over his wide shoulders. 'I do feel good. The only heart that gets broken is my own heart. The only life wasted is my own life.' He smiled at the older, smaller man. 'It's just a time-share. It don't mean anything. Not to them. They safe with me. They know that. Dinner, fuck and goodnight. Everybody needs that at some point. Everybody left at home for months at a time.'

'Hell, Master Chief; it's almost a public service!' Bru dived in to support his comrade. 'And she's an army wife, any case. Not navy. There's a difference.'

Stretch stood silent, towering, distant. The Master Chief walked to him, slapped him on one huge bicep. 'It's not the wives I worry about. It's you, McCann. This latest one is under your skin. And from the pain in your eyes and the strain in your voice she's gone. You going to use your free time to find her, to forget her, to find another, or...'

'I'll use the week to play piano, Chief. Play a lot of that deep south voodoo music to banish her ghost. There's always a festival.' Stretch flexed his hands dramatically; a wide white smile split his dark features. He and both his brother SEALs nudged knuckles and braced forearms. 'And I guess I'll work out some, get some muscle onto these skinny bones. But first I reckon I'll take a drive past a house I know, and check that she still walking and talking ... even if it's not with me. I'm OK with that.'

oOo

Stretch McCann climbed from the cab, slapped it on the roof, rose to his full height as it pulled away. A considerably smaller and younger woman bounced into him, making a theatrical attempt to knock him off balance.

'Sailor!' she sang out.

'How can you tell?' He adjusted his sailor's cap atop his shining black sailor's head, straightened the trouser creases in his sailor's uniform.

'It's a gift,' she said, punched him lightly at belt height. 'A gift. You coming to stay here again? It's been a while. You away a lot. A whole lot.' She smiled. 'But it's sure good to see you again.'

'Ain't no place like home.' Stretch stretched. 'Damn cabs don't get no taller.'

'And you don't get no smaller, sailor.'

'This is true. You been holding the mails for me? Do I ... like ... have some mails? Does anybody remember me?' He laughed. Dropped his kitbag, lifted the smaller woman and swung her around like a child on a fairground ride. 'Hey, Betsy, you don't get no weightier. You not eating?'

She rattled with laughter as he landed her on her feet. 'No more Betsy, sailor Stretch. I'm grown up. Elspeth now please. You need to be calling me Elspeth.'

The big man hefted his baggage, swung them both onto the path to the building before them. 'You gone straight past Elisabeth and all the way to a new name while I been gone? That's cool stuff. Hey, look. I'm an old man, I got no memory left. Can I call you Betsy?'

She laughed some more. 'No. Elspeth.'

'Elspeth it is then, Betsy. Forever Elspeth.'

She grabbed his free hand, pulled on it. 'Come on now, come see Ma. She has your mail, and she'll have seen us and brewed up some coffee, that shittery muck you like.'

'Hickory, babe. Hickory. Your ma is an outstanding lady.'

'Hickory, shittery. Isn't that a poem? You going to call me Elspeth? That's cool. Pops says I'll always be Betsy. Semper Betsy, he says. That's Latin. How come Pops knows Latin? Do you know Latin, sailor Stretch?'

'Nope. Your pop knows it because he's a Marine. They speak Latin. It confuses the enemy. Semper means always. He's telling you that he'll always be there for you. He's a good guy.' He rolled his eyes. 'For a Marine.'

'He says it means I'll always be his Betsy. Makes sense to him, I guess.'

One of the side-by-side twinned front doors opened, a wave of powerful hickory coffee aroma rolled out to meet them, like a welcome mat, and more useful than any red carpet. Elspeth and Stretch swanned into the house, coffee and greetings waiting for them both on the kitchen table.

'Welcome home, Stretch. Long time.'

'Yeah. Hello Evangeline. You look so good. And so,' Stretch skated sugar and cream across the table, 'so does Elspeth.' They all laughed, all three of them.

'Hey mom, this tastes like ordinary coffee. Smells like … hickory. What gives?'

Her mother smiled sweetly at her daughter. 'You hate, loathe and detest hickory coffee, Betsy. Always tell me how much you hate it. You got straight brew. Stretch gets the man stuff. Bagdad special brew, eh Stretch?'

Elspeth was having none of this. 'I'm grown. I am an adult, mother. I can drink grown-up coffee.' She made a little-girl face. 'I can try.'

Stretch passed over his mug. 'Try?'

And took it back. Her face was a picture. Every picture tells a story.

'How old, you?' he asked.

'Sixteen.'

'Old enough then. Time to start practicing.'

'That tastes worse than whiskey.'

'You drink whiskey, huh?'

'Only when I can. Only when mom's not looking.' She looked up. Mother and daughter smiled a shared smile. 'And I know when to leave. You old folk got catch-up to do, huh?' She got up from the table, went on her interrupted way.

The two adults considered each other. A silent stand-off.

'Evangeline.' Stretch sipped and nodded his appreciation. 'What's the haps? All good here? That no-good brute husband of yours off saving the world, or making it safe for the white man or something?' They both laughed.

'Long time, Stretch. You been spending time with someone? A special someone?'

'Been fighting out in the hot lands. There was someone ... someone special to me, but she's gone. Guess I wasn't special to her. Works both ways, huh?'

'Yeah.' Evangeline poured for them both. 'You really taking cream with that now? Your first sign of age, huh?'

'Weakness comes to us all. I'll need to open up the house. Learn where everything is, do cleaning and decoration, maybe some paint...' his voice tailed away. 'Time filling, you know? I'd expected to be travelling a little, tourist stuff.'

'With that special friend?'

'Yeah.'

'Your place is fine. I even watered your plants.'

Stretch rolled his eyes, turned his head half away and gazed at her sidelong. 'I don't got no plants.'

'Sure you do. I had a feeling you'd be home.'

'You did? That's one hell of an intuition. You reading tea leaves? Entrails? Magic woman voodoo?' They smiled together one more.

'It just felt right. And a girl hears tales, stories, especially if she keeps her ears open and her mouth shut.'

'She does?'

'She does. She sure does. Whether there's truth to those tales, only those in the know, know, right? But sometimes if it sounds right then it is right. You hear me, sailor?'

'Uh-huh. You're telling me something, right?'

'Davey Santos.'

'About him? He's Army.'

'Yeah. How well do you know him, Stretch?'

'Hardly at all. Say hi to. We'd bump along I guess. He's Army.'

'Yeah. That makes it all right, I suppose?'

'Speak plain to me now, Evangeline. If you're going where I think you're going there needs to be room for understanding.'

'Can I speak plainly now? Can I?'

A pause settled on their conversation, extended into pantomime coffee drinking, lip-smacking appreciation, sub-vocal murmurs of thanks. Stretch broke the truce.

'OK. Hit me.'

'Davey's wife. You know her better than you know him, I guess?'

'I guess. Rose. She called Rose, she.'

'Uh-huh. Rose is in a home now. An infirmary. You know that, big guy?'

Stretch shook his head. 'No. No I did not.' He closed his eyes, placed his coffee mug gently onto the table. Very gently, as though it was likely to break. 'She's not well?' A question.

'How ... well do you know her? Be honest, Stretch. Remember this is me, not some barracks buddy.'

'She's the special one I thought I'd be spending special time with, Evangeline. Should I drink something a little stronger?'

'Best not. Think you need to be all together now.'

'You knew, right? About Rose. Did you know she was the special one?'

'She's Davey's wife, Stretch. Not yours. A wife is not a girlfriend.'

'Marriage is just a temporary thing, Evangeline. Except for you guys.' He tried to sound light, relaxed. 'Divorce is easy, mostly painless. So they say. She got no kids, no ties. On her own an awful lot. Young woman. Just natural.'

'She's in the infirmary, Stretch. Story goes that you were involved. Storefront stories, you know?'

'Nope. Not at all. I've been overseas, the Navy does that. Never laid a hand on her.' He paused. 'Not like that. Not, y'know, violent. Is that what they're saying? Be careful now, heads break easy. Like eggs. Harder to fix than eggs.'

'No, that's not it. Not what they're saying. It's all hearsay, Stretch, all rumour. No facts. Few anyway. She's been there, been ... unwell ... for most of your tour, and the whole of Davey's tour too. Mostly.' She caught his questioning stare and replied before he could speak. 'Some kind of accident, maybe a breakdown, I think. Maybe two guys was too much, what do you say, big guy? It's only rumours, but the infirmary's a broken brains place, not a place for broken arms and legs and shit. Excuse me.'

Stretch had risen to his feet, as relaxed as a volcano about to erupt, calm as a kettle of over-boiled water. He walked carefully to the kitchen window, gazed out.

'She's special, Evangeline. No word of a lie. The one. The first one for a long time to be special.'

'She knew that? You tell her that?' Evangeline rose, crossed the wide room and stood next to him. Took his huge hand in her own. 'You tell her she's special? Your special one?'

'Reckon so.' He took her small brown hand in both of his huge black ones, looked into her eyes. 'Reckon I did. There's a ring in my kitbag, Evangeline. Diamond ring. Damned ring now, seems like. What you say.' He stepped back from her, releasing her hand gently. 'Guess I need some time. Guess... Guess I'd better check out the house, check on the plants.' He walked to the door, careful, economical in his movements like many huge men, dwarfing their environments. He appeared bigger than he was. Somehow. Evangeline watched every step.

'I'll come knocking in an hour, Stretch. No rushing off. You go unpack, brew up, take no booze, y'know? Not one drop. I'll be knocking in an hour. We'll talk more then. OK? Say OK to me and mean it.'

He stopped in the doorway, turned to face her, though his gaze was on nothing in that room.

'Yeah. OK. One hour. Don't be late. One hour and five and I'll be heading out. There's favours I can call in. I need to see her. Got that, Miss Evangeline?'

'Got it. Be your own friend now, Stretch. Be your own special friend.'

Stretch walked through the out door, turned ninety degrees right, walked a little way, turned ninety degrees right again, and stood facing another front door. His own. The door was unlocked, Evangeline was watching from her window. He turned the handle and entered, left the door open, walked into the hallway and dropped his bags. Gently enough. Walked steadily through the clean rooms, checked that the water was heated, stripped, showered and dressed again. Opened every window. Switched on a radio. Switched it off again. Dug into his baggage, found the diamond ring in its handsome box, opened the lid of the box and stood it on a low table, facing the best guest chair. Found two glasses and a fresh bottle of Jim Beam to fill them. Left the bottle sealed, sat in his favourite oldest chair and waited. Sailors know how to wait. They do it well. Calmly.

Exactly on the hour, the front door opened. The evening was approaching. Stretch sat still, specialist sniper stillness, long night watch stillness. Evangeline seated herself opposite. Broke the seal on the bottle of Beam and poured two glasses. A big fill for him, smaller for her.

'I spoke with Saul.' She paused. 'You want a light on?'

He shook his head. Calm.

'Saul says hi. He told me to give you all I got. About Rose Santos. Nothing more.' They both smiled gently at the shared conceit. Stretch poured another finger into her glass, raised his own.

'OK.' They drank, slowly.

'Betsy... Elsbeth's sleeping over with some friends. I'll keep you company a while. I don't want you alone.'

'Kind but unnecessary, Evangeline. I'm too old and too wise to harm myself.'

'Not you I'm worried about. Getting harmed, I mean.'

'OK. Carry on.' He sipped some more, then emptied the glass in one swallow. Refilled it.

'Rose had an accident,' she began. Stretch maintained both calm and silence. He nodded; she continued.

'Strange thing. She drove her car into a truck down by the mall. Her own fault. Several witnesses. She just drove under the trailer. Straight across the red light, no braking, no skid marks.'

Stretch raised his eyes to hers. 'She driving that old Brit heap she had?'

Evangeline nodded. 'Yeah. The MG. Her classic, she called it.'

'Shit. Hideous toy wheels. Sort-of car substitute thing.' Stretch sat back. 'What happened?'

'You got it already.'

'Yeah. I hear what you say, sweet Evangeline, but what happened? Rose kept the car in top condition, paid that shop out of ... wherever it is. Too much money for a rustbox like that. Brakes fail? Lights fail? It day or night? What? Tell me.' He raised his full glass, looked at it, replaced it still full on their shared table.

Evangeline carried on looking at her drink, like it contained all the answers to questions she knew were here for the asking. 'Car was good. Daylight. Middle of the morning. Clear view and several witnesses.'

'Brakes were OK?' Stretch was doing the dog with a bone routine. 'No sun in her eyes?'

'All good.'

'Damn. Hot damn. Damn it all to hell. And back again.' He raised his glass, put it down again, still full. Then he stood up, suddenly, rose to his full height and towered over the room. Picked up his full glass, emptied it. Refilled and emptied it again. Refilled it and subsided to his seat.

'There's more, Rose,' he said, quietly. 'Give it to me.' He closed his eyes, adding to the approach of evening. 'And where is she now? I need to see her. How is she?'

'I'll lay it to you like it comes to me, Stretch. They say she done it deliberate. That she done it because Davey knew about you and all the pain that followed his finding out was too much for her. That morning he went back to his unit and ... what? ... an hour later she was under a truck.'

'She'd not do that, Evangeline. Not Rose. Far too straight for that.'

'That's the other thing they say. That she was well off her head. Far out of it. Stoned, trippin', somethin'.'

'Nonsense.' Stretch dealt an absolute. 'She didn't use, not at all. Nothing.' He paused, considered. 'And the Army, the Army wives are blaming me? Is that it?'

She simply nodded in reply. Eyes brimming but held in check.

'I can see that. Where is she now? How is she?'

Evangeline told him the name, the address, the manner of institution which contained and maintained her. Told a story of sprains, fractures, cracked ribs and contusions, and the most serious head injury imaginable. Forehead into a steel and wood steering wheel, no airbags and a lap strap rather than a seat belt. Head scissored down and forward; knees the reverse. Easier on the knees than on the head. Brains all shook up. The future was dark. The body was functional. Nobody lived there anymore.

Evangeline wept then. Night fell over them both.

oOo

'Mrs Santos. Mrs Rose Santos.' The huge Navy SEAL towered over the desk. He spoke quietly in a tone of familiar command. 'I would like to visit her.' He handed over his Navy ID, stood relaxed. Vast and relaxed.

'Mister McCann.' The receptionist could plainly read. A valuable skill in a receptionist to an infirmary. 'You're not on my list.' She looked up from her inevitable screen. 'I have a list,' she explained, carefully, as if to an idiot. Stretch was familiar with idiots. He was a Chief Petty Officer in the Navy.

'I'd be surprised if I were on that list, Ma'am.' He smiled. 'I've been in...' he paused for deliberate effect. 'I've been out of the country. In action. Navy service. You'll no doubt hold another list, a no entry list. I won't be on that, either. That because Mrs Santos is an Army wife and I'm a Navy man. Army and Navy. Never talk. You'd not think we're on the same side.' He smiled, sharing the confidential wisdom of the world with the flattered flunkey.

'We're old friends. Go way back. When I was advised of her ... misfortune, I came straight up. Davey – Mr Santos – is on duty overseas, or I'd have brought him too. You got a tough job, Ma'am, and I'm glad to see you taking it seriously.' He smiled. A heart melted and she supplied directions and an address.

He found Rose sitting in a chair by the side of her bed in a room she obviously shared with another woman. The other woman was lying on her bed, sound asleep. The sleep of the drugged or the dying. Stretch removed his service cap and whispered his hello. There was no reply. Rose was recognisably Rose, but not the Rose he remembered. Her face was puffed, discoloured, distorted, her hair short, and shaved in places. He crossed silently to her side, seated himself on the edge of the bed, reached for, found and grasped her hand. It was warm, healthy. He squeezed it gently, then firmly. No response. None.

'Hey, Rose.' He spoke softly, but close to her ear. 'Rose, darling. Come back to me.' She blinked. He reached for, found and grasped her other hand. 'I've come back, baby. Now it's your turn.' She blinked again. Her mouth slipped open and she began to drool. Her eyes looked independently at different portions of wall, but not at him. One of them, the left, wandered off on its own, aimed with no focus at nothing in particular and ceased to move. She sighed, and drooled some more. She'd been doing this for some time, judging by the state of her gown.

Stretch rose, slowly, steadily and without threat, and moved to the open window. Turned back to her, approached her face on, reached out and lifted her, chair as well, turned and walked out the door, mindful of the delicacy of the burden he carried. To an open door and down into the garden. The sun shone down, nature was strong in noisy activity, and he stood the chair where its occupant could take in the view of the wide gardens, the hum of it all and the light. Rose sagged, limp in the chair, her eyes closed.

'She's stable, if nothing else.' A kind voice, a white coat man had approached, a doctor by his badge. Held out a hand. Stretch took it.

'Good idea to bring her outside. She doesn't know anything about it, but it can't do her any harm. You family, sir?'

Stretch shook his head, his attention back on Rose, little interest bar common politeness in the medical man. 'Just a friend. Close for a while. In the military way. Here one day, gone the next.'

'Like life, really. Although hers isn't in any immediate danger, not any more. The child's stable too. Signs normal. Let's hope they stay that way. Thank you for coming. She has almost no visitors, our Rose. Not that she knows anything about it.'

Stretch was poisonous still, like a snake. 'There really is nothing going on in her head?'

The doctor shook his head. 'Nothing. It's always a surprise that the rest of the body can run steadily along with no attention from anyone inside. Needs cleaning and feeding, exercise if there's a purpose to that, but otherwise... no. Flatline. Brain souped by the impact.'

'And she's pregnant?'

'Yes. It's hard to see when she's dressed and seated like that, but yes. Baby's fine. Mother Nature doing what Mother Nature does best. Thinking of the future.' He smiled, turned to leave.

'How long? How long until... how long has it been? The pregnancy?'

The doctor turned back and told him. Produced more words of kindness, sympathy and banality, and left. Stretch stood by the broken Rose, calculating. Counting back the weeks to an inevitable conclusion.

oOo

'May I sit?' The oddly-accented enquiry came out of the sun, polite and pleasant. Most of the other tables at the outdoor jazz and blues festival were packed solid with festive humanity, all bar this one. The questioner was wrapped improbably in biker leather, held a plate of something sizzling and steaming in one hand, a nine-pack in the other. A motorcycle helmet wrapped one elbow. Stretch, a black man cooking slowly in shorts and shirt, looked up at his white visitor's dark silhouette against the sun. He waved agreement.

'Feel free.'

'Beer?' The newcomer split the pack, pulled the ring on the first can and slid it along the table. It rocked a little as it negotiated the wood's grain, but no drop was spilled. 'Enjoyed your set last night. Some excellent piano. Very Dr John indeed. Unusual audience. Quiet. Like they're pretending to be dismal Brits rather than merry Americans.'

'You're imagining it.'

'Not so. Not so at all. They were lively enough for the other acts. You're not a popular man here. How is that, again?'

'And you're uninvited here. Go figure. Thanks, also.' The large man sank half the beer in a single swallow. Belched, appreciatively. 'And I have a do not disturb sign in letters of fire in the air above me. Not see it, white man?'

'Yep. Do you want to talk about it, big bad black man?'

'Nope. Do you?' Stretch absorbed the remainder of the can. The Brit popped another and slid it to his companion.

'I don't need to. I've no worries in this great country of yours.' Sarcasm and irony are indistinguishable in the cold light of afternoon. 'You're the guy who's got the worries. JJ Stoner, by the way. Jean-Jacques. It's French. I'm English. Figure that.'

'Canuck?'

'Nope. Pure Brit. Life's a puzzle, then you die. It was ever thus. American beer's weaker than mouse piss. Talk to me?'

'Yeah. Like you'd know what I'm talking about.'

'Here to help. That's the curse of us English. We always help. Never get the credit. It's a cruel world,'

Stretch stretched his long, glazing stare to his new friend. Aimed an arrow of enquiry. 'And you care why, exactly?'

Stoner placed his motorcycle helmet on the table with exaggerated and studied care. Took a cloth from a pocket and began to polish the visor. Time passed, surprisingly comfortably. Almost companionably. Stoner ceased his polishing, sighed.

'I'm here on a job. Working with a friend of yours. Suggested I might look you up, he did.'

'Yeah? Say who?' Stretch was watching the stage, the sky, the crowd, anything but his new best friend.

'Can't say.' Stoner sipped some weak beer.

'Ah. OK. Him, then. What did he ... suggest you did? Supply beer for ever?'

Stoner laughed a short humourless laugh. 'No. He sends his best. Told me to look you up, listen to you and decide whether I should invite you to work with me next time I have a job in the USA.'

'You need a piano player?'

'No. Not at all. Muscle and the brains to control it.'

'Gotcha. And you need it when, Mr Englishman? I'm still serving Uncle Sam ... unless you know something I don't?'

'No. But our mutual friend reckons that you are a strong and motivated man and that matters of immediate concern to you will compel you to undertake rash deeds which will be incompatible with your continued employment.'

'Fatally incompatible?'

'His exact words. Ain't that a wonder? Care to tell me your story?'

And rather to his own surprise, Stretch did.

oOo

'And she's knocked up?' Stoner's attention was one hundred percent on Stretch. 'Fuck. Yours?'

'The timing's right enough.'

'What's the view of her future, medical-wise?'

'Bleak, my British buddy. Bleak. But she'll carry to term. That is the limit. The absolute limit.'

'And what's the plan? The plan so desperate that our mutual friend worries on your behalf? Is that plan going to bring down the rage of the entire Army upon you?'

'Stop the games, Stoner. What do you want? And what do you offer in exchange?'

'Decisions are yours to make, Chief Petty Officer McCann. If we work together, what I want from you is an alibi. Unbreakable, solid and convincing.'

'In return? And that doesn't sound like much, what you're asking.'

'It is. In return? I'll provide exactly the same. A rock-solid alibi.'

'I don't need one.'

'Not yet, but I think you will. Especially if you want to avoid endless murderous retribution from those Army boys, as well as being cashiered and all that Navy unpleasantness.'

Stretch stretched, yawning to relieve a tension he'd not recognised he felt. 'When,' he asked, 'will you need an alibi? And for what?'

'You never can tell. Soon. You don't need to know why, you just need to agree. You agree?'

Stretch hung a huge hand across the table. 'Yeah. I need an interest in this sad old life of mine.'

Stoner took the hand, gripped and released. 'Consider it a distraction. Do absolutely nothing foolish for the next forty-eight hours. And carry this.' He slid a cellphone across to his companion. 'I'll call.' He cracked open another can of weak beer. 'Any good clubs around here? Playing decent American blues, where I can borrow a guitar, maybe sit in and play a little? Your Army buddies may all hate, loathe and despise you, but you must have a welcome in some decent clubs?'

Stretch nodded, began to speak, but Stoner interrupted him.

'Not today, maybe not tomorrow, but I'll call and then we'll make good music. Bad men can always do that. It redeems them.'

'Amen,' agreed Stretch, reaching for another beer, and smiling.

oOo

The uniformed cops arrived immediately after the plainclothes guys, who'd arrived bang-on synchronous with the obviously FBI guys. A study in suits, suits of identikit anonymity and ever-variable quality, as is the way with suits. The invasion of the enforcement agencies would have been more subtle had there been less of them, but there were a lot of them, and they conspicuously blocked all exits, so their entrance was both dramatic and remarked upon.

The bartender placed a shotgun on his bar. Rested his elbows either side of it and levered himself to his full height. The medusa's stare may have turned the unwary to stone; the bartender's aimed at transforming the newcomers into compost. Fertiliser.

'Gentlemen,' he said, the bartender. 'How y'all doing. And how can we help.' These were so obviously not questions that the lead lawman ignored them. The bartender gathered other friends around him, two men, three women, all muscled, marked and lacking any form of innocence in their demeanour. He placed a baseball bat – a gnarled old slugger of a tool – next to the shotgun. Stared at the law.

The leading lawman ignored the bartender and all his works, gazed around the club, chewing and looking both hard and cool, some achievement given the heat of the atmosphere. Finally, and with a sigh which could be heard plainly over all the jazz and conversation and which might have moved a minor mountain, his gaze drifted to the bartender, an eyebrow raised, and a surprisingly quiet but entirely audible voice cut across the counter.

'Looking for someone,' he said. Finally his eyes met those of the bartender, then passed on, as though the communication between them was unimportant. The bartender nodded. The more huge of his five friends picked up a glass cloth and began delicately cleaning and drying the beer mugs standing at attention in ordered rows by the sink. He passed the first glass to the nearest woman, who looked at it, shook her head sadly and returned it to the huge man, who washed it one more time. Then dried it again. Then passed it back to the woman, who nodded and placed the glass in its place among its brethren.

'Brit,' said the lawman, returning his attention to the audience, to the drinkers. 'I am looking for a Brit.' He reached slowly into an inside pocket, reached across the bar and placed a golden badge in a folder atop the shotgun's shoulder stock.

The music wound down, the four musicians on the stage taking their applause like the men they all were.

'A Brit.' The bartender mused. 'They, like, illegals now? Immies? I should ask all white guys for ID now? Do they have black guys in Britland?' He pointed an impassive gaze at the lawman's gleaming black countenance. 'I've never seen one. Hey!' He lifted the baseball bat from the counter and tapped a female friend on her thigh with it. 'You seen any Brits tonight, Daisy?'

'Oh.' She paused, as though for thought. 'Yeah.' She thought some more. 'Yeah,' she said again. 'Him.' She pointed at one of the two musicians approaching the bar, deep in musicman speak and plainly in high spirits. They also appeared to be well inebriated, with the floating airs of guys who'd been paying attention to the bottle since the break of day; many hours ago.

Daisy danced around the bar, sidled and oozed her way to the putative Brit, took his arm and gazed at the lawman.

'This here,' she warbled, running an everglades patois deep as any revivalist preacher's. 'This here's a Brit. Ain't you, honey?' She swung from the arm she was holding. Her chosen man dropped her grip, swung an arm over her shoulder, squeezed it.

'Right-o missus,' he said in comic Cockney. 'You got me bang to rights.' He laughed, dropped the silly voice. 'Yes. English. Guilty as charged. Now what?'

The bartender joined the conversation. His shotgun had evaporated and he slid a pair of bottles of sweating cold Bud to the musicians.

'This guy,' he waved an expansive arm at the lawman. 'He's looking for a Brit, he says. Him and all his kind, of which we appear to have a minor infestation. They're looking for a Brit. You're it.' He turned back to the lawman. 'Any Brit do for you, or do you need – like – a specific sort? Brain surgeon, Queen of the Scots, that kinda thing?' His growing audience chuckled collectively.

The lawman collected his badge from the counter, turned to the Brit, and sighed once more, this time into an appreciative quiet.

'Relax, pal. I'm looking for a Brit name of Stoner. Don't suppose you know...'

He didn't get to finish.

'That's me,' agreed the Englishman, offering both his hands to the lawman, wrists together. 'JJ Stoner. Do you cuff me now or should I get shot while escaping? How do you handle these things in the USA?'

His substantial companion and fellow musician stepped between Stoner and the lawman, addressed himself to the former regarding the latter.

'This guy's a Fed, JJ. Serious weight. He's gonna tell you his name and his rank, and then he will tell you why he is interested in you.' All traces of intoxication had left the stage. 'He will also suggest that you step outside for a discussion, alone, and we will not permit that.' He towered over the lawman. 'McCann. Chief Petty Officer, US Navy, Little Creek, Virginia. If I can help you, sir, I would like to.' Not a trace of levity. He stood at a relaxed attention, like the serving soldier he was.

'Chief Petty Officer. Little Creek, huh?' The lawman raised an eyebrow and nodded an acknowledgement. 'Let's find a table.' They did that. Stretch sipped at his cold Bud, Stoner and the lawman left their drinks alone between them. Sentries.

'Mr Stoner.'

'Yes.'

'OK. I am Senior Special Agent Travis, and I'm investigating a crime. Your name and identity have been passed to me as the man my agency would most like to talk with in relation to that crime.'

Stoner nodded, picked up his bottle, then replaced it untouched.

'A crime?' He nodded. 'OK. What kind of crime? A serious crime?'

The lawman held his gaze, ignoring Stretch, who was smouldering a little, like a minor volcano with indigestion. 'Can't say specifics at this time, but yes, a serious crime. Can you account for your whereabouts this evening, between, say, seven o'clock and... oh... ten-thirty?'

Stretch erupted, but in a controlled and not particularly destructive way. 'Yeah. Nineteen hundred to twenty-three hundred. He was here. What's this about, agent? Travis, wasn't it?'

Travis waved over one of his companions from the dwindling enforcement contingent. They were leaving in a less dramatic manner than they'd arrived, interest fading with the lack of obvious action and excitement.

'This is Special Agent Doyle. I'd like him to witness your replies, and if things are as you suggest, we'll leave you in peace here.' He smiled. The other agent failed to smile, looking at Stoner as though he were a specimen. He placed a small recorder on the table between then. Switched it on.

'You are Mr Stoner, a British citizen visiting the United States?'

'I am.'

'Your full name, please.'

'JJ Stoner. Jean-Jacques Stoner.'

'The purpose of your visit?'

'Holiday. I'm here on holiday.'

'Can you account for your actions between the hours of nineteen hundred and twenty-two thirty today, please?'

'I was here in this club for that period of time.'

'The Navy officer here can confirm this?'

Stretch McCann nodded. 'Yep. Been here since maybe four-thirty, working up an act for the evening.' He sounded completely serious, no further volcanic activity. 'The staff and the audience can also confirm that. We were on stage from maybe eight, with a few breaks, until just now.'

'Did you leave the building for more than an hour in that time, Mr Stoner?' The Fed was calm, professional, and so was Stoner.

'No. And there were always witnesses. Like Daisy there.' He nodded towards their support troop by the bar. 'If there's a problem and if it concerns me, Special Agent, you should talk to me about it. Here, I think, where I'm surrounded by friends.' Stoner smiled, no mockery whatsoever.

Travis smiled right back at him with a similar sincerity. Kicked back in his chair.

'I do have a problem, Mr Stoner, Mr JJ Stoner from England. I do. And in all fairness it is now a bigger problem.' He fell silent, a thoughtful expression replacing that of undoubted sincerity, smoothly as winter follows fall.

'How so, Senior Special Agent? Is that actually a real rank?' Stoner maintained his amiable good humour.

'You have what professionals refer to as an alibi, Mr Stoner. What we might define further as an apparently watertight alibi. That said, you do appear to have been in two places at once. A neat trick, even for an Englishman.'

'A perfidious Englishman?'

'I could not comment, such is the special relationship, Mr Stoner. Sir.' Travis stood, slowly, smoothly, in an unmistakably non-threatening manner. 'I would like to invite you to visit my local office, if I may. During working hours. You are under no obligation to accept this invitation.'

'In this, for me, there is?' Stoner was still smiling, as was Travis, both of them in an entirely professional and wholesome manner.

'Bureau coffee is among the best in the land, if not the world, and I would guarantee a supply of coffee for my English guest.'

Stretch erupted into volcanic laughter.

'Shit, JJ. The man's acting human. Must be a Senior Special Agent trick, like levitation or weather forecasting.'

Stoner re-targeted his amiable smile.

'Then it would be churlish to refuse.' His eyes caught and held Stretch's. 'Do you have a car, Stretch? And could you drive me to the local FBI retreat?'

Stretch's smile slipped, momentarily. Stoner held his gaze, unblinking.

'Yeah. Yeah I do. I can drive you. Of course I can drive you. My pleasure, my man. Yeah. Just sort out range and elevation, and I'll aim us all at the Feds.' He too rose to his towering upright position, nodded to Travis and left them, heading for the restrooms.

Travis extracted a card from his wallet, passed it across the table to Stoner.

'Shall we say ten, tomorrow?'

'You can say it, but we won't make that. I have heavy holiday-making to achieve this evening ... what remains of it. Can we say three of the afternoon?'

Travis nodded assent, looked around him for support, spotted Doyle chatting to the redoubtable Daisy, clapped his hands above his head to attract Doyle's attention, gestured to the main exit and left, followed by Doyle, who had passed a card of his own to the simpering Daisy, who rewarded his generous attention the moment his back faced her by sticking her fingers down her throat and miming a spectacular vomit.

Stoner finished his Bud, smacked his lips, and moved smoothly through the quietened attentive crowd to the stage, where he picked up the borrowed Fender Telecaster, smacked it a little to confirm the inaccuracy of its tuning, and launched into a spontaneous version of Johnny B Goode set to a strange rolling rockabilly rhythm which found Stretch running, actually running from the restrooms to the stage in what proved to be a successful attempt to save the song from the amused Englishman's attempt to publicly destroy such an important icon of American history.

oOo

Crowd gone. Quiet. Few lights. Stretch was seated once again at the piano, huge fingers coaxing shy notes from the gentle keys. Stoner sat on the floor next to him, chording the borrowed Fender, nimble fingers coaxing wry harmonies from it to accompany the melody of the piano. His eyes were closed.

'Would you care to explain?' The piano had fallen silent. 'Englishman, pray tell this old sailor what the finest fuck is going on?'

Stoner let both hands fall to the floor beside him. The guitar began to croon a rich chord of its own, increasing in depth and volume as it entered the self-abusing world of feedback, until Stoner reacted, lifted his right hand to the volume knob and shut off the signal. A typical late night almost empty bar soundtrack shrouded them. Hums of coolers, tick of moth on light, vacuum cleaners at dawn.

'I asked for an alibi. You provided it. Easy. Thanks, Stretch. Appreciated.'

'There was no alibi, man. You were here all the time. I told the fed that you were here. That's not an alibi. That's just truth-telling. What was really going down there, with the Senior Special Agent and all his many hired guns? You a lawbreaker, man?'

'Not really.' Stoner mused, his eyes still closed. 'Although I reckon as you will be before this time tomorrow.'

'Reckon that how, exactly?' Stretch was on full alert, watching the exits rather than his companion. 'Driving you to schmooze the feds isn't breaking laws.'

'I told you I'd trade.' Stoner appeared to be drifting off to sleep. 'Trade an alibi for an alibi. You've supplied yours; I'll return the favour tomorrow. You do have a reliable friend, don't you? Someone who could pass for you from a distance through tinted windows, which I'm sure are a feature of your car, the very same car which will be transporting me to visit Senior Special Agent Travis in a few short hours' time, driven by that friend who resembles you at least a little. You definitely do have somewhere you need to be while I'm sipping an approximation of coffee, smacking my lips as though it was good and smiling all the while as though I was where I would most like to be. You do need to be somewhere, don't you? Somewhere subsequently deniable. Doing what your situation demands, I think.' He subsided into a convincing impression of a drunken man asleep.

Stretch looked down at him. Said nothing. His features held no expression at all.

oOo

'Coffee, Mr Stoner?' Almost exactly twelve hours later, the FBI man was politeness personified. 'How do you take it?'

'Standing up, like a man,' Stoner collapsed into an armchair, the only armchair in the office. He was wearing sunglasses which only managed to half-hide the no-sleep blues around his eyes. 'And that's that with the attempt at humour. It was a long and most satisfactory night. You should have stayed, officer.'

'Agent. Officers are police. Quaint American custom for you. Black then?'

'What? Oh. Thanks. No thanks. White. A lot of cream and sugar. I need breakfast. Healthy living takes its toll.'

'As I can see.' Travis poured, quietly. 'CPO McCann? Is he ... ah ... similarly worse for wear?'

'He's ... ah ... recuperating in your parking lot, Agent Travis. It might be a kindness if your bomb squad walked on tiptoes around him. He may be a light sleeper, being Navy as he is.'

'Bomb squad? Is that a joke?'

'Yes. It was an attempt thereat. In England, offices like this first of all do not exist, second of all do not have parking lots, and third of all, if they did and if they did, the staff would be checking under parked cars every ten minutes for explosive devices. Leaving the driver in the car – even if he is asleep – would be an indicator that the car is not a bomb. Do I make any sense? It is early in the day, so forgive any incoherence.'

'Do you have the car's number, Mr Stoner?'

Stoner shook his head, rose and crossed to the window.

'That one.' He pointed. 'That huge lorry thing. The red one.'

Travis placed the first of several coffee mugs in front of his guest, took a pair of binoculars from a desk drawer and sighted down Stoner's arm, which moved around considerably, as though in a strong wind.

'Which? There are several.'

'Oh fuck it.' Stoner pulled a cell phone from his pocket, keyed a number. 'Hey, Stretch', he ground out. 'Flash your lights, will you?' A set of lights flashed before them. 'Thank you. Do it one more time and ... what? ... yeah, go back to writing great tunes in your head, man. In England we call that sleep, big man, simply sleep, like babies do. Makes them beautiful.' He closed the phone.

The lights flashed once more, a window wound down and a large black arm emerged, waved twice, aimed a single erect finger at their window, then retracted into the cool of the interior. Travis noted down the vehicle's license plate, put away the binoculars, dialled a number, spoke in a serious voice and replaced the handset into its cradle.

'We have a situation, Sergeant Stoner.'

'Mister, please. Mister Stoner.'

'I was being respectful, Mr Stoner. Nothing more. Showing respect for your service as a brother in arms.'

'Really?' Stoner managed to sound unconvinced. 'This heinous brew is the very finest FBI coffee, reserved for brothers in arms as a sign of respect? Not a rite of passage, a test of manhood? Jesus, but it's violent.' He sipped, grimaced, and sipped again. 'Just the odour of this would strip rust.'

'Thank you. Do we need to do the mister this, agent that routine?'

'No. Call me Stoner. It's easier. And shorter.'

'You don't prefer JJ?'

'My friends, Agent Travis. My friends call me JJ. It helps me work out who is who when all around me is darkness.'

'You had a bad time in Iraq, Stoner, I hear?'

'Don't remember.' Stoner passed the empty mug back across the low table. 'You were saying? You have a situation?'

Travis refilled, replaced the mug.

'Yes. I have a murder.' He paused. 'A shooting.'

'At the time you were so interested in last evening, then?'

'Indeed. Yes.'

'It wasn't me. I was in the club, playing bad jazz on a bad guitar. America is the ancestral home of the Fender Guitar Company – whatever they're called – I'd expected to find good Fender guitars here. That one would have been more use as a cat door. How is that?'

'Pretend to be interested in my investigation, Stoner. We have evidence that you were the shooter.'

'I am interested, Agent. Truly. I am pretending to be uninterested in the hope that you perceive that as a sign of innocence. I truly am an innocent abroad. Please understand that. Then tell me more. Even the FBI cannot place me where I plainly was not. Strangely useless guitars notwithstanding.'

Travis placed three cartridge cases on the desk. Stoner held his hands high.

'I'm not picking those up, so do not even consider asking me to.'

'Do you recognise them?'

'Oh yes. That's cousin Harold and his half-brother Arnold. Of course I don't recognise them. They're empty shells.' He looked closer. 'Point 22, I'd say. Girl's shells. Close range shots then? Hollow points? Head shots, no exit holes?'

'Your prints are already on them.' Travis focused all his attention on Stoner, who looked at his wristwatch and shook his head. 'It's no use. I could do with another coffee.

It's not every day I get accused of murder. Wrongly accused, that is.'

'I read about Iraq, Stoner.' Travis's voice was quiet, neutral. 'No criticism from me or from my superiors. Respect is all there is here. Even so, that still leaves us with this physical evidence. Prints, partials but definite, are on each case, and there are two alternative scenarios before us.'

Stoner interrupted him. 'Either I took the shots – which I did not – or I'm being set up for the job. I've handled a lot of ammunition, Travis. Lots of it. Many calibres. I'd not use a .22 by choice to kill someone. Might as well wrap a baby pistol like that in a sock and apply it as a cosh rather than pretend it's a serious killing tool. If I was asked to suggest a tool for a hit at close range I'd use a SIG, frankly. It's a fashion thing.'

Travis half-nodded. 'I've got to say this to you; I'm unconvinced by the idea you're here on vacation. I know what you do and how good you are at doing it. I know exactly what you are, and I have no problem with that. Nor has the bureau, unofficially.'

'Well, that's good to know. But why say it?'

'It's because I am aware of your ... ah ... professional status that I'm inclined to believe you. Inclined to agree that you've been set up. Do you know why? Who by?'

Stoner drained his coffee and stood, all trace of dozy hangover apparently and miraculously vanished. Leaned across the low table, hands on hips, bending down to Travis and whispering quietly.

'It's unfortunate that you guys record need to conversations like these. It's a shame.' He offered a hand to Travis, who rose his feet and took it, held it.

'Your vacation visa waiver is good for, what, another week – two? You shouldn't over-stay your welcome. But please do drop by if you're passing. We could share another coffee, JJ. Somewhere... quiet.'

Stoner nodded. 'I'd like that. Coffee that's less of a war crime than your own. No offence.' He looked again at his wristwatch. 'Any chance of a short tour while I'm here, a little hospitality from one brother in arms to another? Stretch won't mind waiting. The sleep will do him good. I've often wondered where you G-men live and whether all those tales tell the truth.

'And then...' he stretched, cracked some knuckles, looked past Travis at the closed door. 'Then I'll go catch up with a couple of old buddies, shoot some shit, shoot some targets on a range with some proper guns. Maybe play some more guitar with Stretch. I'd planned on doing a hire'n'ride with some big old Harley-Davidson motorcycle. Ride Route 66, again. One more time before I die. Everyone needs a vacation, Agent Travis, even old soldiers like me. Old ... retired soldiers.'

oOo

MEANWHILE...

The genuine Stretch slouched along the orderly gravel path which ran alongside the main building of the nursing home. A huge black man in loose medical whites. The afternoon heat broiled everyone, the fit and the dying alike, the caring and the cared for. His skin shone, but he felt no discomfort. Suburban heat is civilised heat compared to battlefield heat. He observed a fire door as he approached it, passed it, continued around the next corner of the big air-conditioned building, turned around and traced his own footsteps in reverse. He performed this manoeuvre three times. Finally the fire door opened. He was ready.

Making a decent show of flicking away a secret cigarette butt, Stretch caught the door before it closed.

'Thanks, brother,' he mumbled to the considerably smaller but similarly dressed man who was even then lighting his own stealth smoke. 'Freakin' door closed behind me. Watch it now.' And he entered the building, straightening his wipes and ostentatiously slipping a mint into his mouth.

The heat of the afternoon encouraged relaxation. The staff sat and wrote endless reports, the patients dreamed of recovery and health. Stretch padded down the corridors with the confident quiet of the huge man he was, outstanding and invisible in his whites.

'Baby. Sweet baby Rose.' Rose sat in her chair. She drooled while she ignored him. One of her eyes had rolled sideways, the pupil entirely absent, only bloodshot white on show to the world. She was thin, so very thin, apart from a vaguely visible rounding belly. Stretch took her right hand in both of his; the pallor of her skin against his made his eyes tear up. He sniffed, shook his head.

'Sweet Rose. Sweet sweet Rose. How could Davey do this? Tell it to me, Rose. How?' He stood again, turning his face from her so her blinded eyes could not witness his weeping. Her door was closed, the corridor maze quiet.

'We should've told him straight. You should've told me about the baby. My baby. Our baby. Because it is. We should've done lots of things. How'd he find out about it? Because you told him, Rose. You did. I just know it. Why? What did you think he'd do? Walk away? Come see me with an axe? He's military; he won't start a fight he'd lose. How could he leave you wounded like this? A pay-back for the both of us? He'd know I'd be back. I always come back. He'll have counted on it. He'll be waiting for me somewhere down the road. That's fine. That's not a problem. That's just him and me, Rose; your two men. Me; your child's father. Him; history man. Oh, man...'

Tears came then. Hot and heavy, fat and salt. The corners of his wide mouth turned down towards his jaw. He held her to him, held her as tight as the lovers they were. Relaxed then, turned her face towards him and touched an eye with his gentle finger. It blinked, but slowly. He stared at her, touched the naked eyeball once again. No blink this time. He covered her eye with his huge hand, held it there for maybe two minutes then pulled it away. The pupil had not dilated, did not react at all. Dying tears shone on his cheeks.

He felt gently for the pulses in her neck; thready but steady. Two lives, one half-lived and the other not yet properly started, delicately balanced between his massive fingers. He pressed firmly and held the pressure. There was no struggle from Rose; she slipped into her world of permanent peace so easily and without a murmur. No fuss; she simply stopped. The second tiny life within her ended before it had even begun. Stretch stood, holding her hand for maybe five minutes. The sleeping sounds of the house of the sick and the dying surrounded him. She cooled, slowly. The afternoon wore on.

He left as he'd arrived, nodding to a quietly coughing orderly and leaving that cigarette smoking man to catch the fire door before it locked itself again. They nodded in shared minor criminality as the afternoon's heat mounted and stunned all who stood against it.

oOo

An Englishman on vacation; JJ Stoner consulted his wristwatch, nodded to his companion.

'Reckon I've time for another couple of clips. What do you say?'

'You should be on your way, JJ.' His companion, an older, heavier man with sagging eyes and a slow step, shook his head. 'There's thunder coming.' He gestured to the blackening skies above the range. 'You on the Harley as you are. We do proper wet here in the USA, not gentle summer showers like you make in England. And in any case, you're a real hot shot with that SIG. Surely do not need more practice.'

Stoner laid the empty weapon down on the counter between them and smiled.

'You can never have too much practice, Marty. Never. You know that. Every round takes you closer to accuracy, closer to honesty, closer to survival when all is dark and only the most proficient make it out. And weather's just weather. A little rain never hurt anyone; makes the grass grow, too. You should welcome rain like the English do. Savour it.'

Marty appeared unconvinced, sounded amused. 'Oh why not? There's only us after all. When you leaving? When you heading home? Did you say you were going to ride 66 again?'

'Yeah. I reckon. Need a little riding time to clear my mind, set myself up for the next job. That'll be along soon enough. Set 'em up for me, huh? Reload, too? I need to take a leak. The coming rain affects a man somehow.' Stoner turned and set out for the restroom, stopped as soon as he turned the corner out of view, looked back and watched his shooting companion pulling on a pair of latex gloves before emptying the shell cases from the black SIG Sauer which Stoner had been firing minutes earlier. The older man bagged the spent cases from Stoner's gun, pocketed the bag and reached onto the counter for fresh ammunition, pulling up short the moment he understood that the cartridge box before him was empty. And he looked up to face Stoner, by now standing before him, a single fresh, unfired cartridge held point uppermost between them in his hand.

'Why?' Stoner stood, calm, solid.

The sweating man swallowed, hard.

'Money,' he said.

'That's disappointing, Marty.' Stoner's tone could easily have been mistaken for sympathy, understanding. 'Money? You'd give me up for money? I hope it was a lot.'

Marty shook his head.

'No. Not really. The threat is worse. The money's an excuse, the threat's the reason. You know how it goes, how the song goes.'

Stoner's gaze was steady, his voice quiet, flat.

'No. No I don't. Not at all. Who? And why? Why did they want me framed?'

'Framed? He didn't say anything about … framing you.'

'He?'

'Can't say, JJ. Just can't. Just get it done with.'

With his left hand, Stoner placed the single bullet onto the counter next to the black SIG Sauer. He took the gun, dropped out its magazine and slotted the single round into it, slamming the magazine home into the pistol with no more force than the mechanism demanded. Then he replaced the weapon onto the counter. Marty stared into Stoner's eyes, all too conscious that Stoner's attention had been entirely on him throughout the loading procedure, which was as automatic as breathing. With his right hand Stoner lifted a bunch of keys from a pocket and showed them to Marty, showed him how easily the big old keys fell between his fingers, protruding like steel spikes when he closed his fist. Marty stood wide-eyed and pale, but silent.

No words were required at this point, other than a statement of surrender, which did not arrive.

Stoner shook his head, still holding his companion's eyes with his own, and punched once and hard into the joint, the hinge between Marty's upper and lower jaws, pulled back his hand. Marty screamed and fell heavily to his knees.

'Just tell me, Marty. He won't know you grassed, because you'll not tell him, and I'll not tell him, so anyone close to you needn't worry too much. Who? Come on; I enjoy this almost as little as you do.' He sighed and raised his arm again; Marty spluttered and muttered, nursing his bleeding jaw.

'Don't know a name!' He shrieked suddenly as the pain of speaking overcame his restraint. 'Jeeze, JJ, I don't know. He just wanted shells you'd fired. That's all he wanted. That's all he got. It was the Irishman. The Boston Irishman. Small guy, quiet, dresses like an Italian.' His speech was slurring through the inaccurate articulation of his jaw and from the blood in his mouth. 'Oh, man...'

Stoner dropped into an easy squat, lifting his face close to Marty's.

'An Irishman?' he mused, and the black SIG Sauer spat its single shot upward through Marty's broken jaw. Stoner closed his eyes as the heavy slug exploded in red from the cranium and headed for the black, thunderously boiling heavens. Marty fell, and Stoner let him fall.

He stood, walked to the bench, slowly stripped the black SIG Sauer and cleaned it with extreme and methodical care, ejecting the spent shell and cleaning that, too, before replacing it into the pistol and placing the pistol into Marty's open hand, making some cursory attempt at closing the man's short fingers around the grip in a transparent parody of a set-up, a fake. He left the small plastic bag of empty cartridges where they were, in Marty's pocket, with his own prints intact on the shells but not the bag. A gift for Senior Special Agent Travis to enjoy at his convenience.

Then Stoner stood, shrugged into his heavy black motorcycle coat, lifted his black motorcycle helmet from the bench and walked outside to where the Harley-Davidson leaned, massively black on its chromed kickstand. He stepped aboard, kicked up the stand and fired up the engine, the uneven rhythmic chunter of its tickover providing a steady percussive background, a mechanised accompaniment to the approaching thunder in the heavens. A single fat raindrop hit the dusty coating of the motorcycle's fuel tank, sitting on it proud and quivering, but refusing to run away down the steel slope. Stoner looked at it, shook his head gently one last time, looked back at the shooting range, then forward to the road ahead. Thunder growled, distantly. More fat raindrops joined their brother, rolled together down the tank's black side, regaining their airborne freedom for a final moment before landing on the hot black exhausts and being blasted back to vapour.

Stoner trod the gear lever into first, rolled the throttle and eased the clutch, rolled fast forward into the gathering storm.

Third Person

I'VE GROWN A TAIL. No no. Not one of those handsome prehensile affairs beloved of cats and chimps. I'm being stalked. Followed. There are shadows in the shadows with my own shadow. I'm unsure how many there are, but a little afternoon amusement will soon sort that out. Oh the delight of it. I was feeling sadly anonymous, neglected by everyone in the loud city. A city packed with people. Everyone rushing everywhere at their own speeds, in their own rhythms, their own patterns. Except for tails. They copy patterns. They walk in the patterned footsteps of those they're tailing. Well... they do if they're none too good at what they're doing.

I stagger to a surprise stop at the junction of three roads. Two of the roads continue, one terminates here. Change roads here for connections to ... oh I don't know; anywhere more interesting. The staggering is important. Staggering a little – you're allowed to actually totter if you're a true thespian – makes it all look more realistic, more innocent. Far more innocent than pausing to gaze intently into a shop window, to tie a tight shoelace or to make a fake phone call. I prefer to stagger. I can of course perform those other little tricks, but generally, whenever I feel the hot breath on my collar I prefer to stagger, stumble or mis-step. Staggering provides a great opportunity to gaze around a little in a state of evident confusion.

If an Oscar nominee performance is required, I can even slip and slide off the edge of the pavement, although that carries risks. It's too easy to twist an ankle, to fall over your own feet or to step into something unpleasant. Stepping in something which fell out of an incontinent dog or an inebriate human is never a great experience, especially when a soul might need to don that cloak of invisibility in a closed public space, a crowded shop for example. Hard to maintain acceptable levels of invisibility when your shoe reeks of dog shit. Or worse. Great big spaces tend to open up around the stinker, making the subtle scuttle more of a challenge than it really needs to be, and although hiding in plain sight is every spook's dream it is less amusing if I'm the innocent being spooked by someone else.

There goes the first. His stagger was worse than mine. Amateur. In itself that's suspicious. When I follow someone, as I expect I'll be doing shortly, I'd always rather walk on by than attempt to imitate my target's deliberately provocative meanderings. It's easy enough to turn back, and most non-professional targets tend to look behind them for their followers.

Wonder why-for the tail? The only person who should know I'm here is the person I've come to meet. I know him, he knows me; we both know where and when we're meeting, though I'm not entirely sure why. Let's check and sow a little more confusion. No hurry. Better to arrive a little late than to roll up with a gate-crasher or three.

I dig deep into the leg pocket of my pink and grey camouflage (pink is a camo colour? Who knew?) cargo combat pants and extract a phone. This is the true sign of herd membership in this benighted age. No one looks suspicious if they're thumbing out weary SMS messages on a phone. I text the man I've come to meet. 'Are you having me followed?' and sign off with a row of x-shaped kisses, just to make him feel loved and wanted, that sort of thing. And then I feel foolish, but I can't unsend a text I've just sent.

No reply. I cast my eyes to heaven in the universal language of theatrical exasperation, thrust the silent device into its pocket and make a great show of checking the street names. In a stroke of creative genius, I heave the phone from its pocket once again and switch on a map app. This gives me another opportunity to gaze around me while the app loads. They take an icy age to connect, even with this supposedly zoomy new 3G system. Which of course I have, because this is a company phone. Hey team, this is a police phone. Only the best for the flat of feet. Not that it's much use because not even the biggest city in this Irish isle has decent 3G coverage just yet. Eventually, the map page loads. And at the same time a reply burps into the message box. A pleasant chime tells me this, so it must be true.

'Follow you? No. Why?'

That's clear enough then. He might be lying, but in grudging fairness he rarely does that unless it's necessary, and if it's necessary then it's OK. Or something like that. So I need to perform a little ardent flushing. The tail needs to be flushed. Tails always expect to be flushed – it's all part of the great game – and can become disappointed, disillusioned if they're ignored. Unless they're really good, in which case it's hellish hard to flush them. And of course if resource isn't a concern – if you're a government tail, for example – then you can set up teams of five, three of which are deliberately inept, get flushed, leaving the two good tails to bask in the shared warm glow of the followed believing that they're both smart and unfollowed. This is all just so super-subtle that it can induce a migraine.

I lean against a mysteriously anonymous chunk of street furniture – some kind of big grey metal box with meaningless stencilling adorning its dull flanks – and consult the cell phone once more. With impressive texting skills for one past their early teens, I confirm to the guy I'm meeting that I am indeed being followed. I don't expect a reply. There is no reply. A reply might have been kind. A reply might have helped. Time to do some flushing. Time to try.

I press the little button which demonstrates ringtones. Variously atonal atrocities intended to interrupt your day; a penance for carrying a cell phone, perhaps. The phone immediately rings to demonstrate my flash new ringtone selection, sounding like a minor train wreck for some reason, crashing and cymbals and very loud. I become the immediate centre of attention and loathing. No one but a mentally deformed person would program their phone to make such an appalling sound. Teenagers stare in naked admiration, point me out to their companions as being über-cool. I bellow into the phone, frothing incoherently and start walking in wide circles, yelling about nothing at no-one. A one-sided argument to pretend that I have a distant listener. Teen admiration heightens, I understand the Pied Piper thing suddenly. It is, from a tail-flushing perspective, counterproductive. I want the tails to follow me in my circling. Normal people do not walk in repeated circles. Teenagers playing audience to my performance are however entirely happy to wander circularly, paying rapt and naked attention to my imaginative invective. It's a frustration. But the performance permits me to observe the attentive realities of my surroundings as I argue with silence.

Two men – not boys – are also tracking my perambulations. I mime gesticulating with the inoffensive phone and then needing to repeat my last phrases to my imaginary audience because they couldn't hear it because I'd been waving the phone around. I believe I have a talent for the performing arts. My tails stop, stand and gawp. Then they remember themselves and amble around innocently. I would have made a superior actress.

The phone rings again. The same impossibly adolescent screech. I stop stock still and stare at it accusingly. I didn't dial myself. How dare it ring at me? I'm suddenly worried that I am over-performing. The hell with that.

'What,' I shout, with convincing irritation. I am in fact irritated.

'How many?' he asks, in a tone of considerable restraint. Also prominent patience.

'Two.' There is no point in subterfuge at a time like this.

'Mug the nearest.' Not the advice I was expecting. Mug him? OK. I can do that.

'Wow!' I yell. 'Thanks!' Even the teenagers are now convinced that I am indeed a mad woman and retreat to a safe distance. I close the phone with a theatrical gesture and pedal off at a decent rate to a side street, an air of serious focus wrapped around me, and stride into the narrowness. Then dive between two hugely malodorous wheeled steel rubbish bins, squat to my haunches and wait. And watch. For my dedicated followers. There are two of them. I continue to be insulted by such a tiny number. My reputation has not preceded me. If in fact I have a reputation. How would I know? Life's little mysteries, number one hundred and one.

My lead follower heaves into the small street. He's cool, calm, collected and considerably capable looking. With a flat-eyed determination he flaps a hand behind him, presumably a subtle secret signal to his colleague, and pauses to survey the street before him. He's good enough. No rushing in, foolishly. And too far away from me for me to jump him silently.

Stand-offs are always bad. The enemy can always summon reinforcements. Or you always think they can, which is just as discouraging. We both know we're both here. I can see him and I know exactly where he is. He can't see me, but is visibly calculating the odds on my position. Where he'd choose to hole up were our roles reversed, which they soon should be. Or would be, were my instructions not to mug him. But they are. What the hell.

I stand up, breaking the stand-off. 'Hi there,' I say, walking towards him, brushing imaginary waste bin detritus from my sleeves in a cool way. 'Nice day for a little stalking, huh?' He stops, stands and stares silently at me. He'll speak in a moment. Men are so predictable.

'Hang on,' I say, rummaging around my pockets and person, shaking my head and looking as flustered as I can. 'Here we go...'

This thing may only be a .22, but it still looks like a gun, and guns always take the unarmed by surprise. Tails have no reason to be armed. That's my theory. Unless they're attached to a stingray, but that's unlikely in the present circs.

'Knees,' I say, gesturing. 'As in, on yours. Now.' The silly little popgun spits a little, hawking a hollow-point into flight and flaking off a chunk of his right shoe's sole as it impacts. My eyes do not leave his eyes. He flinches with useful understanding. I can aim a gun using the excellent hand / eye co-ordination which the good lord saw fit to provide. 'Go on.' Encouragement needs to be maintained to be effective. 'Kneecap next time. They're hollow-points,' I explain in a kindly way. 'Make a right mess of a knee. Ruin your running. Probably forever. Praying will be pure pain too. All that kneeling you can't do. Pisses off the priests.' He sinks to his knees and holds up his hands in the time-honoured gesture beloved by movie hoods everywhere. He even tries not to glance at the entry to the side street. Good effort. Fails. His eyes widen. He holds up his hands of surrender a little higher.

The man I've come to meet prods my other follower in front of him as they both walk into our previously private tableau. My two followers – still only two, I'm still a little insulted – try not to stare at each other. They fail at that, too. My manly date tells his unwilling companion to lean against the wall, facing it, to adopt the position. Thugs and cops always say this in movies, and it always sounds comic. Today it doesn't sound comic at all. The second follower coughs a few words past his dry throat. Following a lady can be thirsty work on a hot day.

'I'm not carrying...' he begins, then falls silent as he falls to the floor. Being knuckled hard behind the ear does have that effect.

'Fuck me, Stoner,' I greet my appointee with the traditional insincere invitation. 'Have you killed him already?' This is rhetoric; of course he's not killed him. Stoner is a pro. He's as good as they get, so he says, and no-one sane would argue with that. Why would he kill him, in any case? He turns to me, shrugs.

'Not yet.' He shrugs again; maybe he's having trouble with over-tight underwear. Who can tell? 'Who are you?' He's speaking to the man on his knees, obviously, and that individual is looking more than a little discouraged by his situation. 'Why are you following my friend?'

At that I lose all discipline and fire off a quick stare in his direction. Me? Friends with him? JJ Stoner? Notable lone wolf and Scourge of the Stratocaster? And if you don't know what that is, you don't know Stoner. Discipline regained, I attempt a glower at Mr Knees. Even I'm unconvinced by my glower, and I can't see it. No matter, he's entirely entranced by the company he's keeping. Maybe Stoner's infamy has spread beyond the two-point-five people he counts as friends. Who can tell? I wave the pistol, menacingly.

Stoner shares a weary expression with us both, Mr Knees and me.

'No need for that. You can put it back in your handbag.' His right hand is quite suddenly and impossibly filled with a black SIG Sauer, which is a whole lot more imposing than my own dainty Beretta. I glance skywards, towards an imaginary deity, and disappear the little gun. Stoner's SIG dangles enticingly. Mr Knees gives it his undivided concentration. 'Speak?' Stoner's tone suggests huge volumes of information in a single word. That word includes threats of violence, dire consequence, maybe an ultimatum or two, and certainly a suggestion that if life is to be preserved that day in all its sweaty glory then speaking would be a good thing. A little healthy bean-spilling would prolong active life – that kind of thing. Subtle a SIG is not. Tails are skilled – hopefully – at tailing. Heroism is a different discipline. Better paid. Less popular. Supply and demand, so forth. Market forces in action.

Mr Knees talks. As is often the way, once he starts he enjoys it so much that it's difficult to stop him. This is a good way to obfuscate, to obscure tiny important facts with waves of meaningless enthusiastic waffle. Stoner knows this. He explains gently that he knows this. Mr Knees nods. He appears to heading for a headache. I wonder whether I should offer him a pill; aspirin or maybe acid, either might help.

My attention always starts to sag after a decently lengthy monologue, lots of creativity and the like, very few facts worthy of the description, and I find myself admiring both the brickwork, the architecture of the small street and the fact that it is so considerably quiet. Quiet is both a rare commodity in the mostly United Kingdom, and an undervalued one, I feel. But it needs a cause. Stoner is entirely focused on Mr Knees, and Mr Knees is going nowhere, so I take a walk to do a little exploring. Exploration and the spirit of adventure are what gave Britain both greatness and an empire; I never forget this.

The nearer entry to the street is blocked by a motorcycle. I didn't hear it arrive. Why not? Who cares? It's Stoner's, so it must be a Harley-Davidson. It says Harley-Davidson on the fuel tank. I check the colour. It's black. It's his. He has no imagination at all. A man, of course. I stroll around the bike and inspect the roll-down sign hooked to its bodywork; 'Police. No Entry.' I admire an attention to detail. Who else goes riding around on an iconic black all-American motorcycle with a rolled No Entry sign stuffed down their trousers, or wherever someone like Stoner would hide it?

And the small street really is just a cut-through. In days of old it would have been littered with tradesman's entrances and access to cellars, but in these modern times it's just silent. That silence is quite suddenly damaged by a muffled squeak, presumably from Mr Knees. I don't check that all's OK with Stoner. It will be. Trust me on that. As I walk by the two-man play in one act it's plain that nothing important has happened. True art in drama. Life imitating, as they say. Except that Mr Knees is weeping. Unbecoming in a man. His companion has the preferable alternative position and is still unconscious. Or performing a brilliant impression of unconsciousness. Wise man. Wisdom is rare in this world. He should go far. Live long and prosper. Possibly.

Stoner is talking quietly to Mr Knees, his tone sounds less encouraging than you might have expected. He doesn't look up as I pass, instead he does something mysterious with his trousers. They're black leather biker pants, Stoner being of that persuasion, and he unzips the leather of the lower left leg, reaches inside and lifts a blade from his heavy black leather Caterpillar boot. How do you ride around with a sharp knife in your boot? Seems risky to me. Maybe it's not actually sharp.

Stoner rests the point of the black blade – that would be either plastic or Teflon-coated steel, then – on Mr Knees' left leg, and slices, with little apparent effort. Teflon, then, not plastic. And definitely sharp. Worth remembering. Mr Knees is plainly in distress. I leave them to it, and walk briskly to the other end of the street, where there is another No Entry sign, this one on a neat supporting frame all its own. I marvel at Stoner's attention to detail. And I wonder whether everywhere he goes he carries an assortment of potentially useful traffic signs with him. This would not be the best moment to ask, however, although he would make a most effective traffic cop. I return to the tableau; it can't go on much longer. Five minutes, maybe seven, is about the limit for acts of violence in a public place to be kept quiet.

Sure enough, in my absence the two men have been joined by three others, youngsters by the look of them; hoodies and no body mass at all. Maybe that's the trade this small street is accustomed to; weight loss by epic drug abuse. I walk steadily back to the group, reaching inside my coat for my own blade. Not a black one like Stoner's, but shiny, with decent blood gutters and three sharp edges, Stoner looks up, shakes his head, stands and turns to face the three new players. Three young men, that's plain now. They spread out in a decent combat geometry. They've handled situations like this before. Street lice.

'Fuck off out of it.' Stoner is justly famous for his fine vocabulary. 'Just ... fuck off.' He displays the blade. The lead youth produces a Stanley knife. Looks threatening in a charming adolescent way. Stoner shakes his head again. He manages to look sad. Miraculous acting. I am in range now.

The three young men ignore me. I need to work on my air of malice and menace, plainly. Mr Knees takes what he mistakenly believes is an opportunity and starts to rise, hampered a lot by six or seven minutes spent sitting on his ankles and weeping and bleeding from more than a single cut to his leg. And with an agility which can only be admired, Stoner spins like a ballet dancer and kicks the ascending man in the balls. This is apparently painful for men, although it doesn't appear to produce any discomfort in Stoner, who as soon as his right kicking foot lands back on the ground, half turns and kicks Mr Knees again in the same place, this time using his other foot, the other heavy Caterpillar boot. Mr Knees screams and collapses. Before he lands back on his knees Stoner has got his right foot back into action, his left on the ground again, and plants another heavy leather boot into Mr Knee's throat. Who vomits, spectacularly. Projectile vomiting, they call it. Remarkable to observe. Accurately named.

Stoner turns back to the three youths. He's not even breathing hard, not even sweating so far as I can see, despite his macho biker leather kit. His voice radiates an amiable charm which sounds genuine to me.

'Now will you just fuck off?'

He holds the black SIG Sauer in his left hand, the dark blade in his right. He looks down theatrically and hangs the gun inside his leather biker-boy jacket – all very Marlon, 1950s style – and tosses the blade from hand to hand, adopts the knife fighter's stance. Feet well apart and on firm ground, hips loose and swaying gently, and leaning towards the young men. He gestures with the blade to the kneeling Mr Knees, who is mopping his puke from his clothes and trying very hard indeed to stop weeping.

'It's a money thing. A private money thing.' Stoner points to Mr Knees' still recumbent colleague. 'And I don't do witnesses.' The three hoodied boys finally leave, unbloodied and wiser.

Stoner transfers his attention to me. From the front, he appears very insane indeed. Being on the same side as him is a good thing.

'There's a spare helmet on the bike. Put it on.' He returns that same intense attention to Mr Knees, who is trying to be somewhere else entirely. A physical impossibility. He should know that. 'The next time I see you will be the last time you see anything at all. Got that, hero?' Mr Knees nods, vigorously and in silence, not meeting his eyes.

I'm standing next to the motorcycle before Stoner arrives. He still looks insane, though he unclips his own helmet and zips up his jacket in a controlled conventional way. The trouser leg is already zipped, I observe.

'Ummm...' I say, displaying a fine vocabulary of my own. 'Do you want me to carry your signs? They might come in handy? Again? In case we meet heavy ... traffic.'

Stoner actually laughs. It sounds genuine, too, which is suspicious.

'Hello Bernadette. Good to see you. Get aboard...' he gestures to the small buddy seat at the back of the bike, 'and let's get some of that famous wind in the hair thing. How is life in the Garda?' Before I can answer, the motor's running and we're heading for the highway ... or for the centre of town, downtown Belfast, which will have to do for now.

oOo

'They were tailing you to lead them to me. Fools, then.' Stoner passes me a half-litre screw-top bottle of Union beer, an interesting choice of drink. Not what you're normally offered in a notably nationalist Irish bar. How did he magic this up? Is there no end to this man's unholy talents? I hesitate. 'Go ahead,' he gestures amiably. 'It's perfectly palatable. Strong, too.' He smiles. I tip the bottle and sink maybe half of it, pass it back. Wipe my lips and proffer a gentle ladylike belch.

'Nice,' I share. 'Very nice. Socialist beer in an Irish country garden? In the afternoon? Isn't that all a little decadent for such a worthy drink?'

He just laughs at me. Nothing malicious. He just thinks everyone's stupid until proven smart. Few of us pass the test, and even when we do we're never allowed to forget that it's a continuous assessment kind of test. I adopt the best sneer I can manage and offer it in return for his patronising laugh. It has no effect. No fair exchange here.

'I led them to you, then.' I feel a vague sense of guilt. It's easy to feel uneasy when dealing with Stoner. He wears his hormones on his sleeve – always looks at me like he wants that one simple thing, though I don't believe he actually does. Not always. I think he does it to distract women, and I think he does it because it works. I have no idea why. I am of course immune to him. Mostly. And to his way of looking at you like it's either fight time or fuck time. Time to make life or take life. That's how he looks at you. At me.

He leans across the table, like he's about to pat my hand, patronisingly. In fact he places another bottle of Union beer in it. I feel fooled, somehow. How could he hold a half litre bottle without my seeing it? Legerdemain, no doubt. If I knew what it meant.

'No,' he says. The laughter's ancient history. 'No, you didn't. They set a small trap for me and I walked into it. Clever enough. But I can't see what they got out of it. You were there, I was there, and now we're both not. Did either of them touch you?'

'Excuse me?' He's often obscure. Thinks too much. I try to act blonde, which is not easy for a brown-eyed Irish girl. 'Of course they didn't. I'm a policewoman and I'm armed. Why would they touch me?'

'Then it's on the bike.'

I hate this, though there is a small fascination in trying to figure out where his over-thinking is leading him. Us.

'What is?'

Too late. He somehow produced another pair of bottles of beer from nowhere and left them on the table when he walked away. Now he's approaching his motorcycle as though it's an enemy, which it might be of course. It is American, and he himself is a lot more English than Brit, though he'd deny that. I'm Irish and proud of it. He knows that, too, and makes allowances, he says.

I sip the beer, ladylike, like. Then decide that the taste's good, so I pour the rest of the bottle down my neck and unscrew another. It's pleasant enough. Dilute. Like all beers which are not draft Guinness. Anything else is less, as the adverts remind us. Stoner's lying on his back, staring up at his own motorcycle from underneath. He looks like he's talking to himself, but that's a sign of madness, and I'd prefer that he remain at least a little sane. Then he takes something metallic from somewhere else about his person and uses it to detach something else metallic from the motorcycle. Then he stands himself up – managing that all on his own – and repeats the exercise on the other side of the motorcycle, detaching something else.

He's back, looking mostly unamused and pouring his second – maybe third – bottle of Union beer down his throat. Thirsty work, lying down, plainly. Two small shiny objects sit on the table between us. 'Neat,' he says, which is obviously a compliment.

I know what the objects are, although I've not seen their exact type before. 'Bugs,' I suggest knowledgeably. He nods. 'Just positionals or sound transmitters?' It's always good to appear knowledgeable. I start out on my exploration of my third – maybe fourth – bottle of Union beer. It's getting better by the swallow. Stoner looks up, his face without expression, mostly.

'If I was bugging for audio, I'd not stick the bugs next to a motorcycle engine.' Feeling stupid gets easier with practise. I wait for the patronising smile, but it doesn't arrive. Instead there's another unconvincing impression of deep thought.

'I've no particular place to go.' He's looking unusually blank. 'So they just want to know where I am. I wonder why.'

'Don't we all,' I say. 'We all want to know where we are. It's a teenage angst thing.' He looks at me like I'm deranged. In fact, had I not known better I could have believed that I was approaching a state of inebriation. This is unlikely after three –maybe four – half litres of some pale middle European imitation beer. I usually drink Guinness. Draft. I share this revelation with Stoner. Or at least that's my intention. What actually happens is that I grab his hand and stare into his eyes, speechless for a second. And then I belch. I hadn't seen that one coming.

'Sorry, JJ.' I try to pretend it was a cough not a belch. 'I'd not seen that one coming.'

He just looks at me as though he's a fish and I'm a lure, turns a bottle around and points at the label. Union beer appears to be twice as strong as Guinness. I believe I've had enough practise at feeling stupid now.

'You need a meal,' he says. Gets up and goes inside to get one. Maybe two. That would be one each. Now I feel overpoweringly sleepy. For fuck's sake.

oOo

I wake up suddenly. The reason for the sudden awakening is obvious; there's a hand clamped over my mouth. And I can think of many better ways to wake up, frankly. The hand smells faintly of soap. There's a voice, a quiet male voice. 'Shhh...' it says. 'They're here.' It's impossible to ask who and where and why when you've a hand clamped over your mouth. Instead I tell myself that it'll all be OK and that I'm in good hands. Which may even be the truth.

'You OK?' asks the voice; quiet, male. The correct response is to nod, silently, so the hand over the mouth can be removed and all joy, etcetera can be restored. Instead of doing the correct thing (to be predictable is to be boring) I open my mouth a little and lick the palm of his hand with my tongue. A normal man would react by immediately recoiling and removing the hand at once. Not this man; he takes his time, lifts the hand away so slowly or so quickly – it's impossible to work out which – that I'm uncertain it's gone, then he wipes his palm gently on the top of my head. Stoner; not like other men. Happily.

I'm not sure why this should be, but having a hand – even a friendly hand – clamped over the mouth tends to have the effect, a side effect maybe, of demanding that all attention is centred on that hand. Once the hand has lifted and the patronising head-pat has been endured, renewed wider focus reveals that I'm wearing only my underwear, and I'm lying on a sleeping bag. A decent enough and decently soft sleeping bag, but it's not a conventional bed. So Stoner brought me here. I have no memory of this – little memory at any rate. There were the followers, the street thugs, the bugs, the beer, the bike ride and then... a hand over the mouth. A typically quiet evening for a modern policewoman about town.

Which brings with it another thought. He didn't remove all my clothing. Not only didn't he interfere with me at all, he didn't even take the opportunity for good long stare. Should I feel insulted by this? Patronised? I look pretty good naked; everyone says so. I decide instead that I'll feel flattered. He's treated me as a friend. Stoner has almost no friends at all. Far more lovers – fuck-buddies, as he sometimes describes them – than friends. He's not like other men, as I say. Now I'm unsure whether I'm entirely happy about that.

Time to wake up. 'Who are they, and where are we?' Pretty basic questions I'm completely certain will fail to get a response.

'We're in the barn with the bugs. They're in the farmhouse and I know one of the voices. I think. Hard to tell in the dark.' That's Stoner humour, I think.

'Why am I almost undressed?' We all have our own priorities.

'What? You fell over. Puked up. Got filthy. Your stuff's drying. I washed it.'

'You what?'

'You heard. Now shut up. These guys may be aiming to kill us. Even you can spot the disadvantages of this.'

More wit.

'Stay here.' And off he goes, Sir Galahad, off to rescue a dragon in distress from some dire maiden.

I wonder where my clothes are drying and whether Stoner the all-action hero thought to take my cell phone out of the pocket before washing it with the rest of the kit, and – there's a sudden indescribable racket. Impossibly loud. Real blare blare blare stuff. Think air raids and the sirens and things like that. Heavy fire, bangs and crashes, alarms. Sounds like the blitz. It's coming from another building. Something has kicked off and some kind of alarm is going mental. I consider for a moment what Stoner would want me to do. He'd want... he'd expect me to stay safely calm, quiet and professionally out of the way while he sorts out whatever needs sorting. That sounds... dull. But survivable. I cover my ears with my hands. I scream. I can scream, really well. I grew up during the Troubles here in Ireland. I can surely scream. And before you think I've gone all girly and stupid, remember that I know Stoner very well, better than you think, and that the awful blaring cacophony will be something he's caused. This means he wants the invaders to be distracted. So, helpfully, I'll provide some additional distraction. In case any of them gets the time to look out the window or something.

There's a dim early-dawn light outside, so I run out of the barn, waving my arms around and screaming at the top of my voice – full Irish singer's lungs and maximum pumping effort and I scream for help. I scream rape and murder, terror too. I can do that really well. It's tremendously effective, providing that the only people who can hear it are men. Women just do the despising sneer at the sheer unforgiveable girlyness of it. I add to the visuals by unhooking my bra, dropping it behind me and legging around still screaming for help. Between the sight and screams of a topless decently buxom Irish lass and the mechanical claxon, any decently red-blooded male should be confused to all buggery.

The siren stops. I dive into cover and sit still, wishing I'd not dropped the bra, but only a little. Men know what tits look like.

Stoner calls out, sounding entirely cool, calm and a little bored, just checking that I'm OK. I shout back that I am and ask whether he's OK. It's at this point that pre-arranged codes which reveal whether either shouty party is under duress are a clever idea. We have no pre-arranged codes. I step out into the brightening quiet dawn and head over to the farmhouse, where the lights are now lit and all is presumably under control. Control by the good guys. Who are us, in case you'd not figured that out already.

'That is one fine sight for the morning.' Stoner, always the perfect gentleman, is gazing in my semi-naked direction. 'Bigger than the last time I saw them. Heavier by the look, too. You pregnant?' It's easy to shift from affection and respect to disgust and contempt. Wit is called for.

'Fuck off, Stoner,' I sneer. 'Just fuck off.' I too have a way with words.

There are three people who are not Stoner in the room when I arrive. It's a bit of a squeeze because for some reason Stoner's motorcycle is in there too. Four men, a woman – an apparently heavy woman of course – and a large black Harley-Davidson. One of the men looks very unwell indeed. He's sitting on the floor against the wall by the outside door, and has something stuck through his neck – all the way through; in one side and out the other. It looks like a screwdriver. Unless it was unusually clean for a screwdriver he'll be lucky to avoid some heavy infection from that. If he stays alive, of course. No need to worry about infections if you're dead.

The second man looks worse, if anything. He's lying face down and is bleeding a lot. On further inspection, he might have stopped bleeding; it's hard to tell. There's a handle sticking out of his back, very low down, just above his pelvis. Lots of nerves there. Nasty nasty stuff. I can't see what's on the other end of the handle, but it's plainly done some damage.

'Anything I can do?' Stoner looks towards me and away from the third person, but only briefly, then he looks back.

'Coffee, please, Bernadette. Black might be best.'

So Stoner doesn't care whether the other guy knows my name or not. Several inferences from this. The third person isn't going to survive this; he already knows who we both are; Stoner simply does not give a shit. The latter is the most likely.

'Are there any clothes in the place?' I ask mainly because I feel surprisingly naked, the surprise being that I'm uncomfortable; being naked isn't a problem. I wonder why I feel uncomfortable. 'And what was that fucking awful noise?'

'They fell over the bike. It has a motion sensor and a decent alarm. Anti-theft kit. Really good. More power in the hooters than there is in the engine.' He smiles. He can be odd sometimes. 'Clothes in the bedroom. Think so, anyway. I've no idea who lives here, so I don't know what size they are. Your own kit's back out in the barn, but it's still damp. We need to get on. Could you do with the coffee? Please?'

He turns back to the third person, the last intruder, who is sitting cool as you like in the comfy chair. That is pretty damn chilled; your buddies are gasping, groaning and bleeding out in front of you, you're face to face with topless totty and a nutter killer bastard with a big black SIG Sauer in his hand and a knife in his eyes, and you're sitting there as though there's not a care in the world with your name on it. No wonder Stoner wants a coffee.

'Talk,' says Stoner. The tone of his voice would freeze the air; dry ice. 'You've gone to a lot of trouble…' he gestures around him with his unarmed hand, 'so you must want to talk. Now's your time.'

'Two things.' From the voice, the guy might be female. A woman, not a girl. Deep voice. All three of the intruders are dressed in standard commando black, complete with gloves, tool belts and hats, so it's unusually difficult to tell. To be certain. But it could be a woman. The coffee's going to be instant.

Stoner just nods. Says nothing more.

'First; had to find out whether you're as good as I was told. You are so far. Second; I want a job doing; a sensitive and complicated job, and I want it done properly and completely. You were recommended.'

'The job?'

'If you kill these two,' he, she, whatever, gestured at those less fortunate, 'you'll have done half of it.' The more she spoke, the more I believed her to be a woman. Interesting that Stoner had worked out exactly who to talk to: that the two guys were disposable, and that this mysterious third person was the one who wanted a conversation. Stoner didn't seem wildly inclined to chat for long, however. His need for a caffeine fix was obvious.

The twin shots from the SIG Sauer were perfectly synchronised with the explosion of brain tissue from the body on the floor. An ear-breakingly loud noise in a small room. The woman – if such it was – was spattered a lot, but didn't flinch. Maybe Stoner has a sister, and she's it. But the big guy was well pissed off. No doubts about that. Any minute now he'd say...

'You next. Stop talking shit and tell me who you are and what you want. Nothing more.'

'You don't want to know who sent me?' The third person seemed keen to engage Stoner's interest. 'Who it was who told me about you?'

'No. Hurry up.'

'Do I get a coffee, too?'

'No, and when I finish mine, we're gone, my friend and I.'

'Leaving bodies all over the place, just like that?'

'Sectarian violence. Not so much of it these days, here in the shamrock island, not since that supposedly Good Friday, but maybe there's a resurgence. The Very Real IRA or something.' He sipped at his scalding coffee. 'No doubt some wannabe fools will claim responsibility when the story gets out. Speak now.' He sipped some more.

'I want you to kill someone.'

'Of course you do. I don't do gardening. Who?'

'In good time. You need to know why.'

'No I don't. Who?'

'You...' at last there was some doubt in the voice of the third person, who was now the last man standing. Woman. Sitting. Remarkable; she'd seen two colleagues destroyed in front of her and only now she's having doubts?

'Forget with the acting nonsense.' Stoner looked to be about half-way through his coffee. I pulled a sweatshirt over my head, then pulled another over that one. There was a chill approaching. A cold front. Much cold. And harsh with it.

'The target's a politician. Just back home after a while away in Europe. An influential man. You'll know who he is.'

'A man of God? A church leader? Blessed with a loud voice and a devoted following among his flock?'

'You knew? You already knew?' The doubt had gone, the third person's voice was flat. 'Paisley?'

'The inevitable reverend. Story goes that they're setting him up to be First Minister in the North someday soon. Now why would I want to kill him?'

'Money. There's plenty.'

'Of course there is.' The black SIG Sauer spoke again. The third person snapped backwards into the deep padding of the easy chair. Stoner rose, emptied his coffee, and walked to the chair, placed the muzzle of the weapon beneath the jaw of the body and fired a final shot upward through the skull. The black woollen cap retained most of the mess.

'Do you need a hand getting the bike out?' I asked because I am a helpful soul. Stoner was collecting the ejected shells from his own gun. I noticed for the first time that there were three semi-automatics on the floor, along with a gleaming array of spent shells. He ignored the guns and their detritus, pocketed his own brassware and slipped the key into the motorcycle's ignition lock.

'You could hold the doors for me, Bernadette. Be a dear.'

So that's what I did, we collected everything that was ours, and we left, the Harley's engine booming a lot as the sunshine brightened the fields around us and the cold air warmed before us.

oOo

'Why not? Why not take the job?' Stoner had bought breakfast. He was in a good mood, motorcycle running well in its unquiet way, the Garda's lead car had even flashed and waved thanks when he'd pulled off the narrow country road to let the three of them and the ambulance pass, bright lights but no sirens as they raced to answer the anonymous call about the rural shootout.

'He's protected. Too protected. I would have gone down.' He broke up a lump of pretentious French-style pastry. Chewed slowly, like he was thinking. Maybe he was. Strange things happen after murders.

'I would have died trying.' Sometimes his voice carries an almost-Irish lilt, though he told me once he was as much French-Canadian as English.

'You'd have got him. JJ. You know you would.'

'Not so, Bernadette. Not so. Even if... even if I did.' He sighed, long and deep, and I wanted to hug him. He's far too old for hugging. He's nobody's baby but his own.

'And... maybe I would have, because I'd not come out of anywhere they'd expect or at any time they'd expect. I'd lie to them about that. Everybody lies here. It was a set-up of some sort. Here's how it goes. Paisley's own crew, democratic and unionist to a fault, are doing the set-up here. That's my take on it. My view. Others may be available, but I've seen too many of them in all the tours I did in Belfast. I know how they sound, how they smell, what they feel like. They wanted an English assassin. One they could link to the regiment after I was dead and gone. Can you picture that? They'd already set me up to kill the two losers back there. Paisley's Prots would have taken me down and used the guys back there as proof of English perfidy. Can you read the papers, hear the screaming from the pulpits? I would have died, no matter how smart I think I am. Don't want that. Not at all. I have too much to live for to be dying here. Lots of things to stay alive for.' He stopped. Looked around, then looked back at me. No killer's insane stare this time.

'You look so beautiful with your kit off. I mean that. And if you are pregnant, is there any chance ... any chance at all that the baby's mine?'

I threw the remains of my pastry at him. Of course I did. Then I threw the plate. And then my mug of coffee. He did not duck from the assault. He didn't even flinch. He just laughed. Of course he did.

FOUR CORNERED

'DO YOU EVER WONDER...' the Hard Man swirled the golden gleaming liquid in his glass and stared through it as though mysteries were hidden in its shallows. 'Do you ever wonder whether someone whose only obvious skill involves murdering people should aim to improve himself?' He sipped at the spirit in his glass, grimaced. 'This tastes worse than diesel.' He shook his head and drank the remainder in a single swallow, all pretence at sophistication banished. He looked up. Maybe he did expect an answer. Maybe he was intending to be neither rhetorical nor insulting. Maybe.

JJ Stoner sipped with notable dedication and appreciation at his own glass of the offensive brew. He sipped, swallowed a little; sipped some more and swallowed some more. 'I'm sorry,' he said, looking up at his companion. 'Were you talking to me?'

'There's no one else at the table.' The Hard Man was stating an obvious fact, and he stated it with either irony or insult, probably both. Stoner nodded.

'You want a reply?' Stoner appeared to inhale the remainder of the spirit from his glass. Reached for the bottle which stood between them like a sentinel and filled both glasses again. The Hard Man shook his head, slowly and with caution.

'Yes,' he said. 'Please. Humour me. Treat me as though I was a simpleton and dazzle me with your mighty insights.'

'You've asked the wrong question.' Stoner rasped the knuckles of his left hand across the stubble of his cheeks and spoke with the determined clarity of the very drunk.

The Hard Man nursed his precarious consciousness and offered an approximate smile, maybe as a gesture of silent encouragement.

Stoner sipped again and stared at his drink, speculatively. 'A better question would be to wonder whether noted killers – that would be me, possibly the both of us; I don't know you all that well – are also notably good at anything else. So...' he paused, his eyes wandering around the dim room, its quiet occupants and its pall of smoke. 'So answer a question for me first, then I'll have a go at spearing your calm with icy revelations. Are you also a noted killer?'

The Hard Man's reply was quicker than the relaxed pace of their debate demanded. 'Only in a sense,' he said. 'I rarely killed anyone, but I've caused a lot of people to die. It's not the same thing.' Both men nodded, carefully, in agreement. Stoner poured more liquor into their glasses. Raised his own to a toast. The Hard Man flicked the fingers of one hand, missing his glass entirely but signalling his acceptance of the toast. Stoner drank.

Finally, Stoner replied. 'Killing one person – a single person – is a lot more difficult than killing a few dozen or a few thousand. It's easy to be a general and sit on your big horse on top of your big hill and send the cavalry to attack the guns, or to sit behind your big desk and despatch a fleet of bombers to knock the fuck out of a city filled with millions of unarmed civvies. That's easy. You'd go home to bed and sleep deep after that.

'But to walk up to another soldier – another armed soldier – and separate him from his breath is a personal thing. If they're not a soldier and they're not armed ... it's a more difficult personal thing. You don't go home and sleep well after that. Not unless you're a true sicko. And I don't think any successful professional can do that unless they have a lot more depth. Are you asleep?'

The Hard Man opened an eye and shook his head, so slowly that the simple act appeared to be causing him pain, which may have been the reality of the situation. 'I'm listening,' he said. 'All ears.'

'So your button pusher, your general, whatever, no; they don't need to be better than being able to push buttons, give orders. But your soldier, your private contractor, your very own hotshot hitman, he will already be improved. He'd not survive otherwise. Not for long. Why d'you ask? You intending to offer philosophy classes for jaded murderers? Offer lessons on growing prize dahlias to counteract the killer's angst?'

'Do you get angst, JJ?' The Hard Man appeared to be regaining interest.

'No. Not as such. Do you?'

'How come?' The Hard Man was into asking questions, not answering them.

'Don't know. Don't care enough, maybe.' Stoner up-ended his empty glass, sat back and considered his companion. 'Why the interrogation? Why here?' He gestured vaguely around them at the darkness of the bar, its many shadows concealing more than its few lights revealed. 'There I was, expecting a little catch-up, a checking-in, a how's it going, so forth. I'd not expected the Spanish Inquisition.'

'No one does.' The Hard Man wasn't smiling at all. 'There's an opportunity,' he remarked, slurring only slightly. 'I have a sudden senior vacancy, due to ... early retirement, and if you can ride a bicycle while singing a sweet song, patting your gut and scratching your ear at the same time, you might want to fill it. Might be able to fill it.'

'Like a cavity. Fixing a hole. Unfortunate death in the family.' Stoner was all eyes.

'Exactly. Let's try it. Initiative test. You carrying?' A casual question from the Hard Man. Stoner equally casually laid a handgun on the table next to the exhausted bottle of anonymous spirits. No one else appeared to notice this. It was plainly a world-weary bar. He spun the weapon so its pistol grip was positioned perfectly for the Hard Man to grip it fast, if that was the intention. The Hard Man shook his head and loosened a button of his limp pale shirt. He was sweating, maybe more than their alcoholic consumption would cause.

'I'm going to leave,' he announced, ignoring the gun. 'I think I'm going to throw up. This shit is horrid.' He waved vaguely at the offensive bottle. 'Some... a few tables away from you, behind and to your right, is a guy who's likely to follow me. He's likely to take me out if he can. You up to doing unto him before he does unto me?'

'Why?' The handgun had vanished again, once more invisible in the dark, smoky, alcohol soaked atmosphere. Stoner's attention was on his companion. No looking around him.

'Can't tell you.' The Hard Man looked quite suddenly sad, unhappy, deflated. 'Maybe later. Maybe not.' He rose to his feet, tapped the knuckles of his right hand against the damp wood of their table, and headed for the door. As he'd predicted, a chair scraped wetly behind Stoner and to his right. A man loomed into Stoner's area of lateral awareness. A large man, moving with purpose towards the same door. As the large man passed Stoner's table, Stoner let his head fall to the tabletop, the perfect image of a drunk collapsing into whiskey dreams, and the large man passed by, ignoring the drunk, maybe not even registering his presence. As he passed, so Stoner reached out to him and passed the black blade of a short knife through the Achilles' tendon of his left foot, then his right foot. The blade was sharp, Teflon-assisted, and glided through sock and tendon as though they were no resistance at all. The large man fell forward, grabbing at furniture, drinkers, the scenery, at anything, and he fell in commendable silence, finally breaking his descent with his forearms, and as soon as his balance was restored, stable again on his knees and arms, he turned to look behind him, hate across his face.

But Stoner was gone, no haste in his passage to mark him out from the rest of the drinkers.

oOo

'Who was that? What was all that about?' Stoner found the Hard Man leaning against a wall, wiping his face, a pool of puke at his feet.

'He dead?' A Hard Man of few words.

'Not nearly. Won't walk for a while. No lasting damage; missed the femoral by a mile. He'll think twice before wearing sneakers next time.

'Would you care to explain?'

'No. But I do have a job for you, Sergeant Stoner, retired. Maybe more than one.'

'Of course you do. A little gardening, maybe? Horticulture soothes the mind, they say.' The two men walked from the shadows into the night. It rained a little, unusual for the place and for the time of year.

oOo

Drizzle truly is the worst of all worlds. Riding a large and heavy motorcycle on greasy roads through drizzle is never an uplifting experience. It demands concentration from the rider. Heavy rain can clean roads, transferring their inevitable filth to passing vehicular traffic. Dry roads are a rider's delight. They bring precision, accuracy, reward, and a decent rate of progress. Drizzle dilutes the road's grease, makes its surface unpredictable, unstable, inhibits the inherent balance of the motorcycle and usually frustrates the hell out of the rider.

Stoner found release in riding through drizzle. He revelled in the wobble, the weave and sway of it, the unpredictable shifting of the grip levels between front and back wheels, the way the ride absorbed his attention and removed his tendency to worry about where he was going, what he would find at his destination and how he would be expected to deal with it. The heavy black Harley slipped sideways. Stoner remained relaxed. The tyres gripped again, Stoner's natural balance and gyroscopic effects beyond his control plotted a revised track through the bend, somehow avoiding a sequence of metal manhole covers and their inherent skids, straightening up and slowing as machine and man rolled left, down into the open jaws of a car park, no motorcycles permitted.

Down a single floor, then back up again, such can be the mysterious internal geometries of urban car parks. Four storeys, five floors. The rafters rattled at the bike's passage; quiet it was not.

Silence returned as Stoner rolled the bike to a stop, parking it on a cross-hatching of yellow lines and next to a Do Not Park Here Or Else sign, which was – as always – plainly intended for someone else. Anyone else. He kicked out the kickstand, removed his crash helmet, extracted the keys from the ignition and dropped them into the helmet, following them with his gloves. Sat. Ears adjusting to the clatter and churn of the city, the blare of humanity and the concrete calm of the buildings themselves.

He hung the helmet from a handlebar and walked across the dim space to the open edge, leaned against the concrete wall, raising a little concrete dust, and surveyed the scene below him. Extracted a tubby tube from a pocket of his long leather coat, and extended it, finally raising it to his right eye and sweeping its lenses across the façade of the building opposite. Floor by floor. Window by window. Left to right. Methodical madness.

Third floor, third window, exactly as he'd been told. Trust no one; make your own verifications. Act only on your own judgement. Survive.

Third window. Three figures, one standing, two sitting. The standing figure was in fact walking, talking by the manner of his gestures. The two figures in his possibly willing and appreciative audience showed no sign of movement, and at this range it was impossible to work out whether they were listening, willingly or otherwise, or whether they were asleep, rendered comatose by the oddly dramatic gestures of the walking man. It was a man; Stoner was sure of that, from his build and from his posture. Even in these days of considerable equality in most things, no woman would willingly carry herself like that, nor gesture with such loose drama. The seated figures were stationary.

Stoner watched. The sounds of the city revealed nothing of the monologue, dialogue, full-scale conversation in the room in view. He didn't care. What was being said – or not said – was of no interest to him. He was there to watch, not listen. To observe, not overhear. He was interested only in the three figures. They would, he'd been advised, become four. As soon as they multiplied, which he hoped would be a sooner event rather than a later event, he would make a call.

He reached with his free hand into a pocket of his long, damp, heavy, dark leather coat and produced a cell phone. Placed it on the parapet in front of him. With the same hand he reached into another, inside pocket and produced both a battery and a SIM card. Without losing his focus on the third window on the third floor and the three individuals revealed as its occupants, he flicked the back from the body of the phone. Then he glanced down, briefly, and slipped the SIM card into its slot, following it with the battery, which he clicked into place. He replaced the rear panel of the phone, powered it up and resumed his vigil. Nothing had changed.

The cell phone vibrated, its restrained signal offering no clue to the urgency or otherwise of the incoming call. Eye on the window, hand to the phone, and a quiet 'Hello' as acceptance of the incoming.

'Three,' he confirmed. 'Just the three. One talking and walking, the others seated. No signs of restraint nor violence. The walker has joined in with the sitting. This is not entirely exciting. There are better BBC2 dramas.' He listened, and may have smiled at the reply. Smiled a little. 'Correct,' he said. 'This could be a play by Alan Bennett. A rehearsal or something.' He listened some more. 'No. Can't read their lips. Send me a long mike if you want me to eavesdrop as well as doing the peeping Tommy Gunn impression.' This time he certainly did chuckle, briefly. Finally; 'Yes, he's here.' And he closed the phone.

'Hi,' he said, without taking his attention away from the third window, third floor. 'On time as always. Neat and silent arrival. Gold star.'

'Stoner.' The new arrival knelt next to Stoner, placed a pair of heavy-duty binoculars in front of him, and lifted an identical set to his own eyes. Found the window. 'OK,' he said. 'Got them. Three.'

Stoner stood, collapsed his telescope, dropped it into a pocket, hefted the bins to his eyes, checked their clear readouts for range, light levels and amplification, then rested them back on the parapet, stripped the SIM card and battery from his cell phone and dropped the components into separate pockets of his long biker's coat.

'You are one paranoid fuck,' remarked his companion. 'Every time. Every single time, you strip down that phone. No one's listening. The only guy you might be afraid of is standing next to you, and the only guy you surely should be afraid of knows where you are because he sent you here. Paranoid fuck. How goes it, JJ?'

'Good to see you, Shard.' Stoner smiled with his voice. 'Paranoid? Nah. I have a mysterious wish to see another few more dawns, that's all. Y'know?' He dropped smoothly into a pastiche fighting stance. 'I might be afraid of you?' There was a long smile in his voice. No sneer.

'Yeah,' said Shard. 'Yeah.' He resumed his sighting stare through the heavy bins. 'These magicians say it's 280 feet across the street. Looks more like 300, three-twenty maybe to me.

Stoner leaned against the parapet. 'Yeah,' he echoed. 'I'd go with your guts. 320. You tooled?'

'In the van.' Shard's attention didn't wander at all as he spoke.

'Far away? The van?'

'Two floors down, blocking the up-ramp. Signs and everything. Can't miss it. It's bright orange with white stripes, and is the only van blocking the only up-ramp.'

Stoner passed a hand in front of the other man's bins. 'Gotcha,' he said. 'Keys? Plipper? Alarms? Friendly SWAT team guarding it?'

Shard magically produced a pair of keys and a device and dropped them onto the parapet.

'Golly,' said Stoner. 'That's a device. I recognise it. What's it do?'

'Unlocks the car, soft lad. Nothing else that I'm aware of.'

'That's a worry.'

'There's movement. Want to look?'

'Talk to me, spotter boy.' Stoner was watching the busy street below them. It was doing all the things streets do, oblivious – probably oblivious – of the parallel lives operating above it.

'They're all up and doing,' reported Shard. 'Can't make out what they're doing, but it involves them being up.'

'And doing. You said that already.'

'Yeah. They're looking at things I can't see, and talking about stuff I can't hear. What more do you want?'

'You got an eavesdropping ear in the van?'

'Not sure. Don't think so. Why? You need to hear what's going on in there? Who are they anyway? Why are we watching them?'

'No idea. They're probably terrestrials. That's about the limit of my knowledge. I'm here watching because I was told to come here and watch. You too.'

'Got it. You mean terrorists.'

'No. I mean terrestrials. Maybe the boss is concerned about alien invasion or the like. I would be.'

'You think there's a likelihood of an alien invasion?' Shard's gaze was unflinching, he was plainly undistracted by the prospect of alien invasion. His professional detachment shone brightly.

'No. That would be very stupid. Do you think it's likely?'

'Yep.' Shard shifted his position slightly while maintaining his focus. 'But I am a professional and I am unconcerned. I will be concerned only when I am ordered to become so.'

'Commendable, soldier. Commendable. Keep the faith.' Stoner was interrupted by a loud pocketory vibration. He pulled a cell phone from within his heavy biker coat.

'How's that work?' Shard continued to spot the window. 'You took out the gubbins.'

'Two phones,' explained Stoner. 'That I'll admit to. You can have too much of a bad thing.' He hefted the phone to his ear. 'Chinese laundry. How can I help?' And then he listened for a while, and then a while more. It is not a simple matter to accurately define a while.

He left then, walking with surprising quiet for a big heavy man wearing a big heavy leather motorcycle rider's coat and a pair of big heavy leather biker's boots. But he managed it. Quiet. The phone was still clamped to his ear.

Shard called after him. 'There's a set or two of decent legs, tripods, in the van. Be useful, Stoner.' Stoner walked on; the phone had apparently found a new home by his ear.

And returned, surprisingly quickly and surprisingly quietly.

'That was surprisingly quick,' remarked Shard, eyes painted to the lenses of his bins. 'And surprisingly quiet.'

'Yeah. Be impressed, soldier boy.' Stoner rested a pair of seriously big binoculars on the parapet, leaned a tripod against the wall within easy reach of his companion. 'I do as bid. Anything else, brave voyeur?'

'Only how come is it that I'm working for a civilian now? You being that civilian, formerly sergeant Stoner, and me being what you might call in service. God, Queen, country, whatever else you got.'

Stoner might have smiled. Hard to tell in a dimly-lit concrete car park. 'Soldiers always work for civilians, military man. In the long run. It's the natural order of things. I get paid more than you do too, so spare me the heartache about them as does the work getting the least out of it. Pretend I'm a general. Better yet, an RSM. You'd be real respectful then.' He patted his companion on the shoulder, a wide shoulder, companionably.

Shard shook his head, and after another few moments looked up, as if to speak. But Stoner was gone.

oOo

Stoner walked in the best and most efficient way he could. The large biker coat discouraged running, and the large biker boots prevented a combination of running and silence.

He moved down to the ground floor entrance, moving smoothly and quietly between the infestation of parked cars, oblivious to the irritation of all those – and there were several of them – whose access to the upper storeys was prevented by Shard's so-official van. Then out into the street, crossing the road, keeping out of Shard's sightline and heading for an alley. The phone was safely back in a pocket.

Out of the echoes of the carpark and away from any interested eyes, Stoner ran, the heavy leather of the coat flapping around him.

'You need to see someone about that.' The voice was quiet but somehow perfectly audible.

'About what?' Stoner ran to a standstill, bent down and rested his hands on his knees. Stood again, looked around him. Saw no one, which is what he expected to see.

'You sound like the steam pig come to life,' laughed the voice, and a figure appeared, unremarkably following the words. 'You got lung cancer or something? Sounds like it. Your lungs sound like a sack of dead bellows. Horrible noise.'

Stoner caught the newcomer's glance, held it. 'Yeah, yeah. Spare me all that my body is a temple crap. I get too much of it from Shard. Good to see you here, Mince. If you're here, then it must be a hit and not a watch. Yeah?'

Mince shrugged. They were wide shoulders, they took some shrugging. Shrugging was not a frivolous activity, not for a notably violent killer who was almost as broad as he was tall. 'Don't know,' he replied. 'No idea. You're the sergeant, Sergeant Stoner your worshipfulness, you tell me.' There was no malice to his words. 'You got Shard up there in the gods, then?' He waved vaguely, upward, far away; that kind of wave. Stoner nodded. It was enough.

'My brief is to watch this corner, these two walls, all doors and windows, and to note all entries and exits.' Mince produced a small camera. 'The wonders of technology,' he remarked, still smiling.

'Does your brief include a reporting structure?'

'It does. I report to you in the field.'

'And off the field?' Stoner was looking at the several windows and fewer doors.

'Can't say. You know how it is.'

'OK. Who's gone in since you've been here? Which is how long?'

Mince looked at a wristwatch, a big one, a watch to take on expeditions and into orbit. 'One hour twenty-seven,' he announced. 'Twenty eight.' He handed the small camera to Stoner, who in turn flicked through the images on its screen. Took out his active cell phone and began comparing images.

'Neat,' he announced. Then; 'Nice.' He nodded. 'Thanks.'

'You're welcome.' Mince was a man who shared a belief in a creative approach to language. 'Anyone you recognise? Any of them match?'

'Could do.' Stoner nodded. He returned the camera to his companion, flicked at his cell phone to encourage a little communication, lifted it to his ear and walked out of easy earshot. 'Subjects two and three,' he told the phone, which muttered into his ear. 'OK.' He hung up. Walked back to Mince. 'Stay here,' he suggested, as though this was a debate among equals and that there was room for discussion. Mince failed to reply, returned his silent gaze to his areas of interest. Stoner walked on, briskly, retracing his steps. Back to the carpark, back up the ramps past the confused cars and their drivers, past the parked van.

'You sick or something?' Shard greeted him without lifting his eyes from the bins, perched as they were before him on a neat and nifty tripod, leaving his hands free.

'Sick?' Stoner's breath rasped. 'It's the coat. It's not intended for running in.' He leaned forward, hands to his knees, panted a little.

'You sound like an old boiler, mate.' Shard's tone was disinterested, largely, his attention entirely held by the image in his binoculars.

'Thank you.' Stoner stood upright. Dropped the heavy leather coat. Looked with sudden awareness at his companion. 'What're you doing, soldier boy?'

'What's it look like, former sergeant?'

'Looks like you're jacking off, sergeant. Say it isn't so.'

'I cannot lie to a fellow non-com. Now look away, lest terror reinforce your customary feeling of inadequacy when confronted by a real man, a man in his prime.'

'A man doing what he does best?'

'Exactly so. Care to join in?'

Stoner looked around for the other set of bins, failed to find them. 'I give in,' he said. 'What's giving you this plainly irresistible urge for self-abuse?'

'It's a knocking shop,' revealed Shard. 'Either that or they're making a movie without a camera. Maybe rehearsing.'

'Say again?' Stoner squatted down beside him.

'You heard. At it in there. Four of them. Two guys, two chicks. Multiracial, multi-partner, access all areas, no holes barred. Fascinating to a student of the human condition.'

'That would be you?'

'Correct. I live only for education, education, education. To quote our illustrious Prime Minister, a man well versed in masturbation, masturb...'

'Got it.' This from Stoner, who had located the other set of bins. 'I can see that they're doing something, but not what, exactly,' he mused.

'It's all in the eye of the beholder.'

'What?' Stoner was visibly peering.

'It's all to do with the great righteousness of it all.'

'Horseshit. You've got the better bins is all. You nearly finished yet?'

'Patience, Obi-Wan. If you could just and as it were shut the fuck up for a moment, then seed will be spilled upon the ground and a great rejoicing will arise across the land.'

'You're spilling seed on the ground? I think that was supposed to be about farming, raising crops and the like.'

'Each to their own, JJ. Now be a good girl and shut it for a while and I'll make with the groaning thing and then you can have the good glasses.'

'You carry on this way and you'll need the glasses.'

'I thought it made you deaf.'

'I can see that you might think that.'

Shard was impressively and massively silent for a while. 'You want to take over for a while?'

'Lost interest,' Stoner announced. 'And the phone's going to ring.'

'How can you tell?'

'That Hard Man has a certain knack of calling at exactly the wrong...' his phone interrupted him, buzzing in a persistent way. 'Yeah,' said Stoner, holding it to his face. 'Yeah,' he repeated, with no greater show of enthusiasm. 'It's a knocking shop in there.' He paused, listening. 'No. No I've not seen inside, Shard... Harding's hogged the big bins.' He paused again. 'I am not whining. I am explaining. Harding does not need relieving. I believe he's taken care of that himself.' He listened some more. Shook his head. 'OK,' he said. 'I'll take the sho...'. He stopped again. 'Familiar faces. In the street.' He tapped Shard on the shoulder, passed him the lower-powered bins.

Stoner stood upright, smoothly and without evident effort, walked backwards across the empty concrete and away from Shard. He was plainly absorbed by whatever he was being told. 'OK,' he said eventually. He closed the phone.

'Change hands,' said Shard, enigmatically.

'You're a man of untold talent.'

'They're changing the cast. The guys and one of the girls are prepping to leave, looks like. The faces in the street. They're Irish faces. They're watching the same building. The players should charge for this. It's like a peepshow. What're you doing?'

Stoner hauled back into his heavy leather coat. 'I'll be back,' he announced, inevitably.

'To come back, you first need to leave,' suggested Shard.

'You're quick. Credit where it's due.'

'Where you off to, big man?'

'Can't say.'

'Can't say, won't say?'

'You got me. You're staying here.'

'I am?'

'You are.'

'Great. Maybe there'll be a few encores.'

'You up for an encore?'

'Yep.'

'Respect. Sow more seed.'

'I'll do my best. It's my duty to Queen and country.'

'Oh please.'

'OK. How long?'

'Until I get back.'

'There's cover on other entrances?'

'There is.'

'Anyone I know?'

'Mince.'

'Oh joy unbounded. That under-brained over-muscled fucktard.'

'He sends his love, undying, that sort of thing.'

'He knows I'm here?'

'Yeah.'

'How long, JJ? Make with an answer, less the comedy.'

'Forty-eight hours tops. I'll sort relief if longer. Do you need cover before that?'

'Nah. Everything's in the van.'

'Uppers?'

'Everything.'

'Gotcha. Emergency number's the same. Usual practice.'

'You don't answer, I call your big boss on the number so sacred that only the angel Gabriel knows it. And me, obviously.'

'That one.' And Stoner walked to his Harley-Davidson motorcycle, kicked up its stand, placed his helmet on his head, his gloves on his hands, fired up the engine and rolled thunderously away.

oOo

A country city, dreaming spires, lost in a hopeless pretence that it still was a town, a beautiful historic town noted for education of the highest kind and culture to match. The city aimed to ignore the desperate sprawl of the suburbs, tried to maintain its self-image of a bastion of standards in a declining world.

Stoner rolled his motorcycle to a quiet stop in a leafy lane, some distance from the sprawl, a green space preserved against all odds and the corruption of property development between two areas of older – and therefore somehow better – development. Heavy houses, horsey and well separated from each other and from the real world. Except when the real world – in this instance represented by former sergeant JJ Stoner – trespassed.

He switched off the heavy engine, revelled in the sharply contrasting silence. In just a few moments, birds resumed their interrupted conversations, a dog barked, once, twice. The birds ignored the dog. It bothered them less than did the Harley-Davidson. The motorcycle fitted well into the dusty widening of the lane; one more darkness in a confusion of natural shadow and shade. Stoner dismounted and rolled the machine backwards into further incidental seclusion. Not exactly hidden; not exactly obvious. Behind and to the right of the motorcycle was a stile, a non-swinging gate allowing pedestrian access to the field beyond. In the field, its grass grazed short by ruminants who left ample signs of their presence, stood a single tree; a large, spreading tree, a tree affording shelter from storm and shade from the sun, as on this occasion. Beneath the tree was a spot of vivid colour. Stoner swung his legs over the stile, walked towards the tree, to the colour beneath it.

'Bernadette,' he greeted his colourful companion. She smiled up at him, nodded a welcome. The smile passed, like sun behind clouds.

'What you doing, girl?' Stoner stood before her, crash helmet swinging loose from one hand, heavy leather riding coat shifting as his free hand unbuttoned, then unzipped, then unpopped its several fastening mechanisms. 'You ... that's a rosary? You're ... what? Hail Marys and Glory Bes?' He dropped coat and helmet to the grass, silently. The helmet rolled a little while it found its own balance.

'JJ,' she said, quietly. 'Glad it's you.'

He waited for more, then squatted before her, careful not to interrupt whatever was happening between them.

'I...' he ventured. 'You...'

'We're here to do what our masters have bid us do.' Her soft, dark Irish voice complimented the pastoral pastel sheen of the world they shared. 'It's the last job for me, JJ.' Her long fingers moved a string of beads. Her fingers were dirty, Stoner noticed, quite suddenly. The sight of their grime and the rosary they read moved him to silence. He waved his own hands, powerless and lost before her.

'I'm moving on, Jean-Jacques. It's like ... Gethsemane again. In the garden. Here.'

'It's a field, Bernie. A field blessed with cowshit and flies.' Stoner sank down and sat before her. Rested his hands where she could always see them. She watched his eyes.

'For you.' She smiled. Not a sad smile, not exactly. 'I wish we had time to make love here, Jean-Jacques.'

'Babe.' She was barefoot, and her feet, her toes were dirty like her fingers. Her face, her eyes shone to him, her teeth white and improbably defined in the tan of her skin. Her hair appeared to have set, as though sprayed in some strange commercial for cosmetics. Stoner understood that things made no sense to him. 'Tell me?'

'Hush,' she maintained her smile. 'He'll be here soon, and we need to understand how to approach him. We have a job to do. My final fling, if you like.'

Stoner shook his head, spread his hands again. 'Bernadette, you're sitting under a tree like the enlightened one, grubby as a Sixties flowerchild and with henna in your hair, telling me that you're moving on after you've finished your rosary, and meanwhile we just get on and do the job.' He leaned backwards, dropping his hands behind him to catch his own long body before it fell flat on its back. 'You should... I'm thinking you should... you should stand down and I'll do the talking to the target, the whole thing myself. You don't seem ... you don't seem yourself. Lovely Bernadette. What's doing with you?'

Her smile widened, stretching her lips across the white wall of her teeth. 'I'm out. Leaving the game, the police, the off-the-books squad, the lot.'

'Can you even do that?'

'Oh yes.' She certainly did seem confident. The beads had vanished, some sleight of hand, some deception found her fingers free. As with the beads, so with her smile, disappeared into some safe and secret place. 'Here he comes now, walking the dog. The briefing was right, as usual.'

They both stood, an incongruous couple; Stoner dressed as though he'd just marched from the seat of a Harley-Davidson and exuding his usual aura of mild menace, Bernadette looking sweet as a latter-day flowerchild who would harm no one, no thing. The subject of their attention approached, a shifting set of expressions clouding his features as he spotted them, pondered their likely identities and reached a conclusion.

'You're here, then.' His voice was educated, north country English and quiet. Calm. He gestured to the dog, which sat down at his feet, observed Stoner, considered Bernadette and finally decided upon an appropriate response. It scratched behind an ear, and lay down, observing. 'I should have expected someone like you. Inevitable.'

Bernadette spread her hands, possibly emphasising their emptiness, and possibly not. A disarming gesture, if nothing else. 'Yes,' she replied. 'Dr Kennedy. We know who you are, we all know why we're all here, and you have no need to know who we are ... although you can work out where we're from, who sent us and why we're here to talk with you.'

Kennedy nodded. Stoner walked to the tree, leaned his back against it, lifted one of his feet and rested that against the tree, hands in his trouser pockets, coat lying between the three of them. He looked away from the others, the perfect observer. Of both his companions and their surroundings. Had he been a cigarette smoking man, this would have been lighting up time.

'Sections of the government, including your own employers, are impressively unhappy with the interview you've given to a television network and a newspaper.' Bernadette spoke gently enough, the Irish float of her voice lending it a peculiar threat. She named both the network and the newspaper. Dr Kennedy nodded, observing her as though he were a scientist and she a specimen, which indeed he was, and she was not. 'We're here to ask you to retract both interviews and to deny their publication. Especially those derogatory comments about the dossier.'

'To ask.' Kennedy's mouth twitched a little. It may have been a suppressed smile. He shook his head; denial of something. 'To threaten, I think. Threats would ... appeal more to your employers than a simple request, surely.'

'Maybe. It would certainly look that way, and it could easily end that way if you refuse our request. Which is what it is.' Bernadette's tone was a fine example of reasonable force. 'We're asking you to withdraw your interviews. It would be best – by a long way, Doctor – for all concerned, both directly and indirectly. Publishing your interviews would only harm. Everyone.' She looked up.

Kennedy nodded. 'And now the threats. Thank you for being so civilised. You should know...' he paused. 'Have you read or watched the interviews?'

Bernadette shook her head. 'No. No point to it, we have no interest in it.'

'You're employed by politicians, but take no interest in the politics you support?' Kennedy sounded cynical and weary. 'How can you even know what you're doing here? The interviews are truthful, and the public has the right to know that their government has lied, lied and lied again.' His brief burst of animation faded.

'You're employed by the same politicians, Doctor. You've signed the same paperwork that we have.' She waved to include Stoner, who appeared to be absorbed by something far away. 'You're breaking your agreement with your employer, your contract, your word.' She gestured in Stoner's direction again. 'He's a soldier, I'm police. What we think doesn't matter, what we do is what's important. This country went to war, and part of the justification for that war was a report you were a party to and signed. And now you've changed your mind.'

'Do you know why?'

'No.'

'Don't you even want to?'

'No. Think of it differently, Doctor. Think of the thousands of soldiers who killed thousands of soldiers, civilians and all in between, at least in part because of the reports you were party to and signed. Don't interrupt. I'm appealing to your better judgement, for your understanding.' She waved vaguely at Stoner once more. 'He's a soldier, a sergeant, a very active and senior sergeant who lost several of his own unit in an action your report, your signature validated. Can you apply your doctoral intellect to the current situation in which you find yourself? Can you understand – here comes a threat, look out – can you understand that if the same senior officer who ordered this sergeant to murder a lot of people he'd never met, and who had certainly done nothing wrong and nothing at all to harm him... if that same senior officer ordered him to put a few ounces of lead into a few more heads of people he's never met, and who had done nothing personal to him except get many of his brothers killed... can you see how he would not, shall we say, feel reluctance to obey? To follow his orders? To honour the contract he signed?'

Doctor Kennedy looked at Stoner. The dog looked at Stoner. Bernadette looked at Stoner. Stoner scratched behind an ear and gazed into the middle distance.

'I've been in warzones,' Kennedy announced, with some attempt at passion. 'I don't scare any more. I'm not withdrawing anything. Nice speech, Miss. Is that your best ... shot?' He smiled a supercilious smile.

'No need to decide anything right now, Doctor Kennedy.' Bernadette smiled a smile of her own. An inscrutable smile. 'Come and see us again in the morning. Same place, right here. Sleep on it. Talk with Mrs Kennedy.

Consider Phlebas, if that helps. You'll have no interruptions between now and your morning dog walk. Nothing to distract you.'

Kennedy took a step away. The dog rose smartly to its feet. Kennedy turned back to Bernadette. 'What are you saying?'

Stoner peeled away from the tree, strolled across the grass and stood behind Bernadette, looking directly at the other man for the first time. His gaze was steady, unblinking, his expression entirely professional and neutral. Bernadette spoke. 'I want you to have time to consider. You have candles, and matches to light them. And if you're feeling a chill, you can burn your papers in either of your log burners and use them to light logs. You will be uninterrupted by telephone, television, even radio and the blight that is the internet. A golden opportunity to explain to Mrs Kennedy – the other Doctor Kennedy – why your own sense of self-righteousness and a fat cheque from the media are going to impact on her and upon your daughters.' She paused, looked at her watch, then at Stoner, who may have blinked. 'Neither of your cars is functional, and your employers have closed the roads in any case. A small and entirely professional military unit is protecting you and yours. Enjoy your evening, Doctor.'

She stepped back, slipped her arm through Stoner's, nodded and walked away, back across the field to the lane where Stoner had parked his motorcycle.

'Jesus,' he said once they were well out of earshot. 'Who is this guy? If I need to take him out, tell me. I don't have that order from on high. Did you write all that crap yourself? I was believing you, lady. Seriously. Heavy stuff. Who is he?'

'He's an arms inspector – or was. And he's lots of things. Like everyone. You in a rush?'

'I have another job running, Bernie. You didn't know that?'

'No. I'm not on for a convivial evening, then? No head to head, no heart to heart?'

'Not really. It's a surveillance, but a tricky one. Not enough eyes, not enough discipline. The Hard Man told me to come here and play Mr Muscles for you, but he didn't say anything about time off for good behaviour. And ... and what's with the godliness, Bernie? The rosary? Retirement? And when do we get to talk about the baby?' He stopped, and pulled her to a stop beside him. 'The Elliot quote was masterly, by the way.'

A Range Rover approached them, parked by the Harley-Davidson. Idled in near-silence. Stoner could see the figure of the driver, but no more. Bernadette slid her arm from his as easily as she had pulled them together, nodded to him. 'See you in the morning, then. Seven would be on time; here would be perfect. Enjoy your surveillance, JJ.' She opened a rear door, disappeared inside. The Range Rover reversed, flashed the cannons of its headlights at him just once, turned down a second lane and departed, all in considerable heavy quiet. Stoner watched, motionless, as the small show unfolded for him, then he fired up the motorcycle, wrecking the silence, leaving it idling noisily while he dragged on gloves, helmet and some sense of composure. Turned around in the lane and left the way he'd arrived, just more loudly.

oOo

Fuel. Fuel for both machine and man. An American diner with a petrol station. Early evening. Cool sunlight, promises of romance. A moment of sustenance before returning to the observation. No telephonic urgency. Stoner swung the motorcycle to a pump, satisfied its thirst, considered checking its oil, dismissed the notion as absurd, paid, remounted and shouldered the American machine into a gap between two other bikes. Brit Americana. The wallpaper music pretended to be a Fifties jukebox, the waitresses were American in their friendly attentiveness, and the wall decorations suggested that the diner dining in the diner was somehow transported to an easier time. Stoner smiled at the thought. There had been no easier times. Times – all times – are consistent in their uneasiness.

Menu. He ordered. Coffee arrived and he immediately asked for a refill, raising a giggle from the girl as he drained the coffee hot and black. The first refill followed the original and the second refill held a pause. Stoner pulled a phone from a pocket. Then another.

'Join you?' Polite request from a younger man, owner of one of the other American motorcycles parked outside, at least according to the death's heads and trademark labelling all over his shirt.

'Rather not. No offence.'

The younger man looked confused. He asked a fairly complicated question involving the exact identity of Stoner's machine. But he remained standing, which was a good thing. Stoner looked up, beamed in a poisonous way and shook his head. 'Not a good time,' he shared. 'Maybe later.' He picked up one of the phones with a level of enthusiasm more usually reserved for clasping flaming coals, and waggled it in an apologetic way. 'I need to…'. The younger man smiled, accepting. Moved back to his companionable crowd, a couple of whom raised bottles in a toast. Stoner toasted them back with his coffee mug. It pays to keep unfamiliar friends on your side.

Message from Bernadette. Brief. 'Hurry,' it read. The second message, also from her, said the same thing. Stoner was reaching for his coat before he considered checking the times of the messages. They were before their rural encounter. He sat back and relaxed. Time is always relative.

Message from Shard. Less brief. 'They're all at it. Non stop. Bring your own tissues. Don't talk back.' Stoner smiled.

Message from a withheld number, demanding his whereabouts and ETA. He deleted it. Food arrived and he ate it. The second phone held a couple of domestic niceties; an invitation to a funeral followed by a suggestion that he meet up for a soldierly reunion and tell a few tall tales to cheer up anyone left miserable by burying a friend. Another friend. Conversation at the tables occupied by his fellow easy riders was becoming loud, general movement levels were escalating rapidly and all attention was focussed on the parked bikes.

Outside, as the light leaked away into the bright sky, shadows extended themselves until they met and mated with other shadows, a large saloon car had somehow parked itself in such a way that it not only blocked the motorcycles' exit, should they want an exit any time soon, but it also appeared to be aiming to see how close it could get to the motorcycle nearest to it. The motorcycle collective inside the diner appeared to be at least a little familiar with the characters involved, judging by the hooting, snorting and derisive gestures.

'What's with the comedy?' Stoner joined the younger man, who was part of the general amusement. 'Is this dickless tool likely to knock a bike over? And why?'

'Happens maybe every week or so,' the younger man acted unconcerned. Stoner's understanding was that this was in fact an act.

'Why? He's very close to my motorcycle, and I am an unforgiving man.'

'It's complicated. You don't need the history.' The younger man sighed. A younger woman reached up and squeezed his hand, looked with almost no interest at Stoner, and resumed her watching stance. Stoner wasn't entirely sure, but it appeared to him that the car and a motorcycle had touched.

'My motorcycle is next to the end, my friend. What say I share a word of caution with the driver?' Stoner stood and shrugged his coat over his shoulders, settling it more comfortably.

'I wouldn't.'

'Why?'

The younger woman waved a forefinger at Stoner. 'Because they're waiting for it.' He followed her gesture and observed two marked police cars, lights out, standing in the shadow.

'Really? The plods are ... what? On their side? Unlikely.'

'Rugby club. There's history.'

'Yeah, yeah. The famous history of violence. I'll go chat with plod. If that no-nuts damages my machine I'll break his legs. I need to explain this to the officers.'

'You don't understand!' A cry too late. Stoner was out through the door and striding fast towards the police car. The driver of the big saloon ignored him, and continued to inch forward, inch back, every time rocking the nearest motorcycle a little more. Stoner reached the nearest police car. Stopped. Walked in front of it, in front of its dark lights. He slowly reached inside his long heavy leather coat, removed a phone. Held it in front of the car's windscreen. There was no noticeable reaction.

Exaggerating every gesture, Stoner flicked the phone to life, dialled a number, held the phone to his ear. The police car lit its sidelights, presumably to see this performing clown better. Stoner took the phone from his ear, pointed in a truly theatrical manner at it, then at the passenger side of the car, walked around to that side and tapped gently on the window. Which rolled down. A uniformed hand took the phone. Every two-wheeled eye in the diner was watching Stoner. The invasive car driver and his crew appeared too engrossed in their game of tip-a-bike to bother about anything behind them. They plainly knew that the police were on their side. If there were indeed sides in this strange shuffling non conflict.

The person in the passenger seat of the police car returned Stoner's phone to him. The window rolled up. Stoner pocketed the phone and walked to his motorcycle, looping around the back of the idiots in the idiot saloon car on his way. He stood by his bike. Pointed at it. Shook his head, waggled an admonitory finger at the car, made a shooing motion with both of his hands. The driver ignored him. The car rolled nearer, lifting the motorcycle nearest to it to the point where its balance was precarious indeed. Stoner's machine stood next to it.

He shrugged. Ran very fast, banking around the bikes, lifted something from a pocket of his long coat and shattered the driver's side window with whatever it was. The car stopped. Dead. Stoner reached inside the car, and pulled a head through the window. The car's engine stalled. It was suddenly inert. Whatever window-smashing object Stoner held in his hand he now applied with some vigour and evident enthusiasm to the head and neck he was attempting to pull from the car and possibly from the shoulders of its owner. Heads bleed badly, a fact confirmed by this one, and the blood it bled smeared on the skin and curdled in the short hair of the head protruding from the window. Stoner stopped, held the leaking bloody nose of the injured window dresser until he coughed and groaned. Proof of life.

All three remaining doors of the car opened in no particular order and a total of five men piled into the evening. They may have been shouting a lot, it was hard to tell from inside the diner, where the ersatz jukebox was belting out an ancient Chuck Berry number proclaiming to anyone nearby that he had no particular place to go. The same could not be said of Stoner.

He shrugged his shoulders back, dropped his heavy coat, and demolished the man nearest to him; a heavy kick from a Caterpillar boot applied to the crotch achieves this result. Always. It is unrecoverable, except in the movies. In this case as in real life, the kicked fell away from the kicker, curling around himself and quite suddenly puking violently, coughing through the mess. Out of it. Two men down.

The fallen man had been clutching a bottle. Stoner borrowed it, maybe with a word of two of grateful thanks, politeness always being a virtue, and smashed it into the face of the next man along. The bottle broke, such was the unreasonable force applied to it, and one of the long splinters of brown glass plainly did some terrible damage to at least one of the victim's eyes, judging by the amount of blood and stringy clear jellies which appeared on his cheek. The appearance of the curious blood and jelly mix was accompanied by a sound more usually encountered while skinning a live pig, although most pigs would have had more fight in them. Two to go.

The biker boys from the diner were arriving. Stoner waved them away. 'Just fuck off,' he suggested, not unkindly. Then turned his attention to the two remaining men, neither of them built on the slight side, and neither of them apparently sober.

Stoner spoke. Not quietly, but not exactly shouting either. 'Knives, guns? You guys tooled up? If you are, show me the evidence and I'll show you my answer. If not, best just call an ambulance for your buddies. I'll give you a half-minute. Then I'll come collect.' He walked to his motorcycle, removed something from its baggage.

'Collect what?' Some people can be surprisingly literal in the most unusual of circumstances.

'What you got? Time's up.' Stoner dropped to his ankles like a Cossack dancer and whipped a light chain around the ankles of the nearer man. Who, inevitably, tried to walk or run or maybe fly, and fell down out of control. Inevitably. He yelled and reached for Stoner, who was passing by and who didn't pause his stride as he delivered a nose-breaker to the angry face below him. Less of a kick, more a stomp, but the crunch was the same, and as effective without requiring all that difficult footballer skill. And blood is less intrusive on the sole of a boot than on its uppers.

'You and me, then, huh? You can run away. They won't help.' The last man was looking in an increasingly frightened way at the parked, unlit police cars. As if on cue, one of them fired up quietly and moved away, lighting its lights in a single red and blue salute. 'They're on their break. Everyone needs a break. They'll have called the ambulance by now. Surely. If I was you ... a disgusting notion, frankly ... I'd, like, run away now. Unless you've got a gun. Do you have a gun?'

A shaking of head. Then running. The silent walk back to the diner, through a small and silent band of bikers, collecting the long coat. Subdued. Returned to his booth, the waiting food.

'Uhhh...' A small delegation, beards common among the men, less so with the women.

Stoner looked up from his freshly cooked but steadily cooling American food. 'Go away.' Not unkindly. But not friendly, either. Two ambulances lit the car park with their strobes. Two policemen, from the single remaining car, appeared to be agreeing the contents of statements with the paramedics. A sad tale of friends getting drunk and fighting a bit. Typical Saturday night in the city. Even if it was a Tuesday. In the country. Variety is the spice.

oOo

Night amplifies sound. The heavyweight Harley-Davidson thundered lazily through otherwise silent streets. Intrusively loud and dismissed as simply an irritation by anyone whose nocturnal manoeuvres were interrupted by the shudder of its passage. Stoner rolled the machine into the multi-storey car park, shaking its inner peace like a mongoose with a snake. Past the No Entry signs, their red warning lights lit and ignored. Parked up. Walked up, past Shard's parked van. Had to admit it, a van was more subtle than the Harley. Less manoeuvrable but more invisible. You could also sleep more easily in a van. Something to consider for the future. If there was a future.

'Hey, silent man.' Shard was eye to the lens, nose possibly to an invisible grindstone.

'How goes?' Stoner popped a thermos from his long coat, passed its warmth to his observer, who took it from his hand without breaking his gaze from the glass.

'Interesting,' he remarked, sipping hot black coffee. 'Got interesting now.'

'They all still doing it, doing it?'

Shard's laugh was professionally restrained. 'Picking their nose and chewing it ... you don't mean. No. No, they're not. You'd be wanting what the movies call a sitrep?'

'I would. Also a sip of my coffee. It's cool on a bike.'

'That would be why you brave the cold and ride one, noble man.' Shard passed over the flask. Stoner picked up a set of binoculars and peered. Shook his head invisibly and with small irritation. Shard reported, as promised.

'A crowd. Six. Four dicks and two dolls. All four have enjoyed both, in several entertaining combinations and with some imagination. One of the studs is Olympic class; bonk for Britain, that one, though he is – I think – no Brit. He is familiar.' He paused, waiting for the question, which lay between them unasked. 'No pos ID though. Know the face, I think. You want the long glass? Maybe you can make a make on him?'

'Nah.' Stoner sat back. 'Mince?'

'No sign.'

'Visitors? Here, I mean.'

'None. Nobody loves me, everybody hates me.'

'That at least is true. I'll make a call.' Which he did. 'Fuck.' Then the uneasy quiet of text messaging in the night with a dim screen and cold digits. Again: 'Fuck.' Eventually he snapped the cell phone into darkness and silence. 'The second team of watchers. The street operators. They still there?'

Shard grunted. 'No idea. It's dark. No peripheral. No movement though. They looked Irish. They'll be down the boozer. Wise guys, the Irish. Not like us Brits. Perfidious or not, we surely are stupid sometimes.'

'If they're not still running the marathon shagathon, what've they been doing, active sergeant Shard?'

'Talking. Oh. They're armed. Handguns only, so far as I can see. Nothing heavy, nothing long range.'

'Junk?'

'Excuse me?'

'Dope. They doing dope?'

'Not that I can see. Why?'

'No reason.'

'Papers on the table. Several phones. Much jaw action and telephony. Two laptops. Is this the fabled revolution?' Shard might have been joking.

'Kidnapping.' Stoner wasn't joking.

'OK. Anyone we know?'

'Don't know, don't...'

'Don't care. Yeah, I got that, super sergeant, retired. Don't know shit, don't want to know shit. Gotcha, sarge.' Shard had lapsed into a broad Irish brogue. 'Activity,' he announced, leaning forward further into his lenses. 'Definite activity.'

'Two will leave,' Stoner remarked.

'Two've left,' Shard confirmed. 'Four remaining.'

Stoner flicked open a cell phone, his fingers flew. He watched the screen, nodded finally, his head backlit by the night's vague light. 'Got them.'

'Mince?'

'Uh-huh. Taken them down. One secured, one casualty.' Stoner watched his phone, reading the scrolling text.

'Mince? No knees left to any of the bad guys, then. Hard on knees is Mince. He has a thing. Catholic upbringing.'

'Excuse me?' Stoner failed to sound interested.

'On their knees all the time, Catholics. Affects them.'

'You know this how? You're no Catholic, unless you've had a sudden conversion.' Stoner was still watching the words, and now images to accompany them.

'Got wrecked with Mince just the one time. Savage man. Should have been a priest, that one. Like you, Father Jean. No offence.'

'Put a round into the apartment's entry door, please. You've got clear sight?'

'Affirmative.' Professional. 'Slug selection?'

'Heavy, slow and loud, no frag please.' Stoner took the stronger bins from his companion, zoomed and focussed. Shard took up the rifle, positioned himself, silent now. Balanced his breathing and fired. The unsuppressed report spilled anger, fear into the night. 'Again, please,' said Stoner. Shard reloaded and obliged. The urban environment shrugged off the unusual sound. The apartment's inhabitants did not.

'What's the sight through the sight?' Stoner was scanning the street below them through the binoculars.

'No panic. They're all doing things with their phones.'

'I bet they are.' Stoner rested his opened but unlit cell phone between them. It had nothing to say to anyone.

'You been fighting, big man?' Shard's question distracted neither of the men.

'Just a bit. Why?'

'You smell excited, and you don't smell of sex.'

'Thank you.' Stoner grinned into the dark. 'You're saying I stink.'

'No. Healthy locker room sweat. You smell like you've done a couple of rounds with the feeble. Any reason? Anyone I know?'

'No. Why d'you ask?'

'Just making conversation. Admiring your adventures. You fight a lot for an enlightened man, Father Jean. Always puzzled me. You're not a bar room brawler, so I – just occasionally, it's no obsession – I wonder why.'

'Clears the mind. I get … clogged with rubbish. Like constipation of the brain. Tubes blocked. Violence – a little bit of focus, a little action with a clear result – clears that. I get wrapped up in civilisation … in restraint. Meet too many guys who need slapping but I can't do that for whatever reason. It builds up and I lose focus. Waste time working on self-restraint. So I find some guys who need a slap and I do that for them. Everyone's a winner. They get a kicking, I get calm and clarity. Zen shit a mindless thug like you can't understand. Eat shit, Shard. Be glad you're not me. End of life class. What's the crack, Jack?'

'They're still engaged in confusion. Any minute now there'll be running and shouting...'

'If anyone makes for the doors, pop a knee or a leg or a foot. Not head and not torso.'

'OK master. I hear and I obey. What's going on in there?'

'They're talking with the Hard Man, at a guess.'

'All is explained.'

'All is being explained, most likely. They're four rats, cornered. He'll be explaining their situation to them. They'll be sad and unhappy. Maybe valiant, heroic and similar stupidities.'

The rifle fired again. 'High knee,' announced Shard. 'Doesn't look arterial. Mind you, I am a long way away from the action. And I was right. There's running and shouting.'

Stoner rested the binoculars next to his cell phone. 'D'you have another long gun?'

'Uh-huh. Regular boy scout, me. Always prepared. Light stuff only. Two-two-three hi-vo ready loaded into the old AR15. You want I should go fetch? I could do with a walk.'

'Nope.' Stoner was already walking. He returned, juggling a suppressor onto the barrel of the weapon he'd collected from the van. 'This thing ranged? Zeroed? You ever cleaned it?'

'Nope. Nope. Yep.'

'OK. Count us down from five and put another round near to the door, not into the door or it'll fall apart and they'll escape.'

'Gotcha, boss.' Shard counted down and fired. Stoner also fired, shattering a second window and perforating innocent furniture.

'They couldn't have failed to observe the second gun, then?'

'Not a hope. Certainly not if they're pros.' Shard reloaded, squinted through his sights. 'They're very quiet now.'

'You would be. Holed up in a hotel room surrounded by trigger-happy maniacs with long guns and a plain dislike of hotel furniture.'

'As you say, JJ. Now what?'

'Now one of them will have that smart idea. He'll turn out the lights and close the blinds so we can't see him.'

'Fuck,' remarked Shard, conversationally. 'You can see the future. They've just turned out the lights. Bet they're doing the blinds too, just like you said. I'll switch to IR. I even remembered to fit the fresh batteries.'

'No need. Any moment now they'll put the lights back on.'

'Why? They'll not do that. That would be stupid. OK. They've switched on the lights and left open the blinds. Are they stupid or are they very stupid?'

'Neither. The Hard Man will have told them what happens if we can't see them clearly. He's told them we'll kill them all painfully, other encouraging things like that. Helps them consider, concentrate on matters important, similar things. He's a natural philosopher, that guy.'

'But we can see fine in IR. Your hard guy knows that.'

'We can't see who's who. Can't see our guy. Our inside man. Our mole. The guy who's set all this up for us.

You might shoot him by accident. That would be a bad thing, even for a mean hombre like you, no?'

'Yah. So we, you, he's got an insider, inside?'

'You betcha.'

'You know which one it is? I'd prefer not to shoot the wrong guy.'

'Not a clue. Aim low. Disable, don't destroy. Intimidate, don't eliminate. Sniper school crap like that.'

'I'll pretend I do know what you're talking about.'

'Good man.' Stoner inspected his phones once more. Tapped a message into one of them.

'Now what?' Shard was watching, waiting.

'Now you wait. I sleep. You wake me if anything happens. The Hard Man will leave them to perform a little situational analysis, and then he'll tell them what to do, and they'll either do it or they won't. It'll take all night, most likely. Either way, I got a hot date early in the morning, and I need some innocent babe-like shut-eye to prepare. I'll be out for a while.'

Stoner rolled himself up in his long coat, arranged limbs and rested his head. Instantly asleep, instantly still, and silent. Shard settled himself into the sniper's long watch. Patience and persistence; precision and patience perfected.

oOo

Early doors. Beautiful to some. Sunshine brilliance, the taste of frost, ice on the air. And air so cold and so calm, so still, that it carried sound for a huge distance. Mindful of this, Stoner had parked the black Harley-Davidson some considerable distance from the site of his forthcoming rural assignation with the delicious Bernadette and the confused government scientist, Kennedy. A good bright morning for a brisk walk, followed by polite conversation, an outcome of some kind and a resolution. One way or another, the bright morning would bring a resolution before it warmed into noon.

Figures beneath the tree. They'd no place being there, not yet. Stoner dropped into cover, smoothly and with the ease of long practise in fields more foreign and far less benign than this one. A man, Kennedy, and a woman. Stoner hauled them into focus through his lenses. Not Bernadette. Familiar seen from behind. Familiar in an entirely unpleasant way. The kind of familiarity that makes a chap hope he's mistaken. He checked his watch, everyone was early. An entire and almost exact hour early. Man, woman and the man's dog, arranged at rest, sitting around the base of the tree like some insane modernist *petit dejeuner sur l'herbe* posed for a talentless painter to copy and frame. Time to watch; to wait and to watch. Bernadette would be on time. She always was; neither early nor late, a sort of motto for her to work from. If Stoner's posterior recognition was correct, Bernadette's reaction would confirm it. Stoner checked his apparel. He was indeed armed, and certainly dangerous.

The couple beneath the morning shade of their shared tree were talking. Talking a lot. The woman produced something from the bag at her side and threw it at the dog, which leapt to catch it with every appearance of joy. Kennedy appeared to laugh. The woman threw another something for the dog, which leapt again and caught it again. This is the way of dogs. Their way had never appealed to Stoner. In his world, anyone throwing food around was suspect, not to be trusted. The woman – Stoner was becoming more sure of his identification and less comfortable with what it suggested – threw another mysterious something; the dog leapt about obediently. Dogs are simple. The man looked delighted with the stupidly trusting behaviour of his dog, allegedly his best friend in some sad world entirely unfamiliar to Stoner. Time passed.

Bernadette appeared, walking briskly in the crisp morning air. She stopped short when she spotted Kennedy's companion. Stood still. Then folded her arms. The woman rose – spread her arms wide in a gesture of considerable ambiguity, from where Stoner lay hidden anyway. The woman shrugged, showing her hands to be empty. Bernadette spoke; the other woman pushed her bag away from her with her foot, sat down and petted the dog, which appeared to have fallen asleep. Stoner assumed the sleep would be permanent. He was now positive in his identification. He'd met this woman before, unhappily for all. He'd not expected to meet her again, certainly not in this type of situation. Once is happenstance: twice suggested an employee in the pay of the opposition. Whoever was the opposition at the time. These things do vary with time and perception.

He waited and watched, uncharacteristically indecisive. Rose to his feet and prepared to break cover. Paused and studied the scene before him once more through the long lenses of his bins. The unwelcome woman handed something to Kennedy, Bernadette scrambled backwards, away from them both and rose rapidly to her feet. The something handed to Kennedy was a hand gun. Stoner dropped the bins and ran, lifting his black SIG Sauer from his coat, shedding the coat as he ran, fluid now, indecisive no more. No shouting, no fuss, simply running.

Bernadette had seen him. Her expression came into better focus as he ran towards them as rapidly as his heavy CAT boots could grip the grass beneath him. Kennedy had eyes only for the other woman, who leaned back, away from him, on her knees, arms spread as in prayer before an invisible altar. Bernadette screamed, incoherent at this range, if audible, and as the sound of her scream reached Stoner so Kennedy shot Bernadette, low down in her belly and her scream was suddenly silence, as she clutched herself, his face showing shock, amazement, disbelief and outrage; most of all outrage. She fell back to her knees, holding her hands to her weeping body and staring at Stoner.

Who ran, the SIG Sauer held before him and fired and missed and fired and missed again. And again. He stopped, took aim, and Kennedy raised the handgun into his mouth and plastered his government scientist's expensively educated brains across the dreaming English countryside. Stoner's aimed shot hit him in the gut, purposelessly.

He ran on, reaching them. The unwelcome woman, demure and beautiful in a summer dress and bare arms, empty hands, turned to face him.

'John,' she called. 'You're late again. It'll be the death of you. Come to break up the party, have we?' Her voice was as beautiful as her face. Stoner slowed to a walk, talking distance now, no more shouting.

'Blesses,' he said. 'Fuck. You.' He raised the gun... and stopped. Simply stopped. Stood. Stared at her. Stood. Un-still. Shaking. She held his gaze. He fired. The gun did not fire. His finger was outside the trigger guard. He squeezed unmoving metal. He shook. His body rattled like the tracks of a tank on hard concrete. His mouth hung open and tears pooled around his eyes.

'I think the dog's died, John,' Blesses remarked. 'It's had its day, as dogs do. You too. And I think you need attend to your cow.' She waved a hand at Bernadette, pallid now, sitting cross-legged in the sunshine on the grass, her hands bloody in her lap. 'I think you should drop that black cannon of yours, and I think you should take out your telephone and call for an emergency helicopter. I'll be on my way. Shame about your bastard, though.'

Stoner dropped the SIG Sauer and reached for his cell phone – raging in silence at his inability to disobey, a process entirely unfamiliar and horrible. Blesses smiled, not unkindly, held his gaze as he did as he was told, slowly, robotically.

Bernadette fired once, twice and both of Blesses' knees briefly ballooned red and wet and shattered beneath her as she fell, face down into the beautiful sunlit grassland. 'Call for evac, JJ.' Bernadette was panting, Blesses rolled onto her side, groaning, reaching into her bag and raising her deep wide blue oceanic eyes to Stoner, again.

He kicked her in the side of her head, which snapped around like a puppet's. She fell face down once more, lights out and legless. Stoner tied her hands and her feet with cable ties. Silence. Telephone talk. Weeping and bewilderment. Attempts at sharing, at understanding. At sanity and survival. A helicopter in an unfeasibly short time. Blood and tears.

oOo

'They're about to leave,' Shard revealed over the phone. He sounded distracted, tired, disappointed by the prolonged lack of action. 'Exactly like you said they would. Imagine your boss, Cheerful Charlie himself, talked them into it.'

'Imagine you're right. Wait for stand down. I'll call as soon as I have it. Stay sharp; they may yet develop a set and do their own Butch and Sundance impression.'

'Here's hoping.' Shard cut the call. Stoner watched the exit, unseen. His man Mince was waiting in plain view for the cornered crew to come out. Tense time.

'Do you ever wonder what the big chief said to them?' Mince, reflective. Filling the nervy time with banter. 'Does he, like, threaten them or bribe them or what? I'd not surrender. Mind, I'd not hole up in such a stupid indefensible place, either. What were they doing, anyway? Do you know?'

'Planning a kidnap.' Stoner leaned on the wall, around the corner from Mince, who remained standing in plain view, presumably as agreed with the would-be kidnap collective.

'Kidnapping who? Why?'

'No idea.'

'Guess.'

'No point. Watch your front. I've got your back.'

'Do you never wonder, though?'

'No.'

'I do. It's like we get treated as though we're fools. Know nothing nobodies. Don't like that.'

'It's best that way. Secure.' Stoner was twitchy. He had blood on the hands inside his biker gloves. Bernadette's blood. It was sticking the skin on his fingers to the gloves' linings. He was deciding – slowly deciding, as though it was somehow important – that he'd buy a new pair. Maybe in brown rather than black.

'Look well; here they come.' Mince's interest in the reasons behind things had vanished without trace. 'Four persons. Two male, two fem. And one of them's a cracker.'

Shard's voice grinned into both men's ears. 'That'll be the black girl. I'd like a few choice moments with that. Dirty as they come, that one. Got to be a pro. Moves like magic, body like a whippet. Tall blonde black girl – stuff of dreams.'

'Shut it, please. Stay alert.' Stoner was finding it difficult to maintain focus; his customary sense of detachment was becoming extreme. 'Remember. Courtesy please. One of these four is one of us. I don't know which, neither do you, and that's how it stays. Got it?' Affirmation, five lots of affirmation, which came as a small surprise for Stoner, who'd only been aware of three on his team. The Hard Man, then, slipping in a little insurance in case of ... what? In case of something he might have known about but felt no need to share.

The small group appeared. Stood, hands in plain view. Mince made a show of passing his assault rifle to Stoner, who stepped into the open to receive it. Mince gestured that they should move apart from each other. Two unremarkable military men, both Europeans by their haircuts, two striking women, both blonde, one white blonde, the other black blonde.

'Not something you see every day, black blonde chick. Wonder if she's blonde below, too?' Mince displayed a rare interest.

'Affirmative.' Shard, high up, far away and leaving his station now. Packing up.

Mince took one man, one woman to one side, frisked them both. Stoner took the other couple, did the same. No weapons. Silent. The man in his small party stared at the ground, vacant. The woman, the black blonde, looked him straight in the eye. Arrogant. Young. Very black, shining with health, hair cropped short as filings, very white. Three small blue tears tattooed below her left eye.

Stoner met her glare with mostly disinterest. Then he tapped the blue tears. 'Tell me?'

'You do not need to know, toy soldier. You're just too young.' She was far younger than Stoner. Maybe a decade younger. He turned away. She spat onto the ground between them. He paused for a heartbeat, an eye-blink, moved on, away. Two vans pulled up, men emerged and took away the trophies.

oOo

Hospital. Exhaustion. Bernadette sedated and mostly sleeping. Stoner sat with her. He wanted to sleep, needed to sleep, was in debt to sleep. She opened one eye, slapped the palm of her hand on the bed near to him. He rested his own hand, covered her own completely.

'Would have been a boy, they say.' Then she slept at last. Just slipped away, leaving him in silence.

FIFTH COLUMNIST

'YOU'RE IT, THEN?' The question, or statement or whatever it was, rolled across the desktop between the three of them. The speaker sighed, affecting the air of patient tolerance and condescension employed by top chaps compelled to deal with the lower orders. As some kind of punishment, perhaps. His comment received no reply, either from the woman sitting beside him or from the man opposite them both.

'You're the go-to guy, the it-man?' His air of patience was attenuated to the point of failure.

The woman spoke, suddenly, and the expression of surprise which scrambled across her colleague's face was possibly the first genuine emotion he'd experienced that day. 'You mean hit-man.' Her voice smiled for her. Her face registered no such kindness. 'You made a joke. It's very good.' Her attention was one hundred percent focused on the quiet man sitting opposite, not on her colleague or his alleged sense of humour.

The first speaker spoke again. His tone was exactly as before, a perfected level of detachment, an assumed seniority. 'We have a situation.' He nodded in acknowledgement of his own pronouncement. He considered himself to be smart, that much was clear. He paused, presumably to allow the lower orders to understand the profound importance of what he was saying.

'We are...' he waved an imperious hand to include the woman beside him. She ignored him, watching the man seated opposite. A large man, quiet, calm and breathing an air of competence while contributing nothing to their assembly other than his presence – which was heavy and intrusive. Look, listen and learn, she thought to herself. Her own companion continued.

'We are bounded by the law. We are officers of the law, we must uphold it and cannot break it.' The recipient of this startling intelligence twitched an eyebrow, a tiny movement, entirely unobserved by the serious speaker. His companion, however, stifled a snigger and turned it into a cough. The military man facing them maintained his silence, his gaze past them to the window beyond.

'However, even the most effective of police forces should recognise the importance of complimentary skillsets. These take many forms...' He listed several, not a single one of them applicable to their current situation. And after a while, he wound down. 'For the benefit of Detective Chief Inspector Hannah,' he nodded towards his female companion, 'maybe you could outline your experience and the ... ah ... skills you will be providing.' He stopped, suddenly. 'The skills which may be deemed necessary by the situation ... although that ... ah ... resolution may not of course be required. Let's hope it will not be required.' He stopped, looked up at the figure seated opposite. 'Well?'

The man facing him appeared to awaken from a long and fulfilling sleep. Snapped to alert and shifted his attention from the window to the DCI, who looked right back with a faint smile of interest.

'I am,' he said quietly, 'your last resort. When all else has failed, the forces of law and order call upon us, the forces of lawlessness and disorder. The big hammer. A final solution. Sir. Ma'am.' He nodded to them both individually and said no more.

oOo

'Jack,' announced the lady policeman, the DCI, and offered her hand to the upright man with the military bearing. He took it, squeezed it softly and released it.

'Detective Chief Inspector,' he said, after a pause.

'No need for the formality, sergeant.' She gestured at the chair vacated by the man from upstairs. 'If we're going to work together, we need to get along together.' She smiled. 'I'm Jack. Short for Jackie, short for Jacqueline.' She looked up, smiling some more and waited.

'Sarge,' said the hard military man, slowly and politely. 'Short for Sergeant. Short for Colour Sergeant.' He may have smiled, though only a detective could have been certain.

'No Christian name, sergeant?'

'Not a Christian, ma'am. Jack. Shout 'Sarge' loudly and if I'm in earshot I'll be there for you. Shout it into a radio, and I'll be there, fast as possible. That's how I work with others. You call, I come.'

She leaned her chair backwards onto just two of its four legs. 'What do your friends call you, Sarge? I prefer to work with colleagues as friends if it's possible. Teamwork is always best. So what do they call you, your friends?'

'No idea. Nothing generous, that's for certain.'

'So you're always so formal?'

'You're extremely attractive,' he said, holding her eyes with his own. 'For an older woman. Ma'am.'

She shrugged. 'Good to know. OK. As the pompous jerk tried to tell you, we have a problem, a police problem.'

'Ma'am,' he acknowledged.

'We're going out to dinner this evening. It's formal, so you'll need a smart suit, a club tie, bow tie, something like that, and a full set of table manners. Can you do that?'

'I have a few regimental ties, ma'am, a full dress Number One uniform, if that's what's required. I would need a haircut for that. Number Twos also, less need for the haircut.'

'Civilian, please. That OK? Don't shave. Look stubbly. Can the forces of disorder do stubbly as well as fully formal?'

'I'm a master of disguise, ma'am. I could probably impersonate a human, given enough time to practice a little.' He paused. 'The dinner.'

'You have a concern?'

'If I'm to perform a duty beyond standing around like an over-muscled oaf, I need some background. All successful missions succeed because those involved – preferably just the good guys – have all the available information about the situation.'

'And there I was, thinking you were just a hired gun.' She smiled. He did not.

'You want a gun, ma'am, I'll bring one. I need to know the situation before selecting the weapon.' He cracked the smallest of smiles. 'An RPG is hard to hide in a tux, ma'am. No matter how pleased I may be to see you.'

She was quiet for a small while. Stood. Even standing, she found it hard to look down on the seated sergeant. He was a big man. And hard with it.

'Fully tooled, ma'am.' No trace of a smile. 'My orders are to carry out any tasks required, to take your instructions as I would those of a military officer with the rank of colonel. I also brew up, ma'am, and if I may say so, I could do with a drink.'

She smiled, waved to a table off to one side. 'Drinks are in the cupboard below in case you'd prefer something stronger, coffee in the big jug. You a caffeine addict, sergeant?' She smiled.

'No ma'am. The room is over-heated, talking gives me a thirst. Can I get you something?'

She flicked open her cell phone, looked at its clock, closed it again. 'I'll have a beer.' He rose, poured a beer for her, cracked open a litre bottle of water for himself.

'Can I see your phone?' He delivered the beer, collected the phone from her desk without waiting for a reply. Cracked its back and levered out the SIM card. She watched, intrigued, while he took a device from a pocket, opened it, inserted her SIM card, closed it, and watched its screen. Picked up his bottle and sipped from it. Held up his hand when she began to speak.

'Is this your own phone, ma'am?'

'Yes. No. It's the job phone. Why?'

'Do you have a personal, private phone, ma'am?'

'Yes. I'm not sure where it is, but I can find it. Why?'

'This chip has a splitter. Every call you make is copied to a fixed number. Incoming too, as soon as you press the green button.'

She stared, silent for a moment. Then rummaged through the drawers of her desk. Rose, walked to her coat and shoulder bag, trawled their inner spaces, finally returning with another, older, less sophisticated cell phone, which she passed to the sergeant without comment. He clipped the SIM card back into her work phone, placed it on the desk, repeated the extraction and analysis with her private device.

'It's clean. The battery needs a charge.' He slid both phones back across the desk.

'Can you get the number my calls are being copied to? Can you remove the ... bug ... virus ... whatever?'

The sergeant drank lots more aerated water. Belched and apologised immediately.

'It's not likely to be a phone, ma'am, more likely an IP address on a server somewhere. Impossible to access unless you know the codes – which we don't.'

'Can you remove it?' She was beginning to sound angry. He held up a hand, smiled.

'No. I can't. It can probably be removed by someone with the knowledge, but that someone isn't this someone, and in any case it's better by far to leave it active. You can work out why.' He laid the device he'd used to check the SIM card before her, pulled another device from another pocket, swiped its glass surface until a keypad appeared, stabbed buttons. Her work phone rang at once. A light lit on the test device. 'Answer that, please.'

'How do you know the number?'

'It's on the SIM. Answer please.'

'Yes,' she growled into the phone. A second light lit on the test device, flickering constantly while the first light remained steady.

'Ma'am,' the sergeant spoke firmly into his own phone. 'I need to confirm the time and exact location of the function this evening. Full dress, you said? Civilian dress that would be. And I need to be armed? Confirm please.' He held her gaze while she answered, and she did, her voice cold, clipped, irritated.

'Thank you, ma'am. See you there.' He hung up. The first light, the steady light, extinguished at once, the second light flickered for maybe another second, then died. 'Excellent,' he said.

'Excuse me? My phone is being bugged and it's excellent? Explain that to me. Please. Enlighten me.' She glared at her work phone as though it was a traitor, shook her head suddenly and picked up the coffee. 'Oh don't bother. Now we can sow misinformation to whoever's listening, that right?'

'Yes. More importantly, your phone isn't transmitting all the time. It's not monitoring your face to face conversations. I'll check later to see whether it's sharing your location – if it is, you might forget to take it with you whenever we meet.' He stood, stepped smartly to the side of his chair, took a further step back. 'I'll collect you at 1930 ... from here or from home?'

She stood, conscious that her chair scraped along the floor as she did so and that the sergeant's chair had been silent. Same chair, same floor. 'From home. I'll jot down the address.'

'I have that, thank you.' He nodded, pivoted silently on a heel and left, closing the door silently behind him.

oOo

DCI Jack Hannah opened the front door to her apartment. 'You knocked?' she asked, carefully. 'You didn't use the entry phone? You didn't need to be buzzed into the building?' She stepped back, ushering him into the hallway. And, 'I'm impressed,' she announced, watching as the immaculate man walked silently into the main room. 'The army polishes up well when required.'

'As I said, ma'am, I am a master of disguise. You see before you a humble soldier, ready to die for queen and country.'

'I doubt that. Drink?'

'A drink before the war? How civilised. Always welcome. All professional combat soldiers expect to get hit at some point, and dying is a lot better than many alternatives after then.'

'Holds no fears for you, then?' She poured, whisky for them both.

'No. Half and half with water please. Room temperature if you have it. Out the tap is fine.'

'You're going to meet…' He stopped her, resting a hard dry finger across her lips, removed it and rested it across his own. Pointed to his ear.

'What're you reading?' He gestured at the stacked books on their crowded shelves. 'Any good thrillers there?'

She nodded, tilted her head, regarding him obliquely, an angular approach. 'I prefer history. Why people do what they do and how they work together. Lots to learn.'

The sergeant sighed, a frighteningly honest sound, profound and deep. 'Written history is almost all lies. Read it to understand what the lies are for, remembering who wrote the book and why. History's all good stories, but I prefer fiction. It's more honest.'

'I'll change,' she said, and left him alone with the books and the whisky.

oOo

'Tell me about yourself?' She swung her car expertly through the early evening traffic, gilded sneakers lying in the back along with her dress jacket and bag.

'What do you want to know? There's no point, though. I'd only lie.'

'If you told me you'd need to kill me?'

'Stupid expression. Of course not. It's mostly dull stuff, so I'd liven it up to be entertaining. Military is all about dull. Dull is good. Today no one killed me and I killed no one in return. That kind of dull.'

'OK. So what do you do?'

'Me? Kill people. That's what I'm paid to do. The rest is just hanging around, mostly. You talk – can you do that and drive? Course you can, you're not blonde. Army joke for you there. Laughing is always optimal so long as I'm a sober soldier.'

'How's that?'

'I don't take offence while sober.'

'When you're drunk?'

'Let's see. Tell me about tonight. Your ... situation will be there, I trust?'

'Yes. Both major suspects, both or neither or either of whom is rotting the force from within. You'll meet them both. Form your own judgement.'

'No no. That's not how it works, ma'am. I'm a weapon, the last hammer, like I said. I don't do the thinking thing. I don't judge. You do that. You're the brains, I'm the muscle – deniable muscle. No brains. Simply brawn.'

She carved the car into the driveway of a large hotel, joined a short queue of the others invited. 'Crap, sergeant. You're smarter than I am. I'd value your analysis.'

'There won't be any. Set things up so that the guilty party attacks me, or similar. That's easiest.'

'He won't do that.'

'I don't mean personally. He'll send someone, I'll molest that someone until he, she or other tells me who sent them, then I'll tell you, you'll confer, confirm that there's no admissible evidence and I'll remove your ... situation for you. Hey look, a car parking flunkey. How you successful types do live, huh? Is everyone here a public servant? Does everyone here know what I am, by the way? It helps spook the guilty.'

'The innocent?'

'No one is. They'll spook too. Easiest way is to kill them all.'

'And let God sort them out?'

'Exactly.'

'You do believe in God?' She had the grace to sound more cynical than surprised.

'Of course not. Contradiction is the master of invention. What I believe doesn't matter. It's what everyone else believes that matters to them. Who am I tonight, ma'am?'

'My guest. They'll all assume we're an item, whatever.'

'You're single? There is no Mister Detective Chief Inspector?'

'Long story, let's just say...'

'I'm falling asleep already,' he interrupted, passing her shoes and jacket to her. 'Do I get to beat up on people? Or do I display my knowledge of Kant and my passion for Karl Marx's poetry? That always surprises people, coming from the mouth of an obvious Neanderthal.'

She handed the keys to the attendant, joined him and headed together for the entrance. 'Did Marx write poetry? I didn't know that.'

'Not to my knowledge, but no one knows that he didn't. Confusion will be my epitaph. He may have written that, too, you'll never know. Good evening to you too...' Hands were being shaken, insincerity lathered all around along with the pre-food drinks. The sergeant stood tall, rested a proprietary and very large hard hand on DCI Jack Hannah's shoulder and assumed the expression. No man spoke to her for longer than was necessary before clearing off, while every woman demanded an introduction.

'Rock,' she said. 'This is Rock, not Rocky, not yet.'

'Very clever,' he smiled down at her. 'Rock. I like that. Rock. Hmmm.'

oOo

‘Do you drive?’ DCI Jack Hannah sounded concerned, almost. The sergeant beamed down upon her.

‘Ma’am. I do. I am a one man demolition derby. If you have a car you dislike, or some scenery you find objectionable, I can combine the two with a vigour and a creativity you would find surprising.’ A couple drifted close, staring.

‘Jack.’ The woman spoke, staring at the sergeant. ‘An introduction?’ Her male companion glared, in a civilised way. Jack Hannah shrugged.

‘All work,’ she smiled in a marvellously false way. A lesser woman might have fluttered an eyelash, a lesser man may have winked.

‘No play...’ The conversation died between them. The sergeant switched a full-on Tom Cruise smile upon the latest inquisitrix. She glowed. Her male companion darkened and glared some more. The art of conversation was a lost art, plainly. The couple drifted away again. A small pool of quiet surrounded the DCI and her anonymous sergeant.

‘Ma’am? The driving? Why do you ask?’

‘I want to get drunk. Quite suddenly I’ve had enough.’

‘Feel free, ma’am. I’ll join you. I enjoy being drunk. It’s often a liberating experience.’ He moved, smoothly and suddenly away from her, returning in an unremarkably short period of time bearing two empty glasses and a bottle of an improbably expensive single-malt Scotch whisky. Demonstrating commendable hand : eye co-ordination, he filled both glasses from the bottle, a task which would normally require three hands or a convenient flat surface, and presented DCI Jack with the more filled of the glasses. She took it, pointedly without comment. Sipped.

'If you're drunk, you can't drive.' She emptied her glass, surveyed the room and its shifting shoals of socialites with some malice, and passed the glass back to the sergeant. Who refilled it, and returned it.

'That's a suburban myth, ma'am. Of course I can drink and drive. I drive very well while drunk, in fact.' He smiled in a macho smug way. 'Experience has shown.'

She stared at him. 'What if you get stopped?'

He stared back, sipped from his own glass, smiled. 'Yes?'

'You get a pull, you get to go to...' she sipped some more. 'To a police station, and...' She surveyed the room, focusing on a conversation too far away to be heard. 'The source of my professional unhappiness is over there.' She looked away. He followed her gaze, away from the conversation.

'The problem you have, ma'am...' He filled her glass again, drained his own. 'Your problem is that you are an officer of the law. I...' He refilled their glasses again, the bottle was almost empty. 'I ... am not.' He smiled, poured the last dregs of whisky into her glass, set the empty soldier onto a conveniently flat surface. 'If you get a pull, you get nicked. I ... don't.' He beamed at her, staring intently, plainly intent upon her virtue ... or something. She stared at him.

'I'm watching the source of your unhappiness, ma'am.' He smiled, slid a hard and strong arm around her waist and pulled her to him. 'Look drunk,' he suggested. 'Look happy.' He turned to her and smiled. 'Look into my eyes,' he suggested. She did.

The source of her unhappiness excused himself from his own company, walked over to join them. Smiled. Beamed. 'Jack,' he said. 'So glad you could make it. We don't often see you at these...' he waved around them, encompassing and somehow mocking their company. He looked at the sergeant. Smiled, somehow. Another policeman, a policeman in a resplendent and impressive gold-braided uniform, joined them, seemingly from nowhere.

'Inspector,' he remarked, making it sound like the bastard daughter of Mr Sneer and Mrs Curse, before removing them from his focus, shifting instead to the source of unhappiness and steering him away without further comment.

'You drink, I'll drive.' The sergeant sounded reassuring. 'If we get a pull, I'm not who I appear to be, although my fake identity is genuine. You can't say the same.'

'Say it?' She stared with a focus intensified by the whisky. 'I can't even imagine it. If you crash I'll arrest you.'

'Can't wait.'

oOo

'They're insane. And utterly fucking unprofessional. It's not possible to believe they're adults, never mind the law.' The sergeant was throwing his smart civvi suit around the room. The Dirty Blonde leaned against a table, watching. Smiling.

'You boys,' she said. She looked at a watch, tapped its glass with a long pointed fingernail. 'And now?'

'And now what?' The sergeant prowled the wide room, as menacingly as it is possible to be when clad only in white socks. The Dirty Blonde leaned against the wall, smiled gently, beckoned him to her.

'Time for improvisation,' she said. 'Stress relief. Religious studies.' She smiled some more.

oOo

'You understand our problem, Sarge. Sarge. Christ, I can't call you that. You must have a name.' Jack Hannah attempted to stare down the man with the military stance who stood, relaxed, across from her.

'Sergeant, ma'am. It works fine. You'll get used to the idea.'

'But it depersonalises you ... Sergeant. I prefer to know the people I work with.'

'A noble spirit, but pointless. We simply need to get along while you tell me who and how and by when and I do the method study, then present you with options – if you want them – or simply act at my own discretion and remove your problem. I don't want to know why, or what the problem is. It's better that I don't.'

'You're not curious?'

'As much as a cat, ma'am. I learn from what happens to curious cats. It never ends well. I would prefer to end well, personally speaking. Like all soldiers who've served in the Far East, I prefer the happy endings to any other kind.'

She shrugged, waved him to a seat. 'Or stand, if you prefer.' He sat. 'We have a case meeting in a few minutes. I'd like you to attend it.'

'Why?' Few words, plainly.

'I think that it's important you understand that the case is growing. It's never going to be actionable in court, because some of the methods used to acquire the evidence have been...'

He interrupted, waving a hand to attract attention. 'I really don't care, ma'am.'

'You're being impossible. I care.' She was almost shouting, like shouting at an iceberg.

'Then I'll attend your meeting. You're happy in some incomprehensible way with your colleagues – junior colleagues – seeing me? Knowing what I'm here for, what I do?'

She paused. Calmed. 'It's…' An incomplete statement.

He completed it for her. 'It's an unwillingness to take the responsibility for killing someone. You're unwilling to sign a death warrant off your own bat, so you'd prefer to pretend to yourself that by introducing me to your junior colleagues as some doomy guy murderer killer robot, that your responsibility will be diluted, that approval for your illegal actions will flow like the milk of human kindness and you'll be hailed as some kind of … what? Heroine? That's all nonsense, ma'am. If I weren't on duty I'd say it was just shit. If you can't call the shot, go tell your chief with the funny eyes and go direct traffic or moisten your make-up, whatever.'

She stood in anger. He was not finished.

'I'm a soldier, ma'am. The state pays me to kill people the state doesn't like. It says go here, and I go there. It says, take up this big nasty bang-bang gun and kill that nasty Irish, German, Arab, Russian, Iraqi, Syrian … whatever. I've called time on them all. I…' he stopped. Reboot. 'I am a soldier, ma'am. Task me and I'll complete the task. Put your mark on the order and … job done. It's very simple. This is the law in action. The ultimate sanction. The death penalty.'

'There is no death penalty in UK law.'

The sergeant smiled at her. 'You think?' He waved his hands at her; she sat back into her seat. 'The state kills loads of people. People like me' – he jabbed himself in the chest with a thumb – 'People like me follow orders from people like you all the time, and when those orders are to take extreme action, then that's fine. I'm a volunteer, just like you are. It's just the way it needs to be. Problems arise when the wrong guy gets the long drop. It's then the hypocrisy sets in, the media shitstorm. Weeping, wailing and wringing hands on the BBC news.'

'You approve? The killing? The death penalty?'

'All the same to me.' He shook his head slowly from side to side. 'Do you have anyone in this police palace who could get me a brew? All this philosophy's giving me a sore throat.' An intercom was pressed, an order given, a flask of coffee received almost instantly. He thanked her, poured for them both.

'This guy. The guy you don't like. He's been a very naughty boy, done terrible things, caused ... what? ... deaths, injurious stuff? But you can't pin him down. OK. Send in the troops. Tony Blair sent in the troops, killed untold thousands simply because his buddy Gee Dubbya in the big white house didn't like their leader, the guy in Iraq. You are not in that league, lady. Ma'am.' He drained his drink, looked across the desk with a question. 'Well? That curious cat got your tongue?'

'You make it sound simple. Clear cut.'

'It is. Pretty much. You've got the authority – laughing boy told you that in front of me – so it is simple. You point, I shoot. Whatever. I do the gig and need to believe that you'll not send another version of me after me to clear me off the scene for security reasons.' She stared, silent. He shrugged. 'It happens. I need to trust you guys. Which is why you'll never be my buddy, never know my true name and never get to fuck me, which is a small shame for both of us.' He held up his hand to stop her obvious retort. 'No no, it's OK. I bet you're demon on a mattress, better yet on a desk, huh?' He grinned. 'Only kidding. Ma'am. Relieving the tension a little. Sex does that, they say.'

She stood, stared at him. Shrugged her shoulders and suddenly grinned back. 'Well,' she said. 'Hold that thought. I'll go have my meeting.'

He poured more coffee, a single cup for a single drinker. 'I'll be waiting.' He pulled a device from a pocket. 'Catch up on my reading. Surf some porn. Take your time. I'm in your hands. In a sense.'

oOo

'It's all the hanging around. Does your head in. Mine anyway. It's worse than combat. At least you get to do something when the bad guys are shooting at you. Meeting, meeting. Let's have a meeting about a meeting.' He banged the table once, twice, suddenly. Heads turned. He flagged down a waiter. 'Beer,' he demanded. 'For you too?'

The Dirty Blonde grinned, startling white teeth brilliant in the darkness of her face. 'Yeah,' her grin widened. 'So long as you drink them both.'

'No problem.' The attention of the other eaters, drinkers, watchers and waiters waned and shifted away from them once again.

'Tonight,' remarked the Dirty Blonde in a conversational way. 'It would be very kind if you would give a john unmistakeable confirmation that I never, ever want to see him again. No matter how fat his wallet, no matter how little he actually wants to do with what little he's got left ... I just want him to go away.'

'Terminally?' The sergeant interrupted his beer consumption to ask a simple question.

She shook her head. 'When you've finished all this exciting drinking thing, I'll show you to my rooms, and you can await Mister Money.'

'He's rich?'

'Oh yes. And connected. But he is a radical creep and I want shut. He knows my office hours and – I dunno, maybe he has the rooms watched – he's always arriving when I'm not expecting him.'

'Catches you with your pants down, huh? Ungainly stuff for a ho, honey.' His glass drained, the sergeant stood up.

'Oh ho ho, fucking ho.' The Dirty Blonde also stood, almost the same height as the tall sergeant, but maybe half his mass. 'I so love whore jokes, toy soldier.' She sat down again, catching the sergeant by surprise. 'I think he's either in love with me,' she rolled her eyes impressively, 'or he wants to be my pimp. He talks money all the time.'

'That's what you do it for, honey, for the honey money.' The sergeant held up his hands in plain surrender. 'But I don't care. What you want from me is what you get for free. I'll scratch your itches, you scratch mine. Is he ... let's see. Is he bigger than me, younger than me, faster on his feet than me, better in the sack than me and is he a senior sergeant in Her Britannic Majesty's proud soldiery?' He did preen a little. Maybe a little more than that.

The Dirty Blonde simply rolled her eyes some more. 'I'll pay in advance.'

He grinning. 'In here? With an audience?'

Those white eyes rolled above the black cheeks some more, the Dirty Blonde flagged down a waiter and asked for the check. 'You get free food and drink, soldier-boy, and somewhere safe to stash your bike during the excitement. That's your lot.'

'Good deal.' The sergeant was ready to move. 'Lay on, black puss.' Those eyes rolled again, an elbow dug some ribs, the two of them laughed a little and left the same amount of money on both their sides of the table, covering the check twice and leaving two tips. The waiter was both pleased and confused.

oOo

A door chime, followed by a knuckle knock on the same door, followed once more by the chime. The sergeant opened the door rapidly, suddenly sharing face space with a startled brown male in his middle years, who stammered, stepped back away from the door, only to find the sergeant's clean, strong, hard hands clamped to the lapels of his jacket, dragging him with no evident effort into the lobby.

'This the guy?' asked the sergeant, mostly rhetorically. The Dirty Blonde nodded a silent confirmation into the spluttering conversation. The sergeant, with little apparent effort, propelled the hapless brown man into a more comfortable room, a room with a couch, two chairs, and a low table, as well as music making facilities and a range of unmatched minor furnishings only of interest to people whose priorities for visiting a hooker were sadly confused. The sergeant lowered himself into the larger of the chairs, supporting himself on his arms, and swept the feet of the brown man from under him as he did so, depositing the hapless individual onto an unremarkable rug, although the timing and geometry of the foot sweep were exact and calculated, so the brown man's lower spine caught the corner of the solid wooden table as he collapsed, which provoked a grunt, a sharp intake of breath and an exclamation or two.

'Take the weight off,' suggested the sergeant, radiating bonhomie and brotherly affection. 'Let's a have a quiet chat before you leave. Won't take a minute.'

The brown man attempted a bluster, attempted to rise from his surely uncomfortable position between the hard edge of the wooden table and the proximity of the sergeant's aggressive feet. One of those feet flicked out and kicked away one of the brown man's supporting arms. His revised position was no improvement on its predecessor. 'Shush,' suggested the comfortably seated sergeant, although the brown man had made no comment.

'As I understand things...'. The sergeant had conjured the handle of a knife from somewhere about his person, flicked it and nodded appreciatively as the blade snapped into view. He slid the flat of the blade along the palm of his spare hand, then held that hand out to the sprawled man for inspection. 'See,' he said, conversationally and quietly. 'That's the easy way.' He shrugged, rested an edge of the same blade against the calloused skin of his own thumb, moved the blade only slightly, and shared the vision of the dark drop which immediately appeared with the other man. 'And that... that's the hard way.' He sucked his thumb, endearingly.

'Shush,' the seated sergeant suggested once more. 'There's no room here for debate or discussion. I have a message for you, that's all. It's very simple.' His voice was quiet, gentle, almost friendly. 'My friend here,' he gestured a little to include the Dirty Blonde in the conversation. 'She wants you to leave her alone. Completely. No visits, no calls, no contacts of any kind. That is so easy.' He held up a calming hand, mostly because the other man was struggling a little, either to get less uncomfortable or to speak or both.

'The harder bit is what will happen if you fail to follow my instructions and leave my friend entirely alone. To keep away from her – completely. And forever.' He leaned forward and smiled, showing no teeth, but the blade in his hand shone better than any mere teeth ever could, and spoke eloquently in a voice all its own. 'This is very sharp,' said the sergeant. 'If my friend ever...' he paused, entirely for dramatic effect, '... if she ever tells me that you have made contact, I will apply this blade to your nuts and remove one of them. I've done this before, and although there's a lot of panic, and a lot of shouting, and an amazing amount of blood, the real pain of it comes later, once the shouting, the tears and the stitching have all dried up a bit. They tell me that the pain lasts forever, and that the result of an amateur castration seriously unmans a chap. I can see that. And it doesn't even improve your singing voice, so there's no upside at all.'

'Now,' he leaned forward so that the blade was an immeasurably short distance from one of the other man's eyes. The right eye. 'If I believe you when you tell me that you understand, accept and will keep entirely away from my friend for ever … then I'll not knock you around any, and you can leave. Quickly and quietly. Go home to your … whatever, wife, family, dog. If I don't believe you…' he leaned further forward, though the knife moved not at all. 'If I don't believe you, I'll knock you out now, throw you into the boot of a car, take you somewhere quiet and slice an eye. Just like that. Quick and easy, and makes the point. Don't even pretend to yourself that you could fight me, because you can't, or that you can come back when I'm not here and cause my friend unhappiness. You'd need to kill me first.' He laughed suddenly and sat back, removed the knife from the other man's face, and asked, 'What's it to be, hero?'

'Right. Right. That's it. No harm done. Sorry sorry sorry. Can I…' The visitor looked at the Dirty Blonde, who shook her head, just once, and nodded towards the sergeant, who was standing, towering over the brown man, and glowering, the knife plain to see. The fallen man rose, backing away, holding his hands before him. 'I'm gone,' he announced. And he was. The door clicked fast behind him.

'What puzzles me,' shared the sergeant, quietly, 'is why you didn't just do that yourself?' He turned to face the

Dirty Blonde, who had magicked herself out of almost all of her clothing, and was standing tall and black before him.

'It's a mystery,' she said. 'Except ... he would have fought me because I'm a woman and he has no respect for women; he'd not fight a man, not a man like you ... and you do it so much more ... professionally. You truly are that professional asshole. No man can withstand the professional asshole.' They laughed together, then much more than that.

oOo

'It's a question of understanding your target, knowing how he lives, how he moves, where he goes, how and when; who he sees and why. His routines and habits; where he eats, drinks, fucks and has fun. Lots of shit like that. Tedious detail, and once the detail's established, the devil comes too, and the hit works. It almost does the job itself – like it's the devil doing it, not some guy. Y'know?'

Jack Hannah stared at him. 'No. No I don't know. I don't want to know.' She sounded desperately unhappy, suddenly. 'Are you close to him?' Her eyes were wide, her stare unfocused and general.

'Yeah. What do you think I'm doing when we're not talking about meetings, meeting in meetings, talking about what was in the last meeting and what to do for the next meeting? In between all the talk, all the pointless hot air you guys seem to enjoy so much, I just get on with it. You any closer to confirmation, authorisation yet? I can't pretend I'm enjoying all the sitting around, ma'am. I'm not much for sitting around.'

She smiled, dismally. 'You'd rather be breaking heads, I suppose?'

'No, ma'am. I'd rather be active. Being active is many things to many men, it's not all breaking heads. Right now?' He looked out of the window at the bright day outside. 'Right now I'd like to take my bike up into the Welsh mountains. Breathe the air, drink it right in. You know? No walls, no windows. No people. Just me and my wheels and the power and the glory of it all.'

Jack's wan smile had vanished completely. 'You're serious?'

'Of course I'm serious.' He shook his head in disappointment, maybe. 'You think a smart guy joins the modern army so he can go around beating up on other guys and getting shot at in hot places? That's not true today – if it ever was.' He softened, and turned away from her to look through the bulletproof glass again. 'And then I'd join my brother pongos in Hereford and get ratted. Of course I would. That's tradition. Like bully beef, brass and bullshit.'

'Pongos?'

'Military humour, ma'am. Where the army goes, the pong goes. It is very funny after a dozen or so pints of cheap beer, or after a bunch of lice-ridden ragheads has been trying to ventilate your white British body with their clever bombs and shit.' He rubbed his eyes with the heels of both hands. 'I just want to move on now. When do you give me clearance, please, ma'am?'

She shrugged. 'Any time soon, I think. Maybe tomorrow.' She looked up again and caught the sergeant's eye. 'Can we do a deal?' He raised a querying eyebrow, stayed silent. 'Will you call me Jack once it's done? Can we do some dinner, forget all the inter-department seconded asset nonsense and ... let me see inside the shell, soldier?'

The sergeant held her gaze, and his eyes narrowed, his voice returned to military neutrality. 'You'll not see me again after the gig, ma'am. That's not how it works.' A long, deep sigh. Then: 'If you want to take a drink, drinks are best taken before the war, like I said. If you can get clearance today, I'll stand you a farewell dinner at a restaurant of my own choice this evening. You get to choose the food, I choose the drink and if the spirit of interdepartmental cooperation is strong, then we could make a night of it. For tomorrow we go over the top, and soldiery things like that.'

She stared and smiled and nodded. 'If that's a proposition, it's the most subtle I've ever heard. Shows how little I know soldiers.' She picked up her cell phone, thumbed it to light, read its display and thumbed in a short message. Watched the screen. Then: 'Help yourself to a coffee or ask Theresa out there if you want a nibble. I'm off to see the wizard. Or the Chief Super, who is less interesting. He'll say yay or nay. It's up to him. And if he says yay, then I'm all yours for the evening. Maybe you'll even tell me your name ... sergeant.'

He smiled back, rose and walked to the coffee jug. 'Maybe, ma'am, maybe. You feeling lucky?' But she'd already left, leaving the office door drifting loose behind her.

oOo

She was drunk, no doubt about it. 'I'm drunk,' she laughed, with a delight to it which the sergeant found delightful.

'No doubt about it,' he replied. 'And the night is yet young. The good citizens of the town are heading for their beds and excuses, while us, the masters of the universe, are locked and loaded and heading to hit a club or two.' He grinned. 'You do look pretty good, Jack. For...' She interrupted, laughing some more.

'For an older woman!' She roared with genuine glee, banged her whisky glass down hard on the table, then turned it upside down to match its brother opposite.

'I was going to say that you look damned fine for a policeman, Jack.' The sergeant's expression was of concern, serious, maybe a little worry ... until it too unfolded into a shine of mirth.

'You know a decent club, soldier? Even though you are a stranger in a strange city?'

'Soldiers are famous for their intelligence, ma'am, and the intel I've gathered has revealed two promising establishments, and a couple of more dodgy dives which would do if you enjoy hitting strangers and being hit by strangers. Which would madam prefer?'

'Let's not get hit. You've got a hit coming up ... oops,' she suddenly looked embarrassed. 'Sorry, that was a crap joke.'

He reached across the table, took her hand and squeezed it in his own. Not for the first time that evening. Also not for the first time, she squeezed back, as hard as she could. 'Does your intel also supply a cab?'

'No need, ma'am. Your very own carriage is exactly where we left it. It may even be a smart car and capable of finding its own way back home, should we ... should we need it to.' He may have winked at that point, but the lighting was poor, too poor to be sure.

'You're not worried about getting a pull?'

'Nope. I drive better when alcohol assisted, ma'am. Many soldiers do. Little known fact. It's a habit we pick up when on active service. Helps a guy worry a little less about roadside fireworks, that sort of thing.'

'IEDs, they call them?'

'That's what reporters call them. Soldiers call them fucking bombs ... or worse. Fuck, most of us can only pronounce "improvised explosive device" when pissed up or stoned. "Fucking bomb" works just as well.' They laughed, the sergeant settled the check from a bundle of cash from his 'active service walking out fund,' as he described it to his guest, and they marched grandly out to her Range Rover, where she handed him the electronic passport to its secure electronic systems.

'This is one cool car, Jack. Not entirely like the Land Rovers us soldier boys get blown up in.' He grinned, widely. 'Belt up now, there may be troubles ahead...' he sang. Really... sang.

'It's a Range Rover,' chuckled Jack Hannah. 'Not exactly like a Land Rover.'

'Certainly so. The engine doesn't shake your fillings out for starters. That's a good thing.' He slid the lever into Drive. 'I hate dentists. Especially army dentists.' He swung the smooth machine smoothly into the night, where it cruised the darkened streets, a proud and powerful presence among the dwindling traffic.

The traffic dwindled further as they drifted out of town. The street lighting dimmed and their speed rose. Jack dozed, sliding down a little in her wide cream smooth leather seat, her head settling sideways onto the padded door pillar, where it rested. Such was the smooth power of the vehicle that the sergeant could hear her gentle snores as they flashed through the dark and onto the wide, poorly lit and almost entirely empty dual carriageway; a smooth highway which ringed the entire town. Their speed increased yet more, smooth, silent inside the leather and wood bespoke luxury interior of the Range Rover, which flew unleashed, full throttles for the first time in its short life on the roads.

The sergeant unlatched Jack's seat belt, tightened his own, while the Range Rover's V8 engine sang its off-beat hymn to power, to glory beneath him. Carefully accurate, precision steering placed the nearside wheels onto the lane-dividing crash barrier between an exit and the main carriageway, lifting the vehicle high on one side and tipping it suddenly, violently onto two wheels. The sergeant kept the pedal to the metal, steered into the tilt, until quite suddenly and with a considerable screaming the wild weight and massive momentum two of the vehicle's wheels hit one of the reinforced concrete support pillars, flinging it onto its side and adding a vicious spin to an already chaotic situation. The sergeant released the steering wheel, braced himself against the enthusiasm of the many airbags, and kept the throttle pedal floored.

Jack Hannah was flung face first into the luxurious wooden fascia, then down into the footwell, then was ejected from it by her own airbags before being thrown around as the several tonnes of luxury motor car bounced once, twice across both lanes of the carriageway, before contacting the far barrier at a strange angle, resulting in another bounce, in the opposite direction this time. A screaming of metal, a rapid rotating deceleration; everything in the cabin which wasn't strapped tight was thrown around in a blizzard of paraphernalia. The sergeant had powered his seat up against the steering wheel's cushioning airbag, and was held tight in his place while the world exploded around him. Until it all stopped. The engine idled steadily on, willing, as engines can be.

Impossibly, the vehicle's robust systems were still mostly operational. The sergeant powered down his window, motored his seat back – feeling considerable relief that it would do so – and reached for his companion. Checked for pulses, found none, checked for breathing, found none. No need to manually finish the job. Not this time. Her neck was broken, her face pounded into a permanently glazed expression of wonder. He wound up his window ... which stopped half-way up. The engine stalled, finally. Some lights lit on the dash, while others went out. He pushed open his door, and half climbed, half struggled his way clear, dropping clumsily to the roadway beneath, pulling himself to his knees, to a crawl, checking hands, elbows, hips and knees, finally his face for signs of bleeding. None.

Another vehicle drew alongside, dimmed headlamps fading into the dark of the night. The sergeant reeled and rolled, then collapsed and crawled his way to it, to the dark anonymous VW Transporter van, and gestured for assistance. The driver bounced down from the cab, rolled his wide shoulders, flexed his fingers, then stooped to collect the sergeant, effectively lifting him by his clothing at shoulder and waist and sliding him into the body of the Transporter by way of its wide side door. The sergeant groaned and rearranged himself into cushions on the floor, stretching and complaining. 'This shit doesn't get easier with practice.' He groaned. 'Get me out of here, JJ. Thanks for the extraction.'

The driver gunned up the heavy diesel, reversed a little, before shifting into forward gears and taking the exit where the crash had been staged. 'You're welcome, Sergeant Harding. Job done?' he wondered, conversationally. The sergeant nodded his head – just the once, winced, and strapped himself into one of the jump seats behind Stoner the driver.

'Yep,' he croaked at last. 'Get me to a bath.'

'Check-up first.'

'No need, I'm fine. Shaken and stirred, nothing broken. I'm good.'

'Yeah. And I'm driving, so settle in soldier, and we'll go get you prodded, poked and probed. Debrief, then a seven-day pass before you go back to the unit, compliments of a grateful nation. Or the Hard Man, whatever.'

The sergeant stretched, systematically tensing and easing muscle groups, working against the straps. 'Outstanding. Got a new girlie, need a little ... private time to recover from my efforts on behalf of that uncaring nation.'

JJ Stoner grinned, cruising now with headlamps lit, just below the legal limit. 'New girl, huh? Anyone I know? I should be jealous, me?'

The sergeant achieved a small laugh. 'Nope. No one you know, but boy oh boy is she something special. A delight.'

Stoner tilted his head slightly, listening to an audio feed for his ear only. 'Bravo zulu, soldier, job done. Perfect delivery. Plod is at the scene, tragic traffic accident, drunk driver, death is confirmed. Only one person involved. That grateful nation secretly thanks you for removing another terrorist threat.'

'That what she was, JJ? A terrorist? Doesn't seem likely.'

'They come in many forms, I'm told. There's the muscle, the guys who go bang, there's the brains who build the bombs that go bang, and there's those who tell them where their targets are. That's what she was.'

'So...' The sergeant's speech was becoming indistinct, his head drooping. 'That would make the Hard Man her equivalent; you're the brains of this little op, and I'm the muscle that goes bang. Again.'

'And you've got the gongs to prove it. You'll probably get another one for this, seeing as it's an official sanction. That's why you got to do the interesting bit, super-Shard, and I'm just the taxi driver.' Stoner shot a rapid glance at his battered companion. 'Sleep now, we're an hour away from the safe house.'

'Roger that.' Shard drifted through doze and into sleep. The Transporter droned on through the dark night, hard blues music from its speakers providing a knowing commentary on the night's proceedings and much else.

Special Relationship

'THE PURPOSE OF YOUR VISIT?' The lady with the Homeland Security tags and badges, severe haircut and scowl looked up from her screen. Evaluating, maybe. Maybe not. As well as aggression she also gave every sign of all-consuming boredom. She caught his eye, held it. He stared back. Her boredom achieved a new threshold, followed by a sigh. 'Your visit,' she repeated with almost no attempt at fake patience. 'It has a purpose. A reason. Why are you here, Mr...' she consulted his passport, 'Stoned?'

'For a gig.' English accents were developed in days of empire and arrogance.

'Excuse me?'

'A gig. This is New Orleans, home of the blues, and I'm here to go to a gig.' Stoner smiled at her. She declined to return the favour.

'You'll be staying how long?' She'd stamped something onto a reasonably blank page in the passport, stapled in a single sheet of paper, a skilled task and a crucial task from a notional security perspective, and she looked up again.

'Four days. My return flight's booked in four days.' Stoner smiled once again, a British imperial smile, at the same time patronising and insecure, on every level.

'Have a nice day, Mister Stoned.' She slid the red booklet of his passport across the counter between them, sighed, and waved the next penitent forward for confession and possible absolution.

The Brit rolled his eyes, passed beneath the disinterested gaze of the large men with large guns and largely glazed expressions, headed down miles of aisles in search of his exit. A uniform, professionally helpful, pointed at a sign. 'Baggage reclaim,' he revealed, 'is that way.' Stoner nodded his thanks. 'No baggage,' he shared as in a conspiracy. 'Travelling light this time.' The uniform ignored him professionally.

And at the gate, after declaring nothing, nothing at all, Stoner headed for the rank of cabs, to find himself headed off by an almost huge man, a bigger man than himself, a big black man brandishing a conspicuously large white card with strident red writing. 'BRIT HIT MAN' it announced. Stoner smiled, an uphill smile. 'Subtle,' he shared.

'But accurate, huh? I sure hope so. The man's Navy prides itself on accuracy, always.' The black man, a man in military dress, grinned and folded away his sign. 'Welcome back to the land of the free, JJ. We sure missed you.'

'You did?' Stoner's excess politeness was turning into a habit.

'Nope. Does a dog miss fleas? Welcome back to the scratch, Sergeant.'

'Former sergeant, Master Chief.' Stoner grinned, honestly this time, sincerely, and pounded a large white fist into his companion's much larger black bicep. There was no sign of an impression being made. 'That what you are these days, Stretch? Master Chief?'

'The vehicle is over here. And I am what I am, I'm Popeye the Sailor Man, and that man is hating this crowding. Are you ready for the heat, white boy? That's ours.' He waved at a Humvee, vast in its military implacability, seriously illegally parked and bearing only dirty and obscured unit insignia rather than any form of

DMV identification. A civilian functionary was standing by one of its doors, confused, a big book of citations in hand. Stretch McCann marched to him, dwarfed him, leaned down until his mouth was proximal to the functionary's ear.

'Thank you sir,' he bellowed, quieting the crowd and confounding his adversary in the seniority stakes. 'Classified material in this vehicle. Diplomatic. Weaponry and ordnance.' He waved at Stoner, who produced Her Britannic Majesty's permission to travel without let or hindrance and whipped it past the functionary with a flourish.

'Thank you,' he echoed in an imperial tone so sharp that glass would have cracked and knees would have bent if required. The two men, the two military men, one possibly officially in service, the other probably officially not, swung up into the cool cavern of the Humvee, which roared, squealed wheels and performed several traffic violations with the easy confidence of military might the world over. And especially in the USA.

oOo

The heavy vehicle bulled through the traffic as though it belonged there. Sometimes it was very close indeed to the other competitors in the great city car race, but its battered bulk assured a safe passage. Stretch McCann, a naval man, steered his charge with total confidence and maybe a little unconscious aggression. His voice, however, was soft.

'For a retired military man you pack some heavyweight clout, my friend. I was flown back from very far away to be your own personal driver. Impressed, I am. Also impressed, as I know you will be too, to find myself back in a dress uniform, in the proud service of this grateful nation.' Stretch carved through a chorus of complaint until he reached the freeway lane he wanted, and men and machine uplifted from sea level to a more elevated highway, reaching for the sky and breaking many limits as they did so. Once and once only, the Humvee's siren demanded their priority and cleared a path, the rest of the time the vehicle's sheer presence was enough. They were making progress.

'Why you here, huh?' Stretch had tired of waiting for a response.

'Swampfest.' Stoner grinned, gently. 'Gator burgers, JD and bars. Also music. Loud music.' He reclined his seat, glanced right out of the window and sighed. 'Need some R&R. Woman, maybe two, maybe more. You know how it is. Why are you here, Stretch? Why is a serving Master Chief chauffeuring a foreign civilian in this ... this armoured vehicle, huh?' He paused, swivelled his gaze to take in the gaudy uniform of his vast friend. 'And how come you're in service, brother? Weren't you kicked out? Something like that?' He paused again. 'And among the brass buttons, trophies of war and statements of rank – no unit badges. Lots of gold leaves and no roots. How is that?'

'Because... because those are my orders. Sir.' Both men roared with laughter at the outrageous comedy of the world. The Humvee carved out a powered passage, the steaming heat outside chilled by its furious mechanisms while Stretch powered fearsome music from a sound system lost in the stout steel of the dashboard. Feet stomped. Three feet. The remaining foot was pressing that pedal to that metal.

Catching up took some time, as it always does. And as is the way of military men the world over, walls of need-to-know were encountered, announced and respected. Names were omitted, places too, until the American remarked upon the Englishman's healthy colour – his healthy brown colour. They agreed that his healthy colour was due to the unique heat, the dry heat, of a desert.

'Looks like Libya,' the American remarked, with no pretence at innocence. 'I heard that you guys been ... ah ... active.' He glanced across the wide gulf of the transmission tunnel. 'Am I right?'

Stoner's good humour tottered, staggered a little. 'Not exactly.' He looked upwards. 'Have to assume this thing's wired for sound?'

Stretch shook his head, slowly, then nodded, deliberately. 'Not that I know. Selected at random this morning from a pool of maybe a couple hundred identitanks. But maybe they're all wired. You give a fuck, you?'

'Sinai. Mostly Sinai. Maybe a little Gaza. With a trip or two to confer with friends among some orange groves. Maybe ... higher than that.'

'Golan higher?' Stretch asked, clouded eyes on the highway. Stoner nodded.

'Up that way,' he agreed. 'You can see for miles on a clear day. They have very many clear days that way. Some days you can see clear to Turkey, maybe the Black Sea, maybe even further than that. Crimea, Ukraine. You dig?'

'I dig?' Stretch smiled. 'You truly are a refugee, British man. A refugee from the Seventies, a time when men said "Dig it" and they did not mean a ditch.'

'Or a grave,' remarked Stoner, conversationally. 'And I think it was the Sixties.' He glanced at his mirror, angled his body, stared across his driver to the other mirror. 'Do we have company? A tail?'

'I sure hope so.' Stretch glanced at all the mirrors available to him, then mimed staring upwards. 'But damn, no sign of a chopper. Defence cuts are biting deep. Distinguished British guests only merit ground pounder escorts, no eyes in the skies. Times are hard.'

Stoner relaxed, unwound. Released a sigh so strong that a lesser companion would surely have wept. 'Tell me about this ride, Stretch. What's happening here? Is this a ... y'know ... an abduction? Am I to be held hostage? Like in Beirut or somewhere north of those sunny heights we were discussing, friendly, like?'

'Ask me not.' Stretch shifted lanes, ignoring the protests of softer skinned vehicles, which was all of those in sight, and headed for the off-ramp. 'My orders, and orders they surely are, instruct me to deliver you to your hotel. To introduce you to some of my compatriot colleagues, and then to depart. I have another duty or two to perform while I'm still wearing this so-fancy dress. Lucky old me, huh?'

'We've already passed my stop. I stay at a little place in the Garden District, on Constantinople.'

'Your friendly Uncle Samuel has placed you in a better hotel. Compliments of a grateful nation.' The Humvee navigated its way through a select neighbourhood, finally berthing outside an impressively famous hotel, where a man in a civilian uniform attempted to open its doors, failed, stepped back and waited while Stretch released them from within. The civilian then opened the passenger door and stepped aside, waiting for Stoner to unload himself, which he did, gracelessly enough. He turned back to Stretch.

'You coming?'

Stretch shook his head, smiling. 'Nope. But you are entirely and completely safe here, JJ. Nothing to worry about. Hang on.' Door opening man stood by while the large uniformed sergeant extracted and consulted a cell phone. 'It says here...' He paused for dramatic effect. Maybe he rolled his eyes. 'This kindly device informs me that we will be dining here this evening, you and I, and that I shall be taking you to Swampfest in the morning. I do not – Lord have mercy – I do not need to be in uniform tomorrow. Every day brings a new wonder. Be seeing you, English warrior.' The door of the vehicle shut with a heavy satisfaction, all on its own, no effort required of the occupant, and with a mostly subsonic thunder it pulled down the curving driveway and carved a new hole into the passing traffic.

Stoner watched it leave, turned to the impassive figure of the door captain, standing with Stoner's battered flight bag in his clean hands, and bowed. 'Lay on, Macdonald...'

oOo

'Mister Stoner. Welcome to New Orleans.' Two smart characters in smart suits, standing smartly together, almost at attention, in the smart suite of rooms which were apparently his for an as yet undefined time. Stoner smiled at them, nodded. Said nothing. Dropped his single bag onto a trestle plainly intended for family-sized – American family-sized – luggage and shrugged out of his jacket, a brown leather item which looked as old as its wearer and as though it had lived a long and difficult life – or had been down the road a few times in its own history, which may have been the case. Stoner hung up the jacket, rolled up the sleeves of his sweatshirt, a branded Harley-Davidson item emblazoned with the skulls, flames and exploded engine parts which are somehow and mysteriously connected with the American hyphenated motorcycle, and eased back into one of the suite's several vast and easy chairs. Raised an eyebrow towards his hosts.

The older of the two, a woman of maybe a similar age to Stoner, but who had worn rather better, eased another chair across the carpet until it faced him, Then she sat, smoothly, fluidly and smiled.

'We know who you are, Mister Stoner.' She smiled with no obvious warmth. 'We know what you do, we know who you do it for, we know why you're here and we want you to know that we know. Does that all make sense, sir?'

Stoner smiled back, shook his head a little, stretched out his legs before him.

'Not really.' He held up a hand, forestalling interruption. 'I hear the words and I know what they mean and I'm entirely happy with what you say, although whether or not it's actually true I couldn't say. You'll need to be a little specific. I also know all those things you mentioned, and I also know all the answers to your question, but it is a concern that your understanding and mine may differ. Radically. Judging by the welcome – Master Chief McCann playing cab driver from the airport, this ... ah ... palace – I am concerned that your understanding and mine may be different. And that could be a problem.'

He raised his hands again, both of them this time, and broadened his smile to encompass them all, positively radiating delight with his situation. 'I'm here for the music. For the festival. And the only baggage I carry is that, which you are welcome to examine as you will. No weapons. None at all.' His smile was a gentle smile of innocence.

'You're a musician as well as a murderer, Mister Stoner. We have no problem with either talent.' Again she smiled, a radiance matching his own in its insincerity. 'And we're both of us – all of us – aware that in the same way you'll be able to find an instrument should you decide to play something, so you'll be able to find a weapon should you decide to kill someone. We have no problem with the music. Just the other thing.' Her smile had slipped. She did not bother to refresh it. Silence became her.

Stoner allowed his own smile to fade. 'I'm not here to kill anyone. If you do in fact know why I am here – apart from the music – then you'll know that's the case. If you think I'm here to kill someone, then ... you're dead wrong. As I don't know what you know – or even what you think you know – I can't say much more.' He shrugged. 'So ... what's with the red carpet stuff, huh? You know where I am, where I'm going, all that, so why all the superstar treatment? I'm not complaining. Just curious.'

The man joined his companion, revealing that he too could speak. 'We have no problem with you, or with your being here, or your ... interest in the oil engineer. You're welcome in the United States, and while you're here you're welcome to stay as our guest. We want you to enjoy your stay, to enjoy the festival, the music, gator burgers, JD and bars, and we would not like to see our hospitality – that's our official hospitality – disadvantaged in any way. By a premature death, even an obviously accidental death, for example.' He'd declined to enter into the spirit of the smiling competition and merely frowned instead. It suited him.

'OK.' Stoner reached down and removed his tired Caterpillar boots. 'What now? I've had a long flight. I'd like a shower, maybe an hour's dozing before sampling the nightlife at the side of the mighty master chief. I doubt either of you guys wants to scrub my back – welcome though that would be, of course.' He pulled off his socks, wriggled his toes and wrinkled his nose. 'Shower,' he said.

The woman rose to her feet, her smile held before her like a cloak of impregnability. 'Stretch McCann's taking you out to the Rock'n'Bowl for the evening, I think. Enjoy it. Sonny Landreth and John Lee Hooker Junior, huh? That should be a good night.'

'Maybe you'll be there?' Stoner radiated welcome. 'Standing in the shadows?'

'Maybe,' she agreed. 'Though I prefer music a little more gangsta than the vintage guitar hero thing.' She smiled again, opened the suite's door and held it wide for a moment while warmer corridor air rolled into the cool room. She turned to Stoner and winked. 'Old man's music, huh? Stay tuned, Mister Stoner. Stay frosty.' The door eased silently shut behind her.

Stoner wriggled his toes some more, glanced up at the remaining official. 'Yeah?' he wondered. The agent shook his head, no malice in the gesture.

'Go ahead and shower.' The American walked to a table, kicked out an upright chair, descended smoothly into it, every movement a deliberate confirmation of his physique and fitness. 'I have your back until the SEAL gets back. Take a bath. Take as long as you like. You're a guest of my country. We like to welcome our British allies.' He grinned suddenly, his smooth tones collapsing as his voice somehow drifted far to the north, a New York melody backgrounding his speech. 'And Travis says hi.' He watched the Brit carefully, while his voice recovered its New Orleans leanings. 'And he told me to tell you he'd told me you'd deny even knowing him.' He laughed, undid his tie and unhitched his jacket, all in one seamless motion, shucking the jacket from his shoulders and draping it over a second upright chair in a second fluid movement. Very fit, this one. He rolled sleeves, rose and targeted the room's complex and ritualised coffee machinery. 'You get yourself clean. I'll do the honours with this thing.'

Stoner stayed where he was, watching the performance. 'That's a big gun,' he said, finally, nodding towards his companion's shoulder holster. And he stood. The agent ignored the movement. Ignored the threat in it, and concentrated instead on satisfying the demands of the caffeine device. Stoner walked over to the quiet American, who still failed to turn towards him. Stoner stopped.

'Travis?' The Brit looked innocent, but the single word held something more. Menace? Threat? Simple query seemed unlikely. Finally the American left the coffee machine sputtering to itself in that industrious way and answered.

'He told me to remind you about the Boston Irishman. The Irishman who dresses like an Italian. He told me you'd decline to discuss that guy, but I was to remind you that – and I quote – he still has a live and open contract for you. Can I get some creamer from the refrigerator now?'

Stoner stepped back, bowed a little, walked to the bathroom door, turned back, nodded. 'Thanks,' he said, stripped and entered a world of steam. Then turned. 'And please...' his voice fell to a whisper. 'Be gone now. Tell Travis hi, and tell him I asked for space, just a little space. That OK?' It was.

oOo

Two large men, one plainly an American military man in civvies, the other somehow obviously an unshaven Brit, left their vehicle, an anonymous truck, and walked to the Rock'n'Bowl, its own legend in its Louisiana lifetime. Loud and live music was its own welcome. And a shield, an acoustic shield. Stretch snapped his fingers in front of Stoner's face. They both stopped. The music throbbed, bass guitar and bass drums bouncing the air around them. Slide guitar craftsmanship split everything before it.

'Tomorrow noon. The exact middle of the day. Be visible. Be unmistakeably visible.' Stretch's voice was almost inaudible, his lips masked by his own knuckle wiping his own sweat from his own upper lip.

'OK,' Stoner yelled. 'Let's grab a chilli dog right here before we go inside. Great idea. Thanks for that.' And they did. Two chilli dogs, mustard and fries, all-American heroes. Night followed, as it does in Louisiana.

oOo

'Just leave the money, honey. Then come to momma.' A sweet voice, maybe, from some other throat in some other circumstances. A door had opened, quietly, and had just as quietly closed. At least, a door nearby, if not the actual nearest door. The voice again, a female voice. 'Is that you, honey?' Once again there was no reply. 'Fucking kids,' said the female voice. 'Little noisy fuckers.' A lighter lit, followed by a long cigarette and an even longer sigh. 'Gotta go, sweets. Tonight's superhero will be here any minute. Yeah. Love you too. Yeah, momma'll be with you tomorrow. Yeah, I'll meet you from school. OK, OK, I'll be cool – cool as you, any rate!' She laughed, a dim white light shaded into dark as she closed her phone. A knock.

No response.

Another knock.

A theatrical sigh. A second sighing of silk. Footsteps in the darkness. A door, opening. A voice, quiet, plainly packed with affection.

'You have a key, honey. There's no fee for using it.' She stepped back, a backlit figure against the light of the hallway. 'Or did you lose it, huh?' A second figure, larger, overcoated, hesitant.

'I...' A pause. 'There was a man ahead of me. I thought...' A shuffle and a fumble as the overcoat was slipped gracelessly from its shoulders. 'I thought you might have company.'

She caught the coat, hooked it with expertise onto a rack. 'I have neighbours, honey. And they have visitors – guests, sometimes. This is how folks are in America. Friendly. You know that.' The door closed once more. Their embrace was caught in its own moment, a flash, white as lightning; an electronic illumination, a digital image, a stopped instant. Interrupted by another voice.

'That is how it is in America. Please sit.' They were frozen together, locked arms of guilt, maybe. 'Oh, please. Turn on a light or something. Put the kettle on. Do something useful, why don't you?' As the intruder spoke so the woman hit a switch and a wall light lit.

'Chrissakes,' she said. She stared at the big man, the big white man sitting in her easy chair, legs crossed in confidence. 'You vice? A PI? You sent from his...' – she moved apart from her invited guest – '...his wife?'

'No. I just want to talk to him.' The intruder nodded at the immobile man.

'This a shakedown?' The woman was not giving up. 'I pay protection. Insurance,' she switched suddenly.

'I'm sure you do. It pays to be careful. Always.' He uncrossed his legs and leaned forward, a threat, suddenly. 'Hey, John. Are you happy to talk in front of Black Momma here?'

The customer spoke for the first time. 'John? Who?' He backed up slowly until his back rested against the door. 'What?' he wondered, weakly. 'What do you want? How did you get in? How much to make you go away?'

'Sit down. Momma – I like that. Can I call you that? – Momma, be useful and rustle up some coffee ... and ... I don't like to sound like a threatening cliché, but, y'know ... don't do anything foolish. OK with that?'

She nodded, moved with impressive quiet to a small open kitchen, made with aroma, creamers, cups and silence.

'John. I get you. I'm the john. That right?' The customer walked slowly to a chair, sat down carefully, as though afraid of a whoopee cushion or even worse.

The intruder tilted his head towards the lady of the house. 'OK to talk here?'

The john nodded back. 'I guess.'

'I'm your escort.' The woman in the revealing clothes presented the intruder with a coffee, in a cup, balanced on a saucer.

'That's neat,' she smiled. 'So'm I. So I guess he gets two escorts. One black, one white, one woman, one man.' She smiled some more. 'That's cool. You Brits, huh? Smart. Subtle. So how come you lost your empire?'

Stoner stood, smiling and shaking his head at the same time, extending a hand. 'Do you have the secret password?'

She smiled back, taking his hand. 'Surely I do not. Do you?'

'Nope. But I do have airplane tickets – only two, and both for men.'

'You were supposed to meet us at Louis Armstrong, maybe? The airport? Day after tomorrow?'

'Who can tell? I have a day off tomorrow. Swampfest.'

'OK.'

The john spread his hands, supplicant. The woman placed a cup and a saucer into one of them. 'Will someone tell me what's happening here?' His voice was drifting from confused, guilty towards anger, annoyance. The woman and JJ Stoner shared a smile, but only with each other. And after a quiet moment of confirmation of their mutual understanding, the black woman spoke to one of the white men.

'Seems you are a popular boy. This guy and this girl – that would be me – are here for the same thing.'

The engineer shook his head, theatrically wide-eyed. 'I sincerely hope not.' His original fear had been replaced by calculation. Engineers are calculators, by definition, almost. 'Care to explain?'

Stoner sipped his coffee with every appearance of simple pleasure. 'We're both here to keep you safe. Close protection, it's called. Some protection is closer than others.' He smiled, scanning the room again, and then again. Nodded towards the semi-naked woman. 'Momma here – I do like that, Momma – keeps you close until you check in at Louis Armstrong – that's the airport not a person.' He smiled more at his own terrific joke. 'I take over from there, waiting for you inside security.'

The engineer nodded. 'I'm not entirely stupid. I'm an engineer. I know what an airport is, and ... even what it's for.' Stoner and Momma both nodded their appreciation of his evident brilliance. 'So... you're not a hooker.' He nodded to the woman. 'And you're not a burglar?' A nod to Stoner.

'Oh no,' she said, piling a scandalised tone into her voice. 'I do sex with strangers for money. I most surely am a hooker. But I am a secure hooker. I may not be smart as an engineer, but I can work for two masters. You pay me for sex, and ... someone else pays me to do the sex with you that you're also paying for and they also pay me to keep you safe and keep you close. That is all-American enterprise in action. Then James Bland here takes over. He sits next to you on the airplane, so's he can protect you when some terrorist explodes it mid-Atlantic. Right?' Stoner nodded, smiles all gone now, sipping his drink, cautiously.

The engineer stared. 'You can do that? There's a way to do that?'

'You're the engineer. You work it out.' Stoner turned as if to speak to the woman, deposited his emptied cup onto a small table, turned back. 'You reckon you can still make it with this lady, knowing that she's actually a government employee?'

'Not technically government,' she interrupted. 'More agency than federal. You know how it is.' She turned back to her original customer and widened her eyes so the whites shone like beacons in the black moon of her face. 'And we have plenty we can do to pass the hours in safety.' She wobbled alluringly and turned back to Stoner. 'Why you here, anyway?'

'Just checking up. I'd get the blame if anything happened to chummy here.'

'Gotcha.' She walked to the engineer, who was shaking his head slowly. 'He's good here tonight. Day shift collects him tomorrow.'

'It does? Day shift?' The engineer, confused again.

'You'd call him a taxi driver. He's the day shift, dear. Guardian angels all of us, and if James Bored here had kept away we'd have been invisible and you'd never have needed to worry about it. Let's do some recreational trigonometry, huh? Just you and me.' She targeted her next remark at the big man. 'Clear off, you, white trash.' She smiled, but she meant what she said.

oOo

Swampfest is exactly what it sounds like. A festival in a swamp – or as near as you can get to that quaint notion. The air is hot, the music is hot, the audience is hot, the beer tries but fails to cool the heated crowds. JJ Stoner, a Brit abroad, bounced to the beat of the big sound blasting from the stage. All alone. Watchers none, deserted by all companions, which suited him very well because he was a man at peace with his own company, a man who could delight in inner quiet while wild music wailed all around, and bodies bounced to the same beat, along with his own. And this was one good, loud and lively, band. Zydeco slide at its most proud. Cajun music for the soul. He glanced at his wristwatch. Five minutes before noon. He looked around him and drained the beer from his long-necked bottle, swung it between fingers skilled in the ways of bottles and other blunt instruments. Moved through the living crowd, found a man drinking and drifting to the music, a large man, fat, as was his single companion.

Stoner calculated angles of approach with military precision, careful consideration as he might a thousand-yard sniper shot under fire in bandit country. Trajectory, elevation, velocity and point of impact, maybe not the Coriolis effect, not this time. The correct degree of damage was essential. It didn't pay to kill someone, or inflict unnecessary brain damage, not in a death-penalty state like Louisiana. He smacked his empty beer bottle monstrous hard and with monstrous accuracy against the impact-absorbing rolls of fat at the back of the fat man's head. Who roared, spun and swung, mighty co-ordination compensating for his flab. Stoner ducked, waving his arms wildly and jiving like a fool, a drunken fool, whoopin' and hollerin' crazily. The third man, the buddy of the assaulted American, grabbed him from behind, and Stoner pulled the pair of them to the ground, taking hits from both big, flabby fighters while shouting and laughing and managing to hit them hard without actually doing any damage.

Both Americans were fair fighters. Stoner had chosen them for their great size and entirely domesticated demeanour. He had observed carefully, had estimated, like the professional he was, that they were not carrying concealed, that they were unlikely to be hiding knives, that they were one hundred percent civilians and that they were in fact at the festival to have a good time, not to fight. He was correct in all his assessments.

This family fun activity continued for several minutes before two other men, uniformed men, piled in and pulled apart the parties. 'Hey!' one yelled as the crowd – amused, not hostile – grew around them. 'No need for this.' The music subsided, the audience applauded. 'Be cool,' the policeman said. Stoner hit out at him, knocked off his policeman's hat with his empty beer bottle while somehow managing to avoid contact between bottle and cop, and the affray began once again, ending very quickly this time as the cuffs clicked around Stoner's wrists and the peals of a brightly amplified bell rang down from the stage. Stoner leapt back to his feet, hollering in a wild impersonation of extreme drunkenness 'Midday, more beer!' He lunged for the nearest cop and made as if to kiss him.

'Taser' is a brand name, although that fact is often unfairly ignored by users and victims alike. By means of a cunning use of compressed, environmentally-friendly nitrogen as a propellant, the Taser fires a pair of small, sharp electrodes which are cleverly shaped to penetrate most forms of non-combat clothing. The electrodes remain connected by wires to the body of the weapon, from which a series of very short, very high voltage pulses are passed between the electrodes – conducted through the body of the target. The model of Taser favoured by US police forces is the X26, which peaks its voltage around 50,000 Volts. This is quite a lot more than most vertebrates consider to be comfortable, and the effect is immediate, usually resulting in collapse following the loss of voluntary muscle control.

'Holy flying Jesus!' said Stoner, falling to his knees and dropping his forehead to the grass.

'Twelve noon!' pealed the voice from the speaker stacks either side of the wide stage. 'Happy hour is here again. Two beers for the price of one, for one whole hour. Catch it while you can.'

The crowd dropped all interest in the fighters, the assaulted men shared shouts with the pair of policemen, and Stoner was led away, staggering and unprotesting to a distantly parked patrol car, and onward to a grilling, where he supplied much apology and many promises that similar future rowdiness would not happen. The heat, the beer, the music, the excitement, the heat and the beer, mostly, and he being a visiting Brit and truly contrite and offering whatever restitution his captors deemed appropriate, and it being Swampfest... Stoner walked free by the middle of the hot evening, and walked carefully and with caution through the humidity back to his hotel and its inevitable not-so welcoming committee.

They were Feds again, but different Feds. A different agency. There were four of them. No smiles. No coffee. No special relationship. All men. Suits. Stoner left the door to close behind him, leaned tiredly against the wall next to it.

'What the fuck?' His voice was leaden with tired. 'Guys, guys, it has been one hell of a day. One hell. Of a day.' He observed their absence of reaction with transparent surprise. 'OK. I screwed up. Guess I drank a little too much, too fast. Guess I just ... y'know ... lost it back there, but... Fuck me. Tasered. At my age. I need to sleep for a week. Welcome to America. I feel nauseous. Truly.' He fell silent, walked wearily to the nearest easy chair and collapsed into it, reached down to untie a bootlace ... two of the agents drew their weapons.

'Hold it right there, Stoner. Raise your hands slowly and keep them where we can see them.' Stoner did as instructed, a harder expression, an ugliness spreading over his weariness and waning calm. A little anger. His eyes were still watering and he was conscious that he might be drooling a little. He lifted his hands and laced his fingers together behind his head.

'Happy now?'

An unsmiling third agent patted him down, removed his boots and examined them. 'You need to accompany us, sir,' he revealed. 'I will need to handcuff you. Please stand, slowly, and place your hands behind your back.' Stoner did as instructed, and unsteadily barefoot, the Brit left the building. Many lobby eyes politely looked away, but many more stared in open surprise.

oOo

'I have no idea what you're talking about.' JJ Stoner sat barefoot, facing two other men, one taller, seated, the other standing, pacing, a familiar device to unsettle the interviewee. Who had conducted rather too many interviews of his own to ever be unsettled. He was however manging to present an appearance of mounting irritation.

'Everyone says that, Mister Stoner,' remarked the seated man in a chummy way. 'OK if I call you Jean-Jacques? French is that? Says here that you're a Brit.'

'I am.'

'What?'

'A Brit. You don't care about the rest. Family history. You can look it up. I have a Facebook account. Everything on Facebook is the truth. Every word. The truth is out there. On Facebook.'

The pacing man ceased his limited exercise, turned hard to face Stoner and leaned into him, planting both fists, clenched, onto the tabletop between them. His expression gave a whole fresh intensity to the phrase a steely gaze.

Stoner gazed back, stonily. He did that well. Neither spoke. A small battle of wills winnable only by the party who stays silent longest. The agent stood, glowered, resumed his pacing, still silent. Stoner felt cheated somehow, and turned to face the seated man. He yawned and shook a little, involuntarily.

'What you're saying, Jean-Jacques, is that not only did you not kill Mister Ellory the oil engineer, but that you don't even know who he is?'

'I didn't say the last bit, Mister Agent.' Stoner peered through watery eyes at the man's ID, which somehow failed to reveal not only the interrogator's identity but also his anonymous agency. 'I am aware of who the oilman is, but I most certainly did not...' he paused for emphasis ... 'I did not kill him. Have never been formally introduced, in fact. Not really. Almost a complete stranger. So far as I can see, you guys are holding me illegally. You going to charge me with something? Otherwise I should be ... well ... not here. I need some sleep soon. Please.'

The pacing man resumed his snarl, his crouch over the table, his facial intrusion into Stoner's space. 'We're waiting for confirmation on the GSR. Then we charge you. OK with you, mister lawyer?'

Stoner stared back, impassive. 'I'd kill for a decent coffee. Any chance?' The pacing man stepped back in pantomime disgust. Stoner did not smell entirely healthy, in truth. The seated man, the second agent, was also a patient man. An apparently puzzled man, also.

'Can't really see why you'd kill the guy. Not really. He's off Deeprig, right? He's been heard ... overheard telling some other guy that the failure of the cap on the well was sabotage, deliberate, not any fault of the Brit corporation or their rig, so surely you'd be more interested in keeping the guy alive and chatting, huh?'

'You might think that, brother, and that would make two of us.' Stoner almost smiled. Almost. 'I wasn't joking about the coffee. Got one hell of a headache here. My teeth are itching.'

The pacing man paused in his efforts once again, picked a cell phone from a pocket, grumbled into it about coffee for the prisoner and for his interrogators. He turned to face Stoner once again. 'Your MO. Prints on the ... on the gun. On the rifle.' Plainly he'd worked out that if Stoner was the shooter then he'd know with what he'd shot, so security wasn't an issue.

'I have an MO?' He raised an eyebrow. 'OK. Impressive.' Stoner watched as the door opened and a smart young man delivered three coffees. 'Prints, huh? I'm the sort of guy who offs some other guy – an oil engineer who's presumably on my employer's side in this Deeprig thing – and then what? I leave the gun laying around somehow? With my prints all over it? That's not entirely professional. Let us not fuck about, my friends. You know who I am, what I do for my country, all that, and my my, only yesterday I was conversing amicably with your very own chaps about how I'm here for the music, for Swampfest, and nothing else, and how your very own agency – or one very much like it – has put me up in some shiny upmarket hotel at your very own agency's expense and all that, and now I've just somehow and for no reason gone out and shot some guy.

'Does this make sense? It doesn't to me.' He picked up the coffee nearest to him, drained it hot, then started into the second cup, causing a little confusion.

A cell phone gargled a strangled anthemic rock motif. The seated man flicked it open, looked at its screen, closed it down again. 'No GSR,' he said. 'But the prints are a fine match. Clear. Which will be enough for an arrest.' He looked at his stationary companion, then back to the prisoner. 'OK,' he said. 'Just for the paperwork. Can you formally account for your whereabouts at noon today?' He flicked paper on the pad before him on the table between them. 'At 1207, to be precise.'

'Give or take,' his companion offered. 'A couple minutes either way would be fine with us.' He smiled, venomously enough.

'Think I was in custody. Police custody. NOPD.' Stoner didn't smile at all. 'At noon. Give or take. There was an altercation.' He held up his hands in mock apology. 'It was my fault. I have no idea how it happened. Your boys were justified in frying my synapses. I will not bring charges.'

'Excuse me?' The seated man looked more interested than before. 'Custody? How's that?'

Stoner explained, slowly, carefully. Then he asked for his own phone and for his boots. Which were located and returned to him while both the seated man and the formerly pacing man made calls of their own. Stoner finished first. He drained all the remaining coffee, sat back in his chair. 'A SEAL is on his way to collect me,' he announced. Which was no more than the truth.

oOo

Two men, slowly sipping beer in a Louis Armstrong airport departure lounge. One of them, a Brit by the sound of him, sighed. 'Guess I owe you, Stretch.'

'Guess you do. I will collect. Sooner than you think.'

'Guess you will.' The Brit sighed. 'They're calling my flight. Did you take out the engineer? The inconvenient engineer?'

'Nope. But I guess I know a man who may have done. An old friend.' A carefully blank look replaced all the animation in his expression. 'You really were here to escort the guy – the engineer – to safety ... back to the UK, right? Where he'd have plenty to say about how that spill happened?' Stoner nodded, saying nothing. Stretch let his lips form the curves of a smile, while unhappiness clouded his eyes. 'Looks like you are the world's worst bodyguard, my friend. Please refuse all instructions to protect me, should there be any.' Both men smiled some more, at peace with each other. Both stood. Stretch leaned close to his companion, whispered through barely moving lips, playground style. 'Boston Irish, huh?'

Stoner nodded, once again saying nothing. Being overheard is an occupational hazard, and life itself is haphazard enough. They clasped hands, military style. 'Looks like it.'

'You'll be back, then.'

'You betcha, big boy.' Stoner slung his bag from his shoulder, set out for boarding. 'See you soon. Be good.'

<oOo>

Stoner and Stretch encounter more killer women in the full-length novel, The Corruption Of Chastity

The solitary female sniper squints against the scorching desert sun. Takes the shot. Men die. The solitary female assassin slashes her target's artery. Fades into the Alpine forest. Men die. The betrayed covert operative silences his sadness with the howl of blues music and carnal recreation. What will happen when Chastity, the ice-cold contract killer, encounters underworld investigator JJ Stoner?

Keep reading for an excerpt – and more...

oOo

CHASTITY TURNED to face her uninvited guest. Who was confronted by a tall, well-muscled woman wearing flat-black combat kit, her short tar-black hair frizzing around her skull as it dried, the black camo pancake on the tanned skin of her face streaked where it had been washed and wiped, her eyes bright and white and staring with complete focus and intent at him. Her left hand held a black knife with a wickedly long Teflon-black blade; her right a black pistol, which she elevated slowly and steadily until it aimed with almost no shake at all directly between his eyes.

'You're armed.' Her statement was as flat as the unremitting black of her attitude. Her guest raised both arms until they were clear of his sides, both hands empty of weapons, his pose empty of threat.

'I'm armed.'

'With what?' The gun did not waver, nor did her voice.

'Two Glocks. Thirty-something rounds.'

'Blades?'

'One.'

'Strip. All the way. Throw your clothes and shoes away, like you'll never need them again.'

'That's a threat?'

'It is what it is. It is an instruction. You carry it out or you die. Your call.' Voice and handgun were steady.

'Simeon said you were one hell of a lady.' Her guest was still fully dressed.

'You're still dressed.' Chastity's tone of voice was unchanged. 'It's too melodramatic to do all that "if you're not stripped by a count of five" nonsense, and I'm all out of patience in any case. Strip now or it's bang-bang time.'

He stripped in silence, threw away the clothing and the two handguns and the knife.

'And the pants, and the socks. Let's see what's left. Let's see whether god made you the only black man without a howitzer in his shorts.' No smile, no humour. He obeyed in silence and stood naked before her, a large darkness in the plaster white of the church.

'Satisfied?' He held her gaze, and she held his.

'Only rarely, to be honest. Take a seat. Relax. Tell me stories about who you are, who you think I am and who Simeon claims to be – whoever Simeon is.' Chastity sat on the back of the front row of benches, feet propped on the seat; waved the knife towards an opposite bench where the black man would be visible, vulnerable and too far away from her to pose a threat. He sat as instructed. The gun remained aimed, her expression neutral. He said nothing.

'Go ahead. Entertain me. Time is limited. Much to do. Places to go, people to see. You know how it goes, I imagine.' She sounded bored.

'You have a friend.' The black man spoke slowly, American English, clearly enunciated and without over-emphasis. A soldier delivering a report. 'Your friend is called

Simeon Guest.' He stopped, his expression a question. An ignored question. So he continued.

'Your friend suggested that I should offer to help you if it appeared that you were in need of help.'

'Is that how I appear to you?' The edge in Chastity's voice wavered towards amusement. 'In need of help?' The gun's aim drifted downward, re-centred its one-eyed gaze at the dead centre of the black man's chest. 'A curious interpretation of our current situation. Unless of course you've brought the entire US Marine Corps along with you, they are currently encamped around the lake, all their guns trained on this sweet little old church, locked and loaded and ready to end my short life unless I come out waving a white flag and disarmed by your charm and imposing black toolkit. How am I doing with this?'

'I'm alone.'

'And therefore unwise. If your friend – not mine – Simeon suggested that interrupting this lady at her morning devotions was an activity devoid of risk and that you would not require at least a little support…' the knife flicked towards his groin in a macabre suggestion of humour '…then he may in fact be no friend to you at all. Why are you here, who are you, and what do you want? No jokes, please. I am in no mood for jokes.'

'What? Ever?'

'As I said. We are a little short of time, in case you were working on some prolonged nonsense while your cavalry gallop up. Speak now, or … dream up your own alternative.'

'You'd shoot an unarmed man?'

'Very soon. It's easy.'

'I was instructed to watch and wait here in Bohinj until the action – unspecified in my instructions – took place. I was then to identify the hunter, the operative, and if that operative was a woman and if necessary I was instructed to introduce myself and offer assistance. If required. That's it.'

'That's not it. How was I described to you?'

'White woman, active, five foot eight, ten, blonde. Fast, efficient. Name of Chastity. Nothing more; simply Chastity. That sounds like you, despite the wrong hair.'

'What help do you offer? What do you think I need? And why do I need it?'

'The place is awash with police. Everyone's out to get you. I have a vehicle, resources, facilities. They'll be looking for a white woman. I'm a black man. No-one's looking for me.'

'What's this guy Simeon's interest?'

'You do know him, then. You are who he says?'

'I've no idea what he says. What's he said to you? What's he like, anyway? Another imposing black guy?'

'Never met him. Spoken twice. Can I get dressed? I am not exactly overheating here.'

Chastity shot him, twice in his left knee. Then again, twice in his right knee. He roared to his feet, howling with pain, and collapsed, crumpled back into his seat, hands reaching reflexively for his destroyed joints.

'Maybe the Christian desert god doesn't feel the cold. Who knows?' She walked steadily, unhurried, through the screams of his agony to the small pile of his possessions. Sifted through them, collected weaponry, wallet, keys, sliced through all the seams of his clothing, searching for transmitting devices, found none apart from a cell phone.

'You're not going to survive this.' Chastity spoke pleasantly, calmly. 'This situation is not survivable from your perspective. The best I can offer is to reduce the suffering. Its duration, at any rate. That depends on whether I believe what you're going to tell me, really. You need to understand that I default to distrust. Everyone lies, everyone dies. Got that?'

The black man summoned impossible energies, thrust himself upright, arms providing the acceleration, shattered knees tottering as those long, hard arms reached for her. His eyes were wild, tears and sweat forming twin rivers on his cheeks. She shot him, twice, almost exactly halfway between his navel and his groin, and light left his eyes. He fell back, both knees collapsing into impossible geometries, hunching over his own ruin, weeping now in silence, shaking.

Feedback for the Killing Sisters novels:

'Guns, girls, guitars and scenes of gruesome violence, all shot through with a wit sharp enough to draw blood. With terse and brilliant prose, Westworth delivers a plot that drags you along relentlessly. Loved it, unconditionally.'
R J Ellory, award-winning author

'Serial killings and strange sisters, hard as nails hit men and shady superiors, sleazy blues and sometimes seedy sex... "Charity" mixes grim and dark crime scene action with sticky-floored music venue philosophising in a way that shouldn't work but does.'
Amazon.co.uk

'The writing is clever and inventive, paying few dues to existing genres or styles... There is a hint of Derek Raymond in the more visceral physical descriptions and the sense that we are looking at a dark and dystopian oil painting'
Crime Fiction Lover

'A truly unique reading experience. The author injects style, pace and energy into a witty, thrilling, and sometimes sickening story. The cool, often emotionless Stoner takes you on a roller coaster of a ride right until the very end.'
Amazon.co.uk

'Rich and ambitious, this violent tale plays out with memorable scenes interspersed with writing to savour. A feast of poetic prose wrapped in noir.'
Crime Thriller Hound

'The writing is sharp; we are led deeper and deeper through an often blood soaked, twisting (and twisted) maze of intrigue, betrayal and bloody murder...'
Amazon.co.uk

'There are some sequences which are as satisfyingly testosterone-soaked as any Jack Reacher adventure, and then some which are as bleakly subtle as über-nuanced Japanese noir. For every alpha male with a gun and a hard-on, there's an equal, often opposing feminine force: frequently just as effective and half as smart again. The writing is clever, the plotting is convoluted and the outcome is so utterly unexpected that it caught me completely off guard.'

Goodreads

Frank Westworth has created a cast of characters that are as memorable as they are ingenious and I was enthralled and thrilled right from the start. There are shadowy characters aplenty and a complicated, challenging plot that kept me on my toes throughout.'

Breakaway Reviewers

'Stoner is violent, amoral and cynical... His final speech, when he realises how he has been played, is almost Shakespearean in its bitterness and helpless anger.'

Crime Fiction Lover

'A chilling and fearsome story with many different twists and turns, which take you in many different directions and introduce all kinds of menacing characters along the way.'

Crime Fiction Post-Mortems

'A dark, grievous tale of hanging out with a nihilistic killer and enjoying the ride; it gets under the skin via vivid, sense-filled writing by an author with a unique voice. I'm seduced by Stoner and his world but I want to love him for the right, redemptive reasons. Instead I find myself looking on as a voyeur with a monstrous fascination.

Eden Sharp, author of The Breaks

KILLING ME SOFTLY

Frank Westworth considers creative ways to kill people

KILLER THRILLERS demand thrilling killers, no? I mean ... that's the whole point of them, surely. It is entirely unclear why so many folk are fascinated by creative ways of dying, but we are. Some of us are intrigued enough to write about it, maybe to see how it works, how a murder fits together, how it might feel were the author the killer. Which, usually, is not the case. Usually.

Most deaths – even the deliberate and premeditated deaths which define an actual murder – are pretty mundane. Most professional killers do it in the usual ways: either long range, the most popular and involving missiles, bombs, artillery and the like; medium range, using guys with guns operable by just the guys with the guns, and only occasionally by professionals involved in one-on-one – actual hand-to-hand combat. The latter is pretty rare, research reveals.

Research? Yes indeed. It's not difficult to find a retired (let us pray) killer and ask. I did this, and I assume that other authors of killer thrillers do the same. Look around you; it's statistically pretty likely that you know ex-military types. Maybe well enough to ask them all about the mechanisms. And maybe not.

Creative ways of killing apparently make a book more appealing – they certainly make writing the book more entertaining. I've recently completed a short story which required a surprise person being killed in a surprising way. In a disguised way; a murder disguised as an accident.

And as all parties involved were military or police professionals, that was a fun challenge. Grab a copy of 'Fifth Columnist' if you're interested in the resolution.

Unlike most killings, novels are written to entertain, so maybe the killing ways should also be entertaining. This is plainly a decently bizarre notion, not least because most killings are accidental, for passion or for money – think about it for a second – but I doubt that many killers do it to entertain others. Although...

So I try to provide variety, and even a little originality – entirely to entertain The Reader. So far, in three novels and a half-dozen short stories, methods of murder have included the usual handguns, sniper rifles, a rocket or two, several knives (usually long, sharp and with black blades – I took advice on that) and a couple of one-on-one slug it out fights, although the best advice with the latter is always to strike first, strike extremely hard and carry on doing that until your own life is safe. Talk to a serving soldier, preferably an infantryman.

However, I've also managed a couple of deaths by bathroom furniture, in the shower – dangerous places, hard surfaces, slippery and easy to clean. And for a little variety in one incident the bad guy used a catapult, while in another a nun used an exploding guitar case. It all made sense at the time. The killing I was most amused by – if it's OK for an author to be amused by their own copy – was death by industrial strength Viagra. It was appropriate for the situation, trust me. Also titillating? OK. Maybe a little. A not so petite mort, maybe.

It's not all violence for its own sake, though. When I working up the characters of the – ah – characters, I wanted to portray a couple of them as decent humans, not stone killers, psychopaths or the deviant fruitcakes so popular in the movies and on the telly. OK, so they're killers – that is what soldiers do – but they do not revel in that. Let's take the idea a little further – can you imagine a situation in which death would be a mercy? Of course you can ... probably. There's a great movie called 'They Shoot Horses, Don't They?' which isn't about contract killers in any sense (but is well worth watching all the same) which suggests the desperation which could lead someone – a very best friend, maybe – to do a deed which is entirely socially unacceptable, but which is actually a kindness, a mercy killing. I've told that very tale twice, using different reasons and entirely different characters. It's not easy to write. Not at all. The exact opposite of the alleged 'spree' killers so beloved of so many.

An unexpected outcome of the killer novelist's life is the popularity of the anti-hero. Not the villain, everyone has their favourite villains, from Moriarty to Hannibal Lecter, no; the anti-hero. The character whose view of life can become so bleak that he (or indeed she...) finds it increasingly easy to consider that final kill, that kill of the killer – suicide. One or more of my own characters face this, stare it down, consider it anew, find the idea appealing, so appealing that they need to distract themselves from their own final solution. Distractions? How would an increasingly nervous, distressed and unbalanced person distract themselves? It's not easy, is it? And it's very easy for a killer to kill themself, no matter the means or the method. And surviving a professional killer's suicide would surely be the greatest comeback in killer history, no?

I can't wait to write it...

This blog originally appeared on FullyBooked: http://fullybooked2016.wordpress.com

<< oOo >>

JJ Stoner returns in the full-length novel,
A Last Act Of Charity, published September 2014
Available in paperback and ebook:
www.amazon.co.uk/dp/1909984426/

Look out for the second book in the Killing Sisters series,
The Corruption Of Chastity, published September 2015.
Available in paperback and ebook formats:
www.amazon.co.uk/dp/1910508683/

The final episode of the Killing Sisters series, The Redemption Of Charm, will be published March 2017
JJ Stoner has every reason to kill.
The former soldier, ex-black ops assassin has been betrayed three times over. His enemies brutalised his woman, corrupted his best friend. Stoner's a danger to anyone who knows him. He's isolated. Neutralised. Vulnerable.
JJ Stoner has every reason to die.
Can he find a reason to live?

We hope you've enjoyed this excursion into Stoner's world
Look out for more short stories in the JJ Stoner / Killing Sisters series coming soon

Updates and info at:
www.murdermayhemandmore.net

Or find us on Facebook at:
www.facebook.com/killingsisters

Your feedback and thoughts are very welcome
A rating or review of this story on Amazon or Goodreads would be very much appreciated if you can spare a couple of moments to let others know what you think

<<oOo>>

Printed in Great Britain
by Amazon

17383584R00130